PRAISE FO

MW00533285

"So original and so scary . . . It will be a long time before I sleep as soundly as I did before *Old Fears* . . . A rare and chilling treat."

— WHITLEY STREIBER, AUTHOR OF *THE HUNGER*

"*Old Fears* is a psychological thriller of unusual power . . . I locked the door while reading it."

— DARCY O'BRIEN, EDGAR AWARD-WINNING AUTHOR OF *POWER TO HURT*

" . . . a modern masterpiece."

— C. DEAN ANDERSSON, AUTHOR OF *THE BLOODSONG SAGA*

" . . . the quintessential horror story."

— *THE DAYTON DAILY NEWS*

OLD FEARS

JOHN WOOLEY
RON WOLFE

BABYLON BOOKS

Old Fears

© 2021 John Wooley and Ron Wolfe

Print and eBook editions published by Babylon Books

All rights reserved.

eBook ISBN 978-1-954871-27-4

paperback ISBN 978-1-954871-28-1

No part of this book may be reproduced, or stored in a retrieval system, or transmitted in any form or by any means, electronic, mechanical, photocopying, recording, or otherwise, without written permission of the publisher.

This is a work of fiction. Names, characters, organizations, places, events, and incidents are either products of the author's imagination or are used fictitiously. Any resemblance to actual persons, living or dead, or actual events is purely coincidental.

Portions of this book previously published.

*To the living memory of the
Robert B. Leslie Foundation,
and to what is still to come.*
JW

*To my wife, Jan—I'd be
scared to write without her.*
RW

JOHN WOOLEY & RON WOLFE

OLD FEARS

BABYLON BOOKS

40TH ANNIVERSARY EDITION

FOREWORD

The monster you fear now may be a fake, but there's always the next one.

Case in point: two boys, Dwight and Mike, daring each other to sleep with their arms dangling off their beds, their fingers brushing the floor. You know the feeling? Oh yeah. Me, too.

The first horror movie I ever saw was *The Werewolf* (1956). The poster is right here in my writing room, framed on the wall. "SEE 10,000-year-old horror legend come true!" it says. "SEE man-beast stalk his prey!" "SEE women fight to save their men!" It was a lot to see.

I held up pretty well—even laughed when the hunters wait until the werewolf has taken cover safely behind a rock before they open fire on him. In my innocent crowd, that fateful Saturday matinee counted as a rite of passage, and those of us who could take it left the movies with a whole new sense of fearless manhood. Until bedtime.

That night, I knew the werewolf was under my bed.

SEE 10,000-year-old horror legend lurk under kid's bed at

1310 West B St.! SEE man-beast come after Ronny Wolfe for pretending to laugh at him! SEE women fight to save their men —somewhere else, not here!

Alone in the dark and scared dizzy, I could hear the werewolf growling softly beneath me. And I came to much the same thinking as the boys in *Old Fears.*

You're making this up, I told myself. *You're too old for this! The werewolf is nothing but make-believe, and you can prove it. Just . . . Let your arm slide off the edge of the bed.*

That's right, there you go. Reach down there. And if he's really there, well—he's going to grab your hand and he's going to pull you under the bed. But he's not there. He's not real. You know he's not. So nothing is going to happen to you.

Just . . . reach a little more off the bed. See? Nothing.

Just . . . reach a little more . . .

Very, very slowly, I let my arm slip off the bed, down, down, until my fingers brushed the floor. Nothing happened. Nothing happ—

Something hairy caught my hand, something with claws and teeth. The room flashed white. A bolt of sheer white is what happens when a boy's eyes spring out of this head like in a Tex Avery cartoon.

Then something bit my hand — and those teeth were familiar. I felt the sharp nip that was the signature attack of my family's Siamese cat, Otis. Real funny, Otis.

And so. The lesson.

I learned the werewolf was a fake. The cat was only fooling. But there's always the next one.

My fingers could have brushed a spider down there. Instead of the cat that scared me, it could have been the tornado sirens. A jetliner crashed here last night.

The older I get, it seems, the more monsters I think about—

old fears—and the more they seem real. It's the next one that
worries me.

———————

This will be an introduction of beginnings.

The beginning of a writer: I'm from North Platte,
Nebraska, Buffalo Bill's hometown. My grandmother once saw
Buffalo Bill ride a white horse into a saloon. I wished I could
have seen him, too, until I finally understood that, through her
eyes and through her telling, I did.

The beginning of *Old Fears*: John Wooley and I belonged to a
writers' group in Edmond, Oklahoma, called the Robert B. Leslie
Foundation. (The name is a long story.) He was the founder; I
was the late-comer. Being let in was like getting gold. You could
joke around with anything but writing. Writing mattered.

Mike, Gary, Sid, Norma, Jan, me—we'd sit among the fleas
that infested John's carpet, crack our cheap beers, and read out
loud the stories we'd written. John read with ease and experience; my voice squeaked and my hands shook.

One night, I brought a fourteen-page story called "Goofus,"
about a monster in the cellar. I still have it. The pages look crinkled and sweaty from that nervous reading that was the only
time it reached an audience. It was the first really true thing I'd
ever written.

Mick Winters comes home as a grown man to face the
monster he feared as a child, only to find that the monster has
grown, too—grown bigger than Mick and his Uncle Jack's old
shotgun put together. *"The eyes of the thing emerging from the
cellar glinted cat-like..."* It scared me, not for the cat-like eyes
but for the shivery moment when I had no idea what would
happen next—for the first understanding that fiction is not the

same as make-believe. Goofus knew as much about me as I did about him. John thought the story had something, too.

We struck up a writing partnership, only it was greeting cards at first. I'd sold a couple to Hallmark, and when you figure dollars to words, almost nothing pays better than a greeting card. We looked toward a lucrative contract that would pay us to sit around and do nothing but say happy birthday. Honest. Some people get away with it.

We wrote hundreds of greeting cards. We sold zip. Why? Here is a card that Hallmark thought was too terse:

You? Sick? Damn!

And here is the one that finally prompted the editor to say they'd just as soon not hear any more from us:

Celebrate your birthday like the Wise Old Owl!—Go home and throw up a mouse.

About this time, John moved from Edmond to the country near Chelsea, his little hometown. Mick Winters might have understood. We swapped a few letters, and somehow those letters turned into the collaborative chapters of a novel that took off from "Goofus" and carried us with it. I don't know how it happened. Since then, I've seen whole books written about the collaborative process. What we heard was a third voice.

The book's voice is not John's, and it's not mine. It's spooky. It writes better than we did.

One more beginning, where "Goofus" came from, or the first time I felt the way Mick does in front of that cellar:

I went to my dad for the teaching that every boy needs one time or another. How to handle a big bully.

"Well, you'll probably have to fight him," my dad said. "But you don't have to win. A bully is a coward who likes to hurt people. He doesn't like being hurt. All you have to do is hurt him, and he won't ever fight you again."

After that, he tested how hard I could hit his palm, and he taught me some boxing moves. I was ready for action.

A scrappy little punk who had been picking on me wanted to box in gym class. I faked him the way my dad had shown me, and rocked him one time square in the face before reality set in.

This kid toadied for a bunch of toughs who were looking to kill somebody—me, if I'd whipped any one of them. But I knew, and here was the neat part: *he* knew, I could have. He ducked me the rest of the fight and from then on. He was scared of me.

So now, I was more than ready. I was primed.

The time came as I was riding with my dad in his pickup truck, and on the side of the street, waiting for two-fisted justice, there he was—the big bully. I told my dad to stop the truck.

"That big guy?" my dad said. "That's the guy you're going to fight? How old is that gorilla, anyway? He looks twenty. *Him?*"

And then, he taught me another lesson.

"You stay away from that guy," he said.

———————

Early on, John and I considered tossing in some crazy reason why the book's old fears come to life—a curse or a comet, maybe. But the scariest monsters are those without reasons. Those are the ones that don't quit.

Every kid knows there is something under the bed, something in the closet, something in the cellar. And grown-ups may laugh, but they know in their grown-up hearts that it never pays to reach into dark, cobwebby places, or to fumble downstairs in the dark, or to walk in bare feet when there might be glass in the sand. And in their kid hearts, they know the bogeyman is as real as broken glass.

The bogeyman is waiting, always waiting. Maybe not in the closet, but in the knee that hurts for no reason; in the nights when you wake up and don't know why; in the mirror that gives back some stranger's face, older and sadder than anyone you'd want to know. You never shake the bogeyman.

I think we need him, you and I. He is the possibility so awful that he allows for any other possibility. If he can happen, so can love at first sight. He is the flip side of Santa Claus, and I suspect that he and that right jolly old elf might get together to sneak a drink and swap stories after work some nights.

This book is for the rare, brave soul who not only remembers old fears, but knows that it's better to believe in monsters under the bed than to believe in dust balls and old socks.

In the end, the book is nothing more or less than the best that John and I could write at the time. And that has to do.

Because here's what happened: the oldest fear of all—my dad died. It was about three months ago. He was proud of me and John for selling our books, this and the others. And his approval was more than fatherly; it was that of a writer.

He sold his stories to the early-day *Saturday Evening Post, Liberty,* and *Collier's*—boy-meets-girl stories, funny stories, nostalgic poems about mom's cooking, and he came up with the idea for an episode of radio's *Fibber McGee and Molly.* Heaven knows what he made of our monsters. All he ever said was keep it up.

One night, I was watching *The Tonight Show* with him. A guest comedian recited a verse that got major laughs and a shot of Johnny Carson wiping a bright tear of laughter away from his eye. "Well, I'll be darned!" my dad said. "I wrote that!"

Sure enough, he rummaged in his closet like Fibber and

found the identical poem carbon-copied on an old sheet of onion-skin paper.

John came across the same poem, credited to "Anonymous," in a book of verse. We gave the book to my dad for his birthday with "Anonymous" scratched out and the right name written in.

Since he died, it bothers me that he might have wondered why I never dedicated a book to him. Or maybe he knew. I never wrote one good enough.

But this one comes with a lot of good memories, with a welcome and a key to the town to Tanapah, where I grew up a little, and the hope that all your old fears stay kid-sized the way they should.

And this last line, just before midnight, is the ghost that comes late to pay old debts—this one to Ed Wolfe. Thank you, Dad.

—Ron Wolfe
Little Rock, AR

PROLOGUE

"Dave"
by John Wooley

Mick Winters, eight years old and troubled, squirmed in his bed in the freshly fallen darkness, the subdued thunder rolling persistently around the edges of his consciousness. Chances were good, he guessed, that a storm was headed toward Tanapah, Oklahoma, where he was spending his last few days of summer vacation freedom with his Aunt Lucy before heading back to the city and another year of school.

He wasn't in bed because he wanted to be. Where he wanted to be was on the edge of Tanapah's Main Street, where the Freeman Brothers Combined Carnival was set up for its final night of the summer. Only a few hours ago, he and his friend Jerry had taken the last of at least a dozen rides through their new favorite attraction, the Bloody Tunnel of Terror.

It wasn't bloody, really. In fact, most of it was painted pictures of werewolves and vampires leering from the walls, and one or two dummies made up like monsters with lights shining on them. There were a couple of big fat spiders dangling from strings, and scary noises that screamed from up above them, metallic-sounding and coming with no warning, like police sirens. And there were voices, one on top of the other, moaning and wailing, with a man's rumbling bass cutting through finally to shout, "Flee! Flee before it's too late!"

Then, the car jolted sharply around a corner, and there *he* was.

The first time Mick glimpsed him, fear zipped through his young body like he'd been hit by lightning. Jerry, beside him, actually screamed a little, although later he just said he'd sucked in his breath. Looking back on it, Mick wasn't sure that he hadn't made some sort of noise as well.

And why not? This was the centerpiece of the Bloody Tunnel of Terror, a glowing orange figure dangling from a rope, just high enough above the tracks that he couldn't easily be grabbed by one of the customers.

It took them two or more three times through the attraction before Mick and Jerry realized that there was a voice connected to the body; as it dangled in front of the moving car, an evil-sounding laugh bubbled up, ending with a shouted warning: "Don't end up like *me!*"

And the laughing again, now from behind as the beat-up twin doors opened and the car rolled its passengers back out onto the raised front of the Bloody Tunnel of Terror.

In the course of that Saturday, Mick and Jerry tried other attractions—the Octopus, the Ferris wheel, a couple of rounds of trying to shoot kewpie dolls that only landed them a pair of Chinese handcuffs—but the magnetic force of the Bloody

Tunnel of Terror, right on the very edge of the small midway, kept drawing them back.

In addition to the traveling show, town merchants and organizations had some booths down Main Street, with picnic tables scattered around where people could sit and rest. Mick and Jerry had ridden through the spook house several times before hunger drove them to the Tanapah Volunteer Fire Department stand, where they bought corn dogs and pop from a woman who asked how Jerry's folks and Mick's Aunt Lucy were doing.

After they were seated at one of the tables, Jerry began swirling the tip of his corn dog in twin blobs of mustard and ketchup and then looked up, earnestly nodding his head.

"It's a real guy, Mick," he said. "I *know* it's a real guy."

They had been going back and forth about this topic for a couple of hours, with Jerry coming to believe that the hanging figure was actually a dead human being, coated with some sort of paint or something that preserved him. "Like mummies," he'd explained.

Mick, on the other hand, wasn't so sure. So they'd ridden again, and then another time, hoping to see something that might prove conclusive. They studied the idea like scientists, consulting one another after each ride. But even then, with the apparition growing more and more familiar as they rode through, a thread of fear wove through their attempts at objective research. Too quickly, and at the same time not quickly enough, the old car would wheeze up to and then under and past the figure twisting at the end of its rope, shouting its warning without ever opening its mouth.

"Just think, Mick," Jerry was saying. "Once, he walked the earth like you and me. Now he's hanging in a carnival spook house." He took another bite of corn dog, and then narrowed his eyes like he'd just thought of something. "You think we ought to tell Chief Conner?"

"How come?" Mick asked as he worked over his own corn dog.

"If that guy's dead, *well*, that'd mean he had to be murdered some time, wouldn't it? Or maybe they dug him up out of the grave and hung him up there."

Mick shook his head. "You want to get the carnival in trouble?" he asked. "That nice old guy who takes our tickets and let us have that free ride?"

"Well . . ."

"Seems to me like if he *is* dead, he's been dead a long time," Mick mused. "And if he was murdered, the killer's probably long gone by now. I can't see where it'd do anybody any good to fink him out."

Jerry thought for a moment. "Maybe you're right," he said. "But maybe his soul won't rest until he gets put in the ground for keeps. I think I saw a movie about that on *Fantastic Theater*."

Mick vaguely recalled something similar he'd seen, probably on the same late-night local TV show. It made sense.

"I guess," said Mick, "we could at least be *friendly* to him—just in case it really *is* a guy, and his soul's still in his body, under all that orange paint and stuff."

"Yeah. Next time we ride, we ought to say hi when we see him."

"That's a good idea, Jerry. But you know, it'd be better if we knew his name."

They sipped and ate in silence for a few moments.

"I guess," Mick said, "we could just give him one. It doesn't have to be his real name. It could just be our nickname for him, like Aunt Lucy calls me 'Mickie.' Nobody else calls me that, not even Mom."

"Sure," returned Jerry. "It'll be what we call him every time we see him. And when the carnival comes back next year, he'll know us and we'll know him."

Again, they fell silent, finishing up their meals. And then Mick looked up into the cottony blue Oklahoma sky.

"How about 'Dave'?" he asked, already knowing it was the right name.

———

The clouds had been gathering throughout the afternoon, and by five p.m. the first faint rolls of thunder had begun around the town. By that time, Mick and Jerry had been through the Bloody House of Terror another half-dozen times, including a second one that the jolly old ticket-taker with the missing front tooth had told them proudly was once again "on me." They'd gotten to be friends, the three of them, and when he asked what they liked the best about the Bloody Tunnel of Terror, they told him "the hanging man," but stopped short of sharing the name they'd given him. It just seemed like their secret—theirs, and Dave's.

"Everybody likes that hanging man," said the man as he pulled the metal bar of the car down over their laps. "He seems awful real, don't he? Scared a lot of folks out of their skins."

But Mick and Jerry weren't scared now. Although there may have been vestiges of fear lurking inside them, little thrills of anticipation as the car took them through the doors and into the black-lit chamber for yet another round, all of that was buried by their eagerness to call his name into the darkness, to speak right to him.

And how great it had been to look up and say, "Hi, Dave," when that phosphorescent orange body suddenly appeared above them, dangled from the hangman's rope? As they passed under him, Mick and Jerry broke out in big grins that they couldn't explain. But then again, they didn't need to.

Lying in bed, Mick thought about that, about the glowing feeling it gave him, about how badly he wanted to do it just one more time—to send Dave off to the next little town with a friendly greeting and a promise to see him when he returned to the Tanapah Jamboree next year.

But Aunt Lucy had something to say about that. As per her instructions, he'd returned to her house, only a few blocks away from downtown, for supper, fully planning to return to the carnival and meet back up with Jerry after he ate. But when he opened the door and saw Aunt Lucy in the living room, staring at a TV that showed a weatherman in front of a big Oklahoma map, he knew that things had changed.

His Aunt Lucy was a wonderful woman. He couldn't ask for better. But one thing he'd found out about her in the three summers he'd visited: She was terrified of tornadoes. Likely, before the night was over, she'd be shooing him down into the cellar, to wait in candlelight until the storm blew through. Mick didn't really get it; he was more frightened of the cellar, and the monster he thought it housed, than anything a storm could do to him.

He'd seen the monster—or maybe he'd just somehow *felt* the monster. But it was real enough to tell Aunt Lucy about it, and she'd given that creature a silly name so that it wouldn't bother him: Goofus. Funny enough, that helped, and Goofus never really showed himself when Aunt Lucy was in the cellar with Mick. Even so, he still felt uneasy about going down those steps into the musty darkness, where *anything* could lurk.

Even Dave, Mick thought now. In his mind's eye, he saw Goofus forming out of the wispy darkness, all smoky and swirling like before he was named, and the glowing Dave jumping in and getting him into a headlock like he'd seen the great Danny Hodge do to Skandor Akbar on Channel 6's *Championship Wrestling.*

Thunder cracked through his thoughts. It was a lot closer now.

He'd held out some small hope that the weather would clear and Aunt Lucy would let him go back to the Jamboree after all. He'd call Jerry and they'd meet and say their goodbyes to Dave. He knew by the time he and Aunt Lucy went by Main Street on their way to church the next morning, everything would be packed up and gone, leaving only trash cans overflowing with paper plates and cups and other stuff left by the Jamboree's visitors.

He really had to get back down there, just one last time. It was important. It was, at that moment, the *most* important thing in the world to eight-year-old Mick Winters.

He was in bed because he didn't want to watch TV with Aunt Lucy. She was tuned in to the station that had the most nervous weatherman in the state. He was forever breaking into shows, especially where there were tornado watches anywhere in the viewing area. Mick didn't feel like reading comics, either, although he'd tried. His thoughts couldn't leave the Bloody Tunnel of Terror and its main attraction. Now, as the thunder crashed a little more, a little harder, he closed his eyes and saw Dave, and with every crash Dave swung a little from the end of the rope.

He *had* to go. It wasn't far. All he'd do was head right straight for the Bloody Tunnel of Terror and the nice old ticket-taker, climb into the car, and tell Dave goodbye until next year.

One thing: There was no way Jerry could go along. Mick couldn't call him, because Aunt Lucy would hear, and that would be that. And since Jerry lived on the other side of town, it would take too long to get to his house—and even if he did,

Jerry's own folks might not let him out into the threatening weather.

No, Mick thought, *I've got to do it by myself.*

At that moment, it felt as though he were the last hope, the only one who could make everything come out right—for both him *and* Jerry. He would say goodbye for the two of them—he might even tell Dave, "Jerry says so long," or something like that. And once that happened, just the once, Mick could return home and climb back in bed, with Aunt Lucy being none the wiser.

It seemed that the next thing he knew, he was already on his way to the Jamboree, pulled toward it by the lights that winked like dim eyes under the roiling darkness of the stormy night sky. He barely remembered sneaking quietly out the kitchen door, creeping past the back of Aunt Lucy's head as she sat on the living room sofa, absorbing the latest weather news.

He knew he shouldn't be out there. There was no way Aunt Lucy would understand. She loved him, and he'd never done anything to test that love, to make her not like him. He didn't want Aunt Lucy to think he was a bad kid.

As he approached the edge of the midway, the lump of fear, or conscience, that had been caught in his throat ever since he'd left the house began to grow, spreading through him, flushing his face until what was before his eyes just didn't look right. The naked light bulbs strung on poles looked cheap and dirty; the facades of the game booths, the rides, like things old and badly treated. A few of them had already gone dark, given up, no longer attempting to attract the last straggling members of the Saturday night crowd.

But it wasn't a crowd at all, Mick thought. Hardly anyone was there, and no kids. He recognized very few people; to him, they all looked like the kind of teenagers you saw in juvenile-delinquent movies, the only kind that Aunt Lucy wouldn't let him watch.

The Bloody Tunnel of Terror suddenly loomed in front of him, so dark that he thought at first it was one of the attractions that had already shut down. But then he saw a shadow moving around the ticket booth.

Quickly clambering up the steps, he found not the friendly old guy from that afternoon, but someone else, whip-thin, with greasy hair, his eyes gleaming like an animal's in the near-darkness. He looked, in fact, like the worst juvenile delinquent of them all.

He looked at Mick like he was a mangy dog.

"Shuttin' down," he muttered.

As scared and off-balance as he was, Mick managed to dig into his pocket and come up with a couple of bills and some change.

"Look," he said. "I'll give you all of this if I can ride once."

A flashlight clicked on, the cone of light shining on the money. Then a hand scooped it out of Mick's palm.

"Get in," the guy said, like he was giving an order. The way he jerked back the bar on the car reminded Mick of a movie he'd seen where a guy'd drawn a switchblade knife and snicked it open.

The double doors swung open, and Mick rode into the Bloody Tunnel of Terror, alone and uneasy, with only one thought in mind: to say goodbye to Dave and then to get home before Aunt Lucy found out he was missing.

Past the painted monsters, the spooked-up mannequins, the hairy rubber spiders on strings, Mick Winters rode, and for the first time since he'd discovered the ride, he wanted to be through the exit doors and on his way home. He didn't like the way he was feeling, his aloneness, his guilt about sneaking out—

even the way the dummies stared at him, like they really had eyes.

Then the car clanked around the corner, where Dave waited.

But there was something wrong. Mick knew it immediately. Dave was swinging back and forth, the rope making a swishing noise. It sounded like someone waving a sword. And he was *talking*—already, and not with the words he'd repeated every time Mick and Jerry had ridden past him. These were different. They surrounded Mick, attacked him, even as the car he was in seemed to slow on its tracks.

"You think you can get rid of *me*?" the voice shouted. "You think you can get rid of *me*?"

Stunned, Mick looked up at Dave's face, expecting to see his stony, immobile features. But Dave was actually *talking*! His mouth moved with the words, with the challenge, the lips curling back over white teeth as he spat out the question, again and again.

"You think you can get rid of *me*?"

All thoughts of saying goodbye rushed out of Mick's head. Squeezing his eyes shut, he suddenly was beset by a sickening wash of images, nightmarish in their intensity. There were women, and men, and one man he knew without knowing that had to be him, Mick, all grown up. There was fighting, and screaming, and drinking alcohol just to be drinking alcohol, and geysers of anger that washed over the whole tableau, bathing it in blood-red tints. In an instant, he comprehended that he was somehow seeing his future—or at least *part* of his future—and it was something that seemed completely unlivable. Over it all came the shouted questions from the thing he could no longer call Dave, knowing that on this night, because he had snuck out and disobeyed his aunt and had to go through this one more time, the thing he had once known as Dave would always be with him.

Had the car stopped?

Surely, he should be through this by now. The doors should be opening in front of him, so that he could jump out of the car and run home before the storm, where it was safe and Aunt Lucy would watch over him. But he seemed to be moving along much more slowly than he should be.

He would not look up at the apparition he had, in a more innocent time only a few hours ago, given a name. But he knew he was right under it. He heard it screaming above him.

Wait. Yes. The car was moving. *Thank you, Jesus.*

And in one final gesture, as the shouted question erupted for a last time, a foot of the hanging man scraped across the top of Mick's head.

The juvenile-delinquent ticket-taker was nowhere to be seen when the car pushed through the double doors and out into the night. Mick pushed the safety bar up himself and climbed out, his whole body pinpricked.

Then, a hand grabbed him by the shoulder.

Whirling around, Mick found himself looking into the stern moon face of Chief Conner, the head of Tanapah's police department.

"Your aunt thought you *might* have come back here," he said. "Don't you know we're under a tornado warning?"

Mick gulped. It was like he was reading a comic book, and he and Chief Conner were in one of the panels.

"No, sir," he said, and he had no idea what he was denying.

"Well, there is, and you know how your aunt worries about storms." As if to emphasize what he was saying, a clap of thunder echoed around them, very close. "She was fixin' to go to the cellar and went to get you out of bed. She didn't find you, did she?"

"No, sir," he said again.

"Well, you'd better get home. And you'd better not let me find you scarin' your aunt anymore, all right?"

"No, sir," he said a third time. "You won't."

Chief Conner nodded. "You need a ride?"

Quickly, an image formed in Mick's head about the town police car, siren flashing, pulling up in Aunt Lucy's driveway.

"No thank you, sir. I'll get home now."

"All right. Hurry up, and maybe you won't get rained on." By the time the chief straightened, Mick was already headed down the steps of the Bloody Tunnel of Terror, racing for home —where Aunt Lucy waited. He saw her first as a silhouette, standing at the steps of the cellar in front of the kitchen's dim light, leaning forward as she peered into the darkness. In a moment, he was by her side.

"Aunt Lucy—" he began.

"You can tell me all about it while we're waiting out this storm," she said, an unaccustomed brittleness in her voice. "But you disobeyed me Mickie, you know that?"

"Yes'm. I'm sorry."

She shook her head. "C'm'on," she said. "Candles are already down there. Thank the good Lord the rain hasn't started yet. Weatherman says a twister touched down in Nowata County and may be comin' right for us."

She herded him in front of her down the steps, and instead of the uneasiness he usually felt on his descents into the cellar, this time a strange kind of peace settled over him. At that moment, he wasn't even positive there *was* a monster in the cellar. It sure didn't feel like it now.

Aunt Lucy eased the cellar door shut just as the rain began to pelt down around her. And then, as Mick listened to the storm quickly intensify, slamming sheets of water against the wooden door, he knew why he felt better. That hanged man back at the carnival, the one that had shouted at him, the one who was even now probably lying in the darkness, waiting to be packed up and hauled away to the Freeman Brothers Combined Carnival's next stop—why, his name wasn't Dave at all.

It was Goofus.

—John Wooley
10 May 2021

1

The pickup rolled to a stop, its wheels crackling against the gravel road like the sound of a thousand small bones being broken. Ahead, the midnight darkness was impaled by the yellow-white beams of the headlights. The road was wide enough, barely, for two cars to pass, but the ruts in the center were the farmland's ways of saying *you're a long ways out, boy. Don't look for company.*

"This the place?" Mick Winters intended the question to ring with expectant good humor, but it came out too sharp and too loud. He drummed his fingertips against the top of the steering wheel.

"Up a little more," Jerry Meyers said. He sat with his arms locked straight out, his hands clenching his knees. "Geez, I can't believe we're doing this."

"Look, if it really bothers you, we'll go back."

Jerry lit a cigarette, the glow of the lighter giving his freckled face the look of a Halloween mask. "Nah," he said. "Nah, I'm up for it."

Mick jammed the truck into first gear. It groaned and

lurched. As he slowed it to a coasting speed, Jerry craned to look out the side window.

Jerry was right. It *was* unbelievable, what they were doing. They were two grown men out playing after dark like a couple of ten-year-olds trying to scare each other. And the beer was wearing off. Except maybe for Jerry. Jerry had put away a few more than Mick, and maybe that's why Mick had ended up behind the wheel of Jerry's pickup.

"Divorce is rotten," Mick said, and as the words floated out in the night without further comment, he felt idiotic for saying it. He was grasping for a good grown-up thing to talk about. He was trying to tell the darkness that he was too old now for believing in spooks and goblins, but he was talking to Jerry, and Jerry didn't answer.

The truck crunched ahead over the gravel and past the shifting, rustling sunflowers that lined the road and seemed to watch and whisper. Mick knew if he let his mind go loose, it would convince him that the flowers weren't really flowers at all. He could almost see them massed in the center of the road just beyond the range of the headlights, watching and waiting, and running on wispy feet to take their places on the sides at the last possible instant. And if he glanced into the rearview mirror, he could almost see them fanning out again in back of him.

"Here!" Jerry said.

Mick's foot hit the brake pedal with an exaggerated thrust that made the nose of the truck bob down and the tires skid. It lifted a haze of dust that mixed with the warm, clinging air and sifted into the cab while they sat there, dead quiet.

"Right 'bout here," Jerry said. Finally said. He pointed out the right-side window, leaning away at the same time to keep his arm from going outside the truck. "Over by that clump of trees is where we used to go fishin'," he said. "We'd fool around until near dark and then start home, and we'd always be daring each other to crawl through the culvert. You know how kids are."

Mick nodded. He wanted another beer. He wanted a pitcher, and he wanted Scot to bring it, because everything seemed to make sense when they were back in Scot's Tap with Barbara Mandrell on the jukebox and the Coors sign glowing a dull red over the bar.

"Jer," he said, "we're a couple of nuts out here, you know that? You belong home. You've got a wife and I've got the next best thing. Did I tell you? For a quarter I can make the mattress jiggle."

Jerry took a deep breath and blew it out in deliberate spurts. "It's amazin', isn't it?" he said. "I come back to this place, and I'm just as scared as I ever was. Just like you said."

Mick listened to the rumble of the truck's motor, thinking about what they would do if the motor quit and left them stranded. He felt ice crystals falling and shattering in the pit of his stomach, and he gunned the engine.

"But, shit," Jerry said. "We come this far. Now, I want to see and be done with it. I'm goin'."

Jerry hit the doorlatch and pushed himself out of the truck, the door whining behind him. "There's a light behind the seat on your side," he said.

Mick stepped out, letting the motor run. The firmness of the ground against his feet seemed to flow up into his legs, to straighten his back and clear his head. They *were* making fools of themselves. But that was all. He knelt and rummaged for the battery lantern, finding it alongside a couple of road flares.

Mick straightened and flicked on the lantern. "Show me where," he said.

Jerry stood at the edge of the road, looking down into the

ditch. He didn't have to say anything. His face was bleached in the glare of the headlights.

Mick swept the beam of the battery lantern in a white arc down into the clots of weeds until the light drew a connecting line between him and the mouth of the culvert.

"Dare you to crawl in there," Jerry said. His voice was matched by the quiet stirring of the wind.

Mick looked slowly from the culvert back to Jerry. He looked at that six-foot frame shaped into the natural, lean muscle of thirty years on the farm, and he heard the voice of a little boy. "Dare you," Jerry repeated.

The night wind stirred the grass at the culvert's opening. It was a cooler wind, suddenly, than seemed right for the end of May. It rippled the faint lines of a cobweb that zigzagged the culvert.

For an instant, the culvert faded, to be replaced in Mick's mind by the red-painted door of the fruit cellar in his Aunt Lucy's backyard. He saw the padlock snap open, and the door creak slowly toward him. He jammed his eyes shut to scatter the image.

Jerry scuffed his toe against the gravel. "I crawled through there once," he said. "We rode our bikes out here, me and Frankie Baylor and Tom Gustafson. They dared me, and I did it."

"And what happened?"

Jerry answered with a quick snort of a laugh. "I went in one side, and I came out the other." He kicked at the road, sending a shower of pebbles skittering into the darkness of the ditch. "But I could *feel* it, Mick. I knew it was in there, and it wanted to get me, but it couldn't. And they could feel it, too. We didn't ever come back."

Mick shot a glance at Jerry's eyes, saw them glistening with moisture, suddenly and unexpectedly. "It's like you were saying, Mick. A guy thinks back to the things and the places that scared him when he was a kid, and he wants to be able to say, well, that was a long time ago. He wants to be able to joke about it, I guess. He wants to . . . grow up. But he can't grow up because he's still scared."

Mick continued to look at Jerry across the darkness, measuring the change in Jerry's mood. A few hours ago, Jerry had been buying the beers and punching the buttons on the jukebox in Scot's Tap. He remembered the broad grin of recognition that had flashed across Jerry's face when they saw each other, and marveled that those same features could be tightened and twisted to the shape they held now.

Old fears. It didn't pay to stir into old fears. They were scaly things that seemed dead until they were prodded and brought into the light again, and then the eyes flickered open, and the teeth clicked.

"You know what's in there?" asked Jerry. "A spider. There's a spider so big that it fills the hole. We used to talk about it, and you know what, Mick? We all knew what it looked like. We didn't sit around and make it up and add to it. We just knew."

They met at Scot's Tap, and they could have talked about anything. They could have talked about how Jerry used to tag along after Mick, because Mick was a couple of years older. They could have talked about how Mick's Aunt Lucy would make chocolate chip cookies that she left gooey warm on a plate on the table, and how she would pretend to be shocked and amazed when she came back and found the plate empty. Two guys who used to be boyhood chums, who hadn't seen each other in twenty years, could talk about a lot of things. They didn't have to be out in the dark talking about spiders.

"It's all black," Jerry said. He was staring into the on-and-off flame of the cigarette lighter, snapping at the lighter with his thumb. "It's so shiny black that it looks covered with oil, but if it touched you, it would be dry like old paper. It has—"

"Oh *hell*, Jerry!" Mick said suddenly. "Okay. It was my idea to come out here. Now it's my idea to call it quits."

Mick turned, but Jerry caught him by the arm. "Don't you understand?" Jerry asked. "This'll be over after I go down there and crawl through that culvert. I'll go in one side, and I'll come out the other, and *then* we'll call it quits, Mick. You said it yourself. Tonight, it's me and this culvert. Tomorrow, it's you . . . and the cellar."

The wind dropped, and the clinging air gelatinized around them, bringing with it the stagnant smell of the shallow water in the bottom of the ditch.

"No way," Mick said. "Sure, there's bound to be something inside that . . . thing . . . that would bite you. That's probably what scared you about it in the first place. Or you'll stir up a skunk."

Jerry looked up from unbuttoning his shirt. "Just got this," he said. "It's right out of the package."

He handed the shirt to Mick, but Mick threw it on the ground. "Jerry, what's got *into* you? We were just fooling around . . ."

No. That wasn't right. Jerry had been fooling around. Mick was the one with old ghosts to confront. Mick was the one who had started playing "dare you" and pushed it too far. Didn't you have *some* place, Jerry, that scared the very devil out of you when you were a kid? Didn't you ever wonder, Jerry, what it would be like to go back to that same place now and find out if you'd still be scared? Wouldn't you feel better, Jerry, if you *did* go back, and you *did* face up to it?

"We were just going to drive by," Mick said. "We were just going to take a look at it."

Jerry took a step down the bank of the ditch. "Hand me that lantern," he said.

Mick tried to say no, but he couldn't. It was too late. Mick, the big kid, had called the game, and Jerry was going through with it. And afterward, they would talk about getting together again, but they never would.

Jerry reached up and took the lantern. Mick watched him as he edged down into the ditch. The weeds looked like snakes snapping at Jerry's faded denims. Then, Jerry's head dipped below the line of the truck's headlights, and he became a shadow shape with the lantern light floating in front of him.

The beam moved to the mouth of the culvert, then lowered.

"See anything?" Mick called.

"Nah." Jerry's voice echoed through the culvert. From the other side of the road, something thumped against the metal of the drainage pipe and ran or crawled off into the grass.

"Rabbit, I think," came Jerry's voice.

Mick jammed his hands into his pockets, where they would feel safe, where they might stop shaking.

The lantern light bobbed and circled. The contours of Jerry's face fell into the light, his eyes narrowed, his mouth tensed into a thin straight line.

"It's the same damn feeling, Mick," he said, looking up. "I can see straight through. I can see out the other end. Nothin'." There was a long, lifeless silence, and Jerry looked back into the culvert. "But it's the same damn feeling."

Mick peered at him. "Come on back, then. You've proved everything you can. Or need to."

"Maybe you should dare me, Mick." Jerry's eyes flickered up again, the whites showing a little. "That's what I need to get on with this, I bet. A good dare. C'mon."

"Jerry . . ."

"*Please*, Mick."

Mick took a step over the edge of the bank, as if he were going to suddenly charge to the bottom and drag Jerry back home. But he stopped.

"Okay," he said. "I dare you, Jerry."

Jerry's grin was small in the darkness. "Then I'll do it."

Mick watched as Jerry crouched at the mouth of the culvert, the lantern light splayed out around him. Then the light dimmed as his head and shoulders disappeared from view. Mick could hear Jerry's hands and knees make hollow scraping sounds against the corrugated metal walls of the pipe.

"You okay?" Mick called.

Jerry didn't answer. One foot, then the other, was swallowed up by the culvert, and he was gone. Mick could hear the thudding of Jerry's knees and now and then the clack of the lantern hitting metal. The light became a shifting, faint play of yellowed shapes at the opening.

Mick took another step down the bank, all the time watching the opening. The ground crumbled under his right foot, which was farthest out, and he slid and fell, rolling into the wet, spongy grass at the bottom. He pushed himself up, thinking of leeches, and yelled out at the feeling of his shirt pinned to his body by a mat of sand burr stickers.

Then, the light went out in the culvert.

And from inside there came a silence that crept out on long, thin legs.

"Jer—"

A low, quivering moan began inside the culvert, a moan that built and reverberated from the metal walls, lurching through a series of cries and wailings until it became a scream that abruptly died.

"Jerry? *Jerry!*" Mick ran, toppled, and somehow reached the mouth of the culvert. He fell forward, his hands gripping the hard metal edge, his head thrust into the opening. Inside, the hole was of a black that seemed not only to block his vision, but to invade the back of his mind, slashing a passage and leaving the wound open. And with the darkness came a high, chittering sound, and the rending of flesh, and the thick smell of blood and decay.

Mick's hand closed on the cardboard tube of a road flare. He was back at the truck, scarcely aware of how he got there, except that he must have twisted his ankle in the process. The ankle buckled under him with a pain that burned through his leg and exploded in his knee.

Dragging that foot, gasping for breath, he hobbled to the edge of the road. Half-kneeling, half-falling, he sledded down into the ditch.

"Jerry? Jerry, hang on!"

The black maw of the culvert was impassive.

Scrambling to the hole, Mick struck the flare. The end of the tube sputtered, then caught to a blinding red glare, lancing into the culvert. The walls turned white and silver.

Dumbly, Mick looked down and saw that his hand was not resting in a trickle of warm water at the culvert's edge, as he had thought, but lying in a pool of warm red fluid. He saw boots and blue denim jammed in a heap toward the middle of the tunnel, and beyond that—a darkness that moved.

The darkness was on him.

It touched him, covered him, and it felt like old, dry paper.

2

They were playing lovers' moon that night. Bob had his big brother's candy-apple-red Ford Mustang with the mag wheels and the "Boomer Sooner" horn. He hit the horn, blaring the first four notes of the University of Oklahoma's football fight song, and Ginny slipped into a fit of the late-night giggles.

"Shhh!" she cautioned. "We're trying to *sneak* away, remember?"

"Two sneaks in the night," he agreed. The car wanted to rumble and roar, but he convinced it to roll quietly out of the parking field. He didn't turn on the lights until they could barely hear the dull thump of a slow dance from inside the Tanapah High School gymnasium.

Bob flipped his snap-on bow tie over his shoulder into the back seat and loosened his shirt collar. He rolled down the driver's side window, leaning his elbow out the window and steering with his right hand lightly fingering the wheel. "The rules of this game are very simple," he said.

"Tell me." She turned to face him.

At that moment, if Bob Wortham had been asked to name the most exciting sound in the world, he would not have said the crack of lightning or the scream of a fire siren. He would have named the sound of a yellow chiffon party dress rustling against a white imitation leather bucket seat.

Ginny's auburn hair was an amazement of curls, each fashioned the way a jeweler would shape gold. Flecks of light from the dashboard dials played in her eyes and against the carefully applied gloss on her lips.

"We chase the moon," he said. "We chase it until we catch it, or until you have to be home, whichever comes first."

Main Street was empty. The marquee lights on the old Chieftain Theater snapped off as they drove past, but nobody was walking out of the movie house. The town of Tanapah, Oklahoma, had gone to bed, or to the prom. At Main and Elm, the downtown's one traffic light hung over the intersection, blinking red in all four directions and garlanded with a row of dead Christmas lights that hadn't seemed worth the bother of taking down. Ahead, at the edge of town and to the left of Main, the crescent moon was balanced on top of the water tower.

The moon was a sickle with knife points and a bright, clean edge. "Like you could reach out and touch it," Ginny said. They were outside the town limits now, and she laughed and leaned her head against his shoulder.

Prom night. To Ginny, it had been meeting with the senior prom committee three months ahead of the big night and choosing "Cherry Blossom Time" as the prom theme and folding little white flowers made of crepe paper until the tips of her fingers felt like pincushions. It had been sending away through the Sears catalog store for a white full-length dress that, when it came, didn't fit, and driving an hour and a half into Tulsa to go dress shopping. It had been the magic of watching the high school gymnasium became a time machine, transporting its passengers to a never-never land of rose-colored lights and soft music.

She didn't try to tell Bob what the night meant to her. She just told him she wanted to go.

Bob took the wheel with his left hand, and with his right discovered that Ginny's hair felt oddly stiff, like something that didn't want to be touched. The whole night had felt hardened with hair spray, he thought; but then his fingers found a curl that had escaped being preserved for the ages, and he concentrated on playing with that one.

Chasing the moon, they took the old state highway, then swung onto a farm road stretching due west.

"How much trouble would you be in if your folks found out you left early?" Bob asked.

"It would be better if they didn't find out," Ginny replied. "But they trust me."

Prom night. To Bob, it had been two hours of watching the punch level go down until he could see a red, grainy floor of Kool-Aid granules at the bottom of the bowl. It had been shuffling in time to the band, feeling the crinkling softness of Ginny's breasts pressed against him. It had been sneaking glances into the bleachers where the parents were sitting and wondering if Ginny's mom and dad were *ever* going to go home.

Now, here she was talking about how much they trusted her. In another minute, she would be talking about how much they trusted *him*. Bob downshifted to third to take a dip in the road.

"Whoo! Didn't that make your tummy feel funny?" she said.

"Tummy? You mean right . . . there?" Bob tickled her in the

ribs. She squirmed appropriately. His hand slid down against her thigh, and she didn't say anything.

He took his hand away.

At school, the other guys had been prodding him to tell how far he'd gotten with Ginny, but he never said. She called him a gentleman and made him feel proud of himself and ashamed at the same time. Sometimes, he ached for a sin to keep secret.

The blacktop gave way to the rattling ride of a gravel road.

Bob stole a look at her. The problem was, there were two Ginny Adamses. There was the Ginny he fantasized about, who would beg him to have a man's way with her, and then, there was the Ginny sitting next to him, who passed him half a Snickers bar across the aisle during study hall.

"I want to tell you something, Ginny," he said. "You remember the game against Bushyhead? We had 'em by one basket. One of their guys was going for a layup that would have tied the game, and I shot him an elbow to the side, so he missed. And I didn't get caught."

She sat up, stirring a breath of honeysuckle perfume. "You still feel guilty over something that happened six months ago?" she asked.

"No." Bob shook his head, and the stiff white collar of his dress shirt made his neck feel as if it were poking out the end of a stovepipe. His hands, extending from the crisp, white cuffs that his mother had so painstakingly ironed, seemed to belong to someone else entirely. They were a man's big hands.

"No," he said again. "I mean, afterward, I tried hard to be happy about it, because we *did* win. If the ref didn't see me, that was his fault, not mine. But it's not that way. I mean, not being seen doesn't make any difference."

The car hit a pothole and jounced. "We're going pretty fast,

Bob," Ginny said. "If you want to talk, maybe we should pull over."

Bob slowed the car until the wind from the side window changed to a slow breeze laced with the smell of cut grass from where a county crew had been working on the sides of the road. The cut strips along the road looked pale yellow in the headlights' glare.

"No, I don't want to pull over," he said. "That's what I'm trying to tell you." He shrugged jerkily. "Ginny, I got you out here . . . Well, I did want to get out of that place, like I said, but that wasn't all of it. I got to thinking. I got to thinking about how it would be having you out in the dark in the country, and I got real stupid about it."

Ginny pointed to the right down a crossroad. "The moon," she said, "is over that way."

She sat with her hands clasped in her lap. Grandmother Adams' opal ring, borrowed for prom night, winked up at Bob from her hand like a conscience made of old silver.

Bob made the turn. The moon was coming down now. It was a curved blade arched toward the heart of the world.

"Naomi Peterson nominated me for prom queen," Ginny said. "I said no, that being the queen wouldn't mean as much to me as it would to some of the other girls. But that wasn't the reason." She was staring into her lap, sliding Grandmother Adams' ring back and forth on the third finger of her right hand.

A moth flitted in front of the car. Its wings turned the white of the moon as it was caught in the headlights, then it dissolved into darkness.

"The reason," Ginny said," is that the prom queen couldn't have left early. And I knew you would ask me."

"Wow," Bob said, making the word sound as if he were whispering in the library.

"Are you scared?" she asked. "I am."

He nodded. "Yeah, I . . ." Hs mouth felt full of dry leaves. "What are we going to do about this?"

"Chase the moon, I guess," she said. "And see what happens." She leaned against his shoulder again, but stiffly, like she was being held for the first time.

"How did you know, Ginny? About me. I mean, asking."

She snuggled against him. "I think we've got a lot to talk about, Bobby," she said. "High school's over, and if we don't do . . . something . . . it's going to be over for us, too. Is that what you want?"

Bob thought of her going away to OU in the fall and felt an increasingly familiar lump begin to burn in his throat. "No," he said.

"Nobody cares what we do out here." Ginny's voice was light and flat. "This is moon country." She licked her lips, forcing the words from her throat. "Are you sure you don't want to pull over?"

But the road wouldn't cooperate. It stretched on, seemingly to the end of creation, without so much as a widening for a mailbox.

Bob's hand found the zipper on the back of her dress. He worked it like a combination lock. He opened it like a burglar.

Ginny felt his hand slide hesitantly around her waist, and trembled slightly as the rough, warm fingers moved to cup her breast. She felt them searching, then finding a way under her bra, brushing like feathers and needlepoints against the tip. And like Bob, she sat quietly and looked straight ahead, as if the big excitement was to watch for rabbits.

Bob thought he was never going to stop growing. He thought it was going to keep growing and growing and stand straight up until Ginny would leap to the far side of the car, pointing and demanding to know, "What's *that*?"

The sunflowers rustled and nodded at the sides of the road.

Bob let his hand coast down in a hot, satiny slide to the barrier of an elastic waistband. He glanced at Ginny and caught her glancing back at him. Her face was impossible to read.

She turned and looked out the window on her side. "Where are we, anyway?"

"We've been zigzagging a lot. I'm not sure."

"Oh."

His fingers slid under the elastic. He touched her. There.

"Oh God!" She jerked away sharply. "Oh God!" she cried. "Stop the car!"

Bob pulled away from her like he was five years old again, caught touching his big brother Frank's balsa wood model of a Piper Cub. He looked at Ginny the way he had looked at the bits and pieces of that beautiful little airplane scattered and broken on the floor, all because he didn't have sense enough to keep his hands off.

"Hey, Ginny," he almost shouted, "I didn't mean to—"

"*Stop* the *car!*" She twisted to see out the back window, past the OU parking permit sticker and the KATT radio decal, out into the darkness. "There was—I think there was—a man!"

Bob pushed the brake down, shifting to second. The back lights spilled a red haze into the settling road dust. "I don't see anybody," he said. "You mean walking out here?" He eased the clutch out. The crackling of gravel under the tires was a hoarse whisper, reminding him, suddenly, that they were a long way from town.

"*No!*" Ginny caught his arm in a tight hug. "Not walking. He was crawling, Bob . . .up . . . out of the ditch, and his face was all . . ." Her voice caught in a sob.

Bob felt a blade of cold glass in his throat. "You picked a great time to play spook-out," he said.

"Bob, I'm not playing. I *know* what I saw."

Ahead, suddenly, a black mass at the side of the road took shape as a parked pickup truck, its taillights glowing the color of blood and candlelight. Bob stopped the car. The pressure of his foot against the brake pedal put a shake in his knee. Ginny had already rolled up the window on her side and hit the door lock, and Bob did the same.

Closing the windows, they sealed in a smell of decay that filled the car like a bloated, stirring thing.

"We'll get the sheriff out here," Bob said.

"But . . ." Her voice was high and tight. "Bob, we can't just go off and leave somebody hurt."

Bob glanced backward. "You're *sure* you saw a man hurt in the ditch?"

She nodded, biting the tip of her thumb.

He shifted the car to reverse. The lever locked in place. "Probably some ol' boy got looped up and drove himself off the road," he said. "But the truck doesn't look like it hit anything, so he's probably not hurt—just sick."

"I saw blood on his face, Bob."

"Well . . ." Bob started to back up. "We'll find out." As Ginny pressed against him, he put his arm around her and was startled to discover that the back of her dress was still open. He felt like Saint George—until the car stopped, and then he was plain Bob Wortham again, his heart pounding like a ball against the court.

"I still don't see anybody," Bob said.

Ginny pointed. Her fingertip left a small misty smudge against the window glass. "He was right there."

High grass and weeds dipped and beckoned at the side of the road, hiding the ditch.

Bob fumbled the glove compartment open and found a flashlight. "Ginny, let's just play it safe," he said. "You lock the door behind me, and then you get down, okay? If I don't come back in a few minutes, you get out of here."

"No, Bob, let's just leave. Now."

He shook his head. "You were right the first time. We can't go off and leave somebody in trouble just because it's dark and kind of spooky out here. We're not kids."

"Then I'll go with you."

"No. You do what I said." Bob stepped out of the car. He shut the door. Ginny's hand, reaching toward him, fell instead against the lock button.

She turned to watch him, but he motioned her down. Slowly, she crouched into the seat, then into the space in front of the seat, under the dashboard. The rumbling of the car's engine played against her knees.

Don't think about it. Ginny clasped her arms across her chest. She tried counting. *Don't think about it.* But she hadn't grown up. *Don't think . . .*

Under the house again. Ginny Adams and Marcie Randall were under Marcie's house where the ground was always cool and the sound of footsteps in the kitchen above them was like the devil's heartbeat. They were telling ghost stories in the shadows on a Saturday afternoon.

"Now, this one's not a ghost story," Marcie said. Almost seven, she wielded the authority that came with being two years older than Ginny. "This one is true."

"Aw, how do you know?"

"Because it happened to my sister's best friend's cousin," Marcie said, and her eyes went wide. "That's how."

Ginny swallowed and tugged at the hem of her skirt.

"See, this girl and her boyfriend were out driving la-a-te one night," began Marcie. "And they didn't know there was a maniac loose in the country. And the car broke down, and the boyfriend said, 'You stay in the car. I'm going to get help.' And he didn't come back, and he didn't come back . . ."

The story ended with the girl getting out of the car the next morning, looking up, and finding her boyfriend hung from a tree branch just overhead, dangling from a rope, the rope connected to a hay hook that had been stuck through his back, right between his shoulder blades. And his throat had been cut.

The story also ending with Ginny running home crying, and with Marcie's dad nailing a big board over the crawl space, so there wouldn't be any more ghost stories, at least not there. It ended with Ginny starting to cry again whenever she was taken in the car at night and crying uncontrollably if her daddy got out of the car.

Now, twelve years later, she was crying again.

Don't let it rain, she cried in prayer. *Just don't let it rain*, because in Marcie's story, the girl had been listening to rain on the car top all night, only the rain was her boyfriend's blood.

The door latch clicked on Bob's side.

Ginny gasped, looking up. The side window framed a void of black space and stars.

"Bob?" she called softly. "Bob, don't fool around with me."

The latch clicked again, again, again—with a tugging each time that made the car dip a little toward the driver's side.

"Bob, it's locked, remember? Is that you? Do you want in?"

Ginny wanted to melt into the car. She wanted to be steel and plastic and not alive.

There was a scraping against the outside of the door.

Then—a hand hit the glass. The palm was flat against glass, pressed flat and cold white, the nails long and curling under. It hit with the sound of a butcher dropping a slab of red steak on the counter.

Ginny tasted a salty warmth flooding into her mouth, unaware of how badly she'd bitten her lip.

A second hand followed, splatting flat against the glass.

Rising between them, the head appeared. Tight, hairless skin the color of sour milk stretched over the top of the skull. The head rose. The eyes came over the window rim, eyes narrowed, then suddenly wide and glowing with moonlight and murder at the sight of Ginny.

One of the hands clenched into a fist and came down against the window.

Ginny screamed until her throat scalded, but the glass didn't shatter.

The face, still in the window, had become a thing of mist and imagination. It was a face seen in a cloud, a face twisted in utter rage, the mouth forming dark and silent words, the eyes staring at her . . .

And then, it was gone.

"Ginny! Ginny, open up."

It was Bob. She felt the flashlight beam on her face, heard his voice yelling: "What's the matter? C'mon, Ginny."

She opened the door and fit into his arms like the last, perfect piece in a jigsaw puzzle.

"Hey, now." He stroked her prom night curls. "I found him down there, Ginny. Lord knows who he is or what he's doing out here, but we've got to get him to the doctor. I need you to help me get him out of the ditch."

She was up and out of the car before she knew it, following Bob, clutching his hand, walking through the wall of weeds that bordered the road, then down.

The man was sprawled face down at the bottom. The back of his white shirt was ripped open and mottled red. Beside him, a circle of yellow-white light was reflected against the dark, rippling surface of the shallow water.

They had caught the moon.

3

S unlight, warm and reassuring as a mother's smile, picked its way through the kitchen window, playing off the hanging basket of ivy and the chrome fixtures of the sink. The little stained-glass bird and butterfly that hung opposite each other in the sun's path caught the light in miniature explosions of sparkling, bright color.

The kitchen itself—spacious, orderly, warm—blended into a dining room, and the sun sought out the dining room too, trapping swirling phantoms of cigarette smoke from the ashtray on the table.

A woman sat at the table, staring down at the coffee cup cradled in her hands. She was thirtyish, blonde, and freshly dressed, with an aura of quiet, tired authority about her. Her crisp light blouse looked almost stiff in the morning sun. Next to her sat a little girl, a miniature carbon copy, in front of a half-eaten bowl of cereal.

"Mommy?"

"What, hon?" the woman asked softly, stubbing out her

cigarette and rubbing her temples with her palms, suddenly realizing how good it felt to close her eyes.

"Mommy . . . I'll be real quiet."

"Good. You do that."

The little girl hesitated, swishing a spoon around in her cereal bowl. Without looking up, she said: "I mean . . . I'll be real quiet if I can just . . . um . . . go get Christy."

The nerve endings of the woman suddenly leaped, died, and left a throbbing echo. Her hands stiffened at her temples, and she squeezed her eyes together harder, fighting the impulse to scream.

"Annie," she began, her voice a velvet hammer. "I said you couldn't go in there. Not yet."

"Mommy . . ."

"I'll *get* your doll for you, Annie. In a minute. But I just have to rest a little longer, until I get my third or fourth wind."

Silence. In the blessed silence, the woman felt the dirty metallic taste of nicotine burning at the base of her tongue, thickening in her throat.

Then: "But I'll be—"

The woman's head snapped up, tensing but only for a moment. It was patience-testing time, she knew that, and she had to fight, to maintain control, to act calm and rational. *You can give it away with your eyes.*

"Is it because somebody's in there? Is that it, Mommy?" The little girl smiled up at her. "That's it, isn't it?"

The phantoms were floating all around him, like sooty black cotton, making it hard for him to take a breath. He was drowning in them and when he opened his mouth, they stuffed it full of steel wool and jammed it down his throat, making him swallow it. He lay on his back on Aunt Lucy's kitchen table, and his friends—Cheryl and Jerry and Aunt Lucy—gathered around him, looking down, and he couldn't move and couldn't breathe because the phantoms were there and other people were there too, bearing down on him, suffocating him with their weight. Then he was up and mingling with them, looking down at himself on the kitchen table and he turned into Aunt Lucy lying on the table in her dotted Swiss church dress, and the phantoms had metamorphosed into a crowd that milled and murmured in dark voices around him. He looked again and Aunt Lucy was Jerry and Jerry was him and everybody was on the table at the same time, lying stiffly, eyes open, but all in one body, a swirl of images about him, he saw Cheryl, standing off to the side by the refrigerator, a smile on her face as she nibbled on a chocolate chip cookie and looked at him/Jerry/Aunt Lucy on the slab table, and it frightened him, a fright that breathed a hoarse promise of horrible things to come.

Then—suddenly—he was alone, alone and lying on . . . a cold, wet table in the cold . . . wet. . . dark. . . cellar. And he couldn't move.

───────────────

"We brought Mr. Winters in late last night," said the woman, in slow even tones. A new cigarette burned in the ash tray. "Remember when I came in and told you everything was all right?"

The little girl nodded.

"He was hurt very badly. He had to have stitches."

The girl's eyes widened. "How many stitches, Mommy?"

"A lot. On his back. He was hurt other places, too. I put bandages on him and put him to bed."

"Why didn't he go to the hospital where your other people go?"

The woman remembered the cigarette, reached for it, and took a long drag before continuing. "It's a long way to the hospital, and it's very crowded. I thought I could take better care of Mr. Winters here. Besides"—and for a moment, just a moment, she turned her eyes away—"Mr. Winters and I used to be friends, a long time ago, when I was a little girl."

"Like Jim Bill and me?"

"That's right."

"Jim Bill's my boyfriend." The little girl paused. "Was Mister . . ."

"Winters."

"Was Mr. Winters *your* boyfriend?"

The woman smiled. "I guess so."

"Did . . . um . . . did you have to give him a shot?"

"Yes."

The girl made a face. "Oooooh. I don't like shots."

"I know you don't," said the woman lightly. She stood up and stretched. From somewhere had come a tiny burst of new energy that she knew to be adrenalin. It would help, would get her through another hour or so, and then maybe some more coffee. She would last as long as she could last, and then she would sleep.

There was a flash in the kitchen window. A car was pulling into the driveway outside her house. Quickly she went to the window and looked out, watching as the light-blue late-model Ford with "County Sheriff's Office" stenciled across the side lurched to a stop. More adrenalin. She pulled the curtain back across the window.

"Who is it, Mommy?"

She turned to her daughter. "Go see if Mr. Winters is

awake yet. Open the door quietly and see if his eyes are open. I'll be there in a minute."

When the little girl left, Dr. Cheryl Stanton stretched again, a longer one this time, and went to the door to let Herb Jeffries in.

———

W hite.

The white of pain and suffering and cleansing and it's all over now. The white that movie screens fade to when everything's over and the lights come up and it's time to go home. Mick Winters saw all white and suddenly knew he was lost, away from home and lost, looking up at a dead white ceiling, smelling the whiteness. He bolted upright and immediately felt white pain tear a swath through his back. He groaned, falling back onto the bed and squeezing his eyelids together hard.

Taking a couple of long, deep breaths, he waited for the pain to subside before opening his eyes again. He was in bed, the weight of a crisp sheet on his body. He raised his head a little and looked down the length of the bed, past the foot and across the room to a large, shaded window. Behind the shade, he could make out angular pieces of colored glass. He saw the pale sun through the shade and the glass, the light broken down into pastel pinks and oranges and blues.

Mick slowly turned his head to one side. He was wearing a white hospital gown, starched and crisp like the sheets. He shrugged his shoulder and the gown rustled.

There was a noise to his right, and he moved his head toward the sound. A door opened, and there appeared a small girl, all blonde and white and clean. Her mouth was a dainty, surprised O that matched her eyes.

Cheryl, he thought, looking at the girl, and the dream washed over him like quicksilver, weighting him back down. He opened his mouth to say something, but the door whispered shut and the child was gone.

Mick felt the soothing touch of the pillow caressing the back of his head. The dream residue clutched at him with icy, liquid tendrils, clasping his temples and pulling. He lay back hard and breathed heavily, giving himself up to the weight as his mind struggled.

What *was* it? What had happened?

"Mick?" The voice shocked him, a jolt away from the dream weight and into the white light. He opened his eyes and saw the face of a woman.

His lips moved. His mind raced. The word, the name, came out unconsciously.

"Cheryl?"

The woman nodded. "That's right. How do you feel?"

"I—fine. No. Lousy."

She nodded again and withdrew her face. The face in the dream. Mick struggled to one elbow and, trying to ignore his pain, watched her as she walked around the room, raising shades on windows. She was beautiful, always had been, grown up now—but why was she here? With him and the white sheets and the white ceiling and the dull pulsing white pain?

"You're Cheryl Mallis."

She paused and turned to face him. Behind her, the sunlight blazing through the window nearest her picked up the blondeness of her hair and gave it little gleaming edges, just like all those golden summers ago when they ran and played together in the backyards and vacant lots of Tanapah.

"That's right, Mick. Actually, it's Stanton now. Cheryl Stanton. I'm a—your—doctor." She paused, and her eyes flashed to the doorway. "I think you can come in now," she called.

Mick had started to say "Doctor?" to Cheryl, but the word froze in his throat as a man entered the room and walked around to the side of the bed where Cheryl stood. He had on a white shirt and gray slacks, bootcut, so that his highly shined cowboy boots would fit under the cuff. There was a cowboy hat in his hand, and he wore a gun belt with a big, pearl-handled revolver in its holster.

"This is Herb Jeffries," said Cheryl. "Sheriff's office."

"Hello, Mr. Winters." The voice came out slow and deep and old, a *basso profundo* that sounded like it should belong to a horror movie actor instead of the thin young man. "Could I ask you a few questions?"

Mick started to speak, and then something, a strong, deep, black, awful something washed through him, and he clenched his fists. A memory thrust itself back against his body, insistent and overwhelming, dark and empty and confusing. He was out in the night with Jerry, his old friend Jerry, and they were half-drunk and intent upon something. He was at the wheel, but it was Jerry's pickup, and they were talking . . .then the culvert, and Jerry, and something about a dare.

Yes, that was it. A dare. And then Jerry taking off his shirt ("Just got this. It's right out of the package.") Mick throwing the shirt down. Jerry in the culvert. Jerry—!

"About Jerry?" Mick asked suddenly. "Questions about Jerry?"

Cheryl and Jeffries looked at each other, and then she said, "Yes, Mick. About Jerry."

"What's happened?"

Silence.

Mick felt their eyes on him, and he raised himself more, pushing the pillow back against the head of the bed and inching up, the effort of it weaving more white threads of pain across his back.

"What's *happened* to Jerry?" Mick asked again.

Cheryl moved quickly in front of him, toward the door. "I'll get some chairs," she said.

Jeffries nodded and looked back at Mick. "Mr. Meyers is dead, Mr. Winters." His low bass rumbled. "He's awful bad dead."

The words detonated right behind his eyes. Mick wanted to double up and clutch his stomach, but the pain in his back held him taut. The bar, the truck, the gravel road, Jerry. . .

"He was dead when we got there."

The shirt, the culvert, I dare you, dareyou dareyou. . .

"Maybe you can tell us how."

Mick forced his eyes open, and the eyes of the lawman pinned him, a tight stare shot through with accusation, bewilderment, and even fear. Once again, as in the dream, Mick felt gripped by a dark force, an evil, living, breathing, suffocating force. He broke himself away from the eyes and lay back in bed, closing his own eyes and drowning in the memory. It was at first a wild confusion of images—country darkness, the smell of dry weeds and sunflowers, and gasoline fumes, and the bloated feeling of too much beer. He fought it, but the dam was crumbling and it all rushed back.

He heard Cheryl come back with the chairs, heard the swishing of clothes and the scraping of chair legs on carpet. He opened his eyes. The light through the stained glass reflected patterns on the ceiling. When he finally spoke, it wasn't to Cheryl or to Jeffries, but to the ceiling and the colored sunlight that made it look like church.

"He's . . . dead."

"Yes." Cheryl's voice, this time very near him, on the other side of the bed.

"We were at a bar. Scot's Tap. I ran into Jerry there . . . I've just been back in town a day . . . my aunt's place."

"Go on, Mick."

"We . . . had a few beers. Talked about the old times. Got around to what we used to be scared of. When we were kids."

An image of the cellar door appeared before him. Alone in the cellar, alone and damp and . . . he closed his eyes, opened them. A breeze from the window stirred through the room, making the lights on the ceiling move a little, like sunlight on a lake.

Mick let the air out of his lungs and continued, feeling the presence of their faces beside him, the weight of them.

"We got in Jerry's pickup and drove out . . . there. I know it sounds . . . but we were out there looking for the . . . whatever . . . that scared him. In the culvert."

Dark clouds of pain gathered around Mick's back, and he tried to squeeze in his shoulder blades together. Outside, far away like some distant memory, he heard the laughter of children.

"About what time did you leave the bar, Mr. Winters?" It was the low voice of the lawman.

Images of Scot's Tap. The Coors sign, the pool table. Peanut shells crunching under his feet.

"Must've been eleven . . . no . . ." He forced himself to remember, to concentrate on the trivial things, blocking out the greater horror. "Eleven thirty, maybe eleven forty-five."

"Go on."

The pain was a vise now. Tightening, the pain of memory and the physical pain. Mick went limp on the bed, thinking: *If I lay perfectly still, everything will go away, and I'll be through with this and I won't want to scream anymore.*

"Something . . . touched . . . me." He closed his eyes, opened them, and turned slowly until his eyes met theirs. Their faces hung over him, as heavy as overripe fruit. His pain increased, and he felt moisture beginning to form around the rims of his eyes. "Something touched me," he said again, his voice cracking.

He lay back down, not caring about anything but the pain. Dimly, he heard their voices, but he couldn't follow their conversation and didn't care. He had a lot of questions, but they were spectral and unformed. They hovered outside, on the periphery of his brain, vaguely threatening shapes like the half-seen figures on lonely, dark city streets that don't become frightening until they step into the light.

Tears squeezed out and slid down his cheeks. They, too, were vague, leaving little drying salt trails as they rained. The pain was the only reality for him now. He felt his arm being lifted and was hardly aware of alcohol being rubbed into the fleshy part of his bicep and the needle going in. The pain soon dulled to slow tendrils, crawling and flexing, sliding under the skin and through the muscles of his back like sightless, thick worms.

After a time, he heard Cheryl ask, "Better?"

His tears had dried and only the salt remained, tiny, microscopic crystals that tightened the skin of his cheeks. Cheryl's hand slipped into his. He tried to open his eyes but couldn't. Through the haze, he heard himself say, "I . . . had a dream, Cheryl. I had a dream, and you were in it. And Jerry and Aunt Lucy. But then you were gone. All gone." He heard his voice change then, to a little boy's, slipping away from him.

"Don't leave me, not here, it's so cold here. Don't let him get me. *Goofus!*"

4

M ick drifted in dark clouds that rolled through his mind, a storm of nightmares.

He fought to escape, and . . . *there!* A window. A lace-curtained window and blue sky beyond it.

Her reached toward the window. His fingers trembled inches from the sunlight-sparkled glass. But the clouds overtook him.

The window was boarded over, and the boards were thick and splintered and painted red. And behind them . . . from behind them, he heard a grating sound, a clawing sound, ripping the wood.

And he screamed.

He screamed.

Hattie Redmiller, working in her flower garden, glanced up toward the window on the second floor of the Stanton house. She could see the lace curtains ruffling slightly in the warm breeze. Beyond that, nothing.

But that sound . . .

It could have been the television. She hoped it was the television.

But she'd seen the Hardage Funeral Home ambulance arrive at the doctor's house late the night before and had watched from her own bedroom window as a man was carried inside on a stretcher.

She set the hoe aside.

She brushed her hands.

A pie. She would go to the kitchen and make a lemon chess pie to take next door. It was little Annie's favorite. It might help somebody.

It couldn't hurt.

Herb Jeffries was home late. On Saturdays, he usually closed the office around noon. He had promised to take the twins fishing.

Herbie met him at the door, looking up at him silently. Then Jill. They were two little four-year-old pools of betrayal.

"How's it goin', cowboy," Jeffries said, and reached to give Herbie a tickle, but the boy scowled stubbornly.

"They don't understand," Donna Jeffries said, appearing behind them. She lifted Jill and kissed her. "You could have called, Herb. I know you were busy with poor Mr. Meyers being hurt, but—"

"He ain't *hurt*. He's *dead*."

Her eyes shot down to her children and then back up at Jeffries, accusingly. "Herb, the children are listening."

"Murdered, I think," he said.

Herbie pointed a finger at Jill and yelled: "Bang! Bang! Kill 'em."

"Your supper's cold," said Jeffries' wife. "You can heat it yourself."

M atthew Simmons was tired. The ache had started in his head and spread all the way to his fingertips, like it always did when he worked too late. But it was done—at least *this* story.

That was the trouble with stories, he thought, pulling the last sheet out of the typewriter and looking at it absently. When you got rid of one, there was always another to do, and then another, stretching out into infinity. You took it down and got the facts and knocked it out until it was in neat columns where it made some sense—and then, the next one.

Matthew Simmons ran a hand through his hair. It was like that the mythological beast—the Hydra—where you lopped off one head and two took its place, he thought. Only the heads were people and places and things and events, and you always thought maybe, just maybe, the next one would be different.

He'd be finding that out soon enough.

Simmons scanned the copy, put it down, and thought about having a drink out of the bottle in his desk drawer. He decided against it. Too much to do.

And he knew that whatever he found out, after he had put out the lights in the *Tanapah Herald* building, shut the door, and taken the four or five block walk, he would take the facts and bend them and sanitize them and run them through his typewriter, and they would come out in palatable and easy-to-digest form for the people of Tanapah, his readers.

Like the story he had just finished—all that anybody needed to know about the services held for Oscar Bradley, the town's late mayor who had died in bed. A simple story, to the point, and perfectly right for the town and its paper.

Simmons could have said that the mayor's principal accomplishment during his year and a half in office was getting a mercury vapor lamp installed just down the street from his own yard. He could have said how odd it was that Mayor Bradley had died in bed, his eyes open, of no really known cause. He could have even talked about the squabble that was sure to come about in the city council when it tried to appoint a next-in-line.

Instead, the reported facts were simply that Oscar had died, had been buried, and would be missed.

Matthew Simmons stood and stretched, snapping off the desk light. And now, another story. And not a very good one, any way you cut it.

It was Saturday night, and he felt special, in the way he always felt special whenever he had to work late to get the job done.

But he couldn't rest. There was another story, and he had to check it out.

For almost three years now, Saturday night had meant only one thing to Dwight Braden, and that one thing was *Nightmare Theater*, which came to him at eleven thirty every week over KTLU-TV, Channel 3. Forget about parties, or running around, or the nightclubs and discos that lay somewhere out in the darkness beyond Tanapah like man-made, unreachable stars. He didn't care, didn't think, didn't wonder about anything else, it sometimes seemed, except Count Downe and his corny jokes and the glow of the television tube in a living room with all the lights out.

And the movies. Especially the movies.

He had seen mummy movies and vampire movies and one movie about this tree on a faraway island that came to life and killed people. Werewolf movies and creature-from-the-sea movies and all the Frankensteins and lots and lots of others.

He loved them with a deep and trusting love, never analyzed, only felt. In his waking hours, he and his friends talked about them, bought magazines about them, and even borrowed Jeff Conover's dad's movie camera one time and made a monster movie of their own. Jeff had forgotten and opened the camera in the daylight, so a lot of it didn't come out, but what they had was really good, they all agreed, and someday they would write a real script and do it again.

Except that things had been changing lately, and Dwight sometimes wondered if they ever really would do it again. It frustrated him, made him mad to think about some of his friends, their sudden lack of interest in what they all had shared together. But it was there, and it couldn't be helped.

His friends were growing up. In the past year alone, several of the guys that used to watch the movies at each other's houses had decided that Count Downe was dumb, and they didn't mind telling Dwight at all. One time Danny Lane started teasing him at school, right in front of Mary Alice Lambert, and Dwight just got redder and redder in the face and Mary Alice laughed and he felt like a kid, the littlest, dumbest kid on the face of the earth. He went home and for days he thought about showing Danny a thing or two. There would be a fire at the school, and Mary Alice would be caught under a pile of collapsed rubble in the middle of it; she would be coughing and crying for help, and everyone, even Danny, would be scared to go in after her, but Dwight would grab up his shirt and wrap it around his face and run through the blaze, his eyes burning, and dig Mary Alice out, carrying her in his arms to safety. Or the communists from Cuba would invade Tanapah, and have the police and everybody cornered in Summer's Grocery, and Danny and Mary Alice would be there, the Cubans getting ready to shoot them all—and Danny would be whining and blubbering, "*Please* don't shoot me," and just as they raised their rifles, Dwight would shoot from a rooftop with his pellet gun and knock the first Cuban down, and they would all come after him and the people would escape.

He didn't talk much about Count Downe to his friends anymore, and he wasn't quite sure why, except he felt a gnawing fear that they might embarrass him, and he was twelve going on thirteen and embarrassment was worse to him than almost anything else he could think of, if only because he had to deal with the threat of it every day.

This evening, he was on his way to his friend Mike Henshaw's house. Mike was probably his best pal, even though he was only a fourth grader and that bothered Dwight a little. But Mike was smart, and knew his monster movies, and they had a lot of fun together.

Dwight walked along in the dying rays of the sun, down the sidewalks when there were sidewalks, and along the edge of the street when there were just yards. He passed his English teacher's house and saw her husband out in the yard, coiling a hose, cut through Mrs. Floyd's backyard, past the neat rows of pansies and geraniums turned black and white by the dusk, and came out by the Fishers' old rock house with the rotting gazebo in the back that looked in the dark like the skeleton of some giant animal.

On the way, he thought about the summer vacation that was coming up, and the trip to Grand Lake he and his folks had planned, and about Mary Alice and how the silky fine hair on her arms sometimes looked in math class when the sun slanted through the windows just right, and then he thought, for the hundredth time or more, about his special fantasy, a fantasy that was forever undergoing tiny revisions and embellishments, like the adjustments a watchmaker would make on a delicate and expensive timepiece. He and Mary Alice would meet each other at the Chieftain Theater, like they did almost every Friday night, and he would go to get some popcorn between features, and when he came back some teenage thugs—he thought they were probably motorcycle guys on marijuana or something like that—would have moved in and gotten fresh with Mary Alice. He would race down the threadbare carpeted aisle of the theater just as they were dragging her, kicking and screaming, out the rear exit. Before anybody else did anything, he would dive into them, feeding them knuckles in a bloody and protracted melee, taking them on alone, banging them against trash cans and walls until the fight was gone out of them and the police had roared in.

It was a good fantasy, one he hardly ever tired of. As he walked, he played certain scenes over in his mind again, especially the one with Mary Alice holding onto his arm as the police and people gathered around him, calling him a hero, and he had almost gotten to Old Miss Roe's place before he realized he hadn't thought about the horror movie at all. And it was supposed to be a good one, too, Boris Karloff in *The Body Snatcher*.

He sighed as he passed the old woman's tiny home, her pigeons cooing from the roof into the evening air. It seemed like the movies just hadn't been as good lately. They didn't seem to have that warm magic, that special something, that the old ones did. He really hoped that tonight would be better. Even Count Downe wasn't looking like he used to. Used to be, thought Dwight, he was real scary and funny at the same time. *Now he just seems tired, like my grandpa, and his jokes aren't very funny anymore.*

Before he realized it, Dwight was almost upon the old house.

He slowed his pace just a little and gazed up at it. An old three-story white house with gray curtains webbed across the windows. It was always dark, and the windows were always closed, the sooty panes clamped down tight. Around the house ran a tall picket fence, the whitewash streaked with age and blotched by the brown wood that showed through in dirty patches.

And he remembered the story.

You walk by a picket fence, after dark, and there's a monster on the other side, watching you through the spaces between the slats. If you look, you can't see him because he's too quick, but he's there, pacing your steps, walking the same distance you walk, and when you get to the end of the fence, quick, like a spider grabbing a moth, he leaps out and wraps his arms around you . . .

His friend Mike wouldn't walk by that fence. He'd go across the street.

It was almost completely dark now. The fence jutted through the settling night like white buoys on a lonely ocean.

Dwight walked past the first slat. His foot landed hard on the old WPA sidewalk, Johnson grass and weeds sprouting up through the cracks.

Second slat.

Dwight shot a glance at the fence, but he couldn't see anything.

Behind it, the dark house, the old house of forbidden

secrets, where people lived who never opened their windows or turned on their porch light. A dark, nasty house.

Third slat.

He looked up at the moon. A quarter moon, almost. He felt like it was looking back at him, making him feel like the only living person in Tanapah.

Fourth, fifth, sixth slats.

The nearest streetlight was two blocks away. He saw it in front of him, glowing dimly atop its pole, like home free in kick-the-can, a place where he'd be safe. He wanted to run.

What would Mary Alice think?

Seven, eight, nine, and ten, and he could see the end of the fence, where it met the corner of the sidewalk. He heard the sound of his breathing, loud in the heavy spring air, coming out in little ragged spurts. There was a lightness in his head. A dog barked from a yard in the distance, and the bark turned into a long howl. The black, colorless thickness of night had replaced the brown of dusk. He felt himself sweat.

Five more to go.

The monster shuffles along beside you, behind the fence, his hands dragging along the grass, looking, always looking, his dead face scraping along the wood as he watches you. You.

Right before the end, he drew up short, almost paralyzed, trying to think of anything but monsters. He tried to start his fantasy with Mary Alice, to fall back on it, but it wouldn't come. Images came to him: how she looked in the summer, her ponytail tied back, her freckles, the way she laughed when he did a wheelie on his bike in front of her house.

Dwight heard something move behind the fence. A rustling. A scraping. The dog began to howl again, like a lonely coyote.

He took a step. And then another.

The rustling stopped.

His foot hit the angle of the sidewalk just underneath the end of the fence. He looked down at his tennis shoe like it was no longer a part of him. And suddenly he was sprinting, head down, past the end of the fence and into the blacktopped street. In the middle of the street, he whirled around and faced the fence's edge, ready to take off again.

Nothing. There was nothing there at all.

He stood for a long moment, the breath dying in him. He stared behind the fence, at weeds trailing up into the cracks, at old concrete blocks and bricks and a garden someone had started a long time ago. He looked again at the house, the dark house where probably some old people lived who just couldn't get out much and didn't feel like opening their windows.

Dwight started to smile, and then the smile dropped. Looking at the house and the fence, he felt relieved, mainly; but mixed in with the relief, washing through him deeply and thoroughly, was a little sadness, an ache, a vague longing for things that would never, could never, be the same again. Standing there in the deserted street, he suddenly, stupidly, wanted to cry.

But he didn't. He stared at the old fence and the old house there in the dark for a while longer, and then he turned his back on them and continued down the street to his friend Mike's house, thinking about summer vacation and Mary Alice Lambert and not thinking much at all about the horror movie he was going to see that night.

5

It was a six-block walk from downtown to Matthew Simmons's home, if he took the shortest way. In wintertime, he would follow the path of his own footprints through the snow: in spring, he would watch for new bird nests in the elm trees that lined the sidewalk.

The old town tried not to show its age, he reflected. There were new fronts on some of the stores. Hell, there was even a new motel at the edge of town, with a restaurant that had lured the Kiwanis Club away from the Wide Awake Café downtown for the first time in seventeen years. One thing about the town of Tanapah, though, that tipped off its years and that couldn't be repainted or fronted over, was that it had sidewalks.

He passed the Redmillers' house and glanced over to see the dark figure of Otis Redmiller sitting on the front porch.

"'Lo, Matthew," Otis called. "Workin' late I see."

Simmons waved and replied without slowing down, "No rest for the wicked, Otis."

Behind him, he heard Otis Redmiller chuckle, "Guess not," followed by the protesting squeak of the screen door and Hattie

Redmiler's voice. "That man has just *got* to learn to take it easier. Him, at his age."

And from Otis: "Shoot. Wish he wasn't in such a hurry. I was fixin' to ask him . . ."

The voices were lost, then, to the sound of Matthew Simmons's shoe heels hitting the sidewalk in the quick one-two rhythm of a man with business to see about. Home was another two blocks away, but he began to slow his pace.

He felt good, and he shouldn't have. He ought to have been aching over what had happened to Jerry Meyers, as the rest of the town was doing. He would have ached, too, if he had let himself recall the young Jerry, pedaling up to the front door of the *Herald* building on a red Schwann with training wheels and asking for a paper route, or the page one announcement of Jerry's wedding, or last week, even—the picture showing Jerry with a stringer of six catfish he'd caught. Three of those fish were wrapped in tinfoil in the freezer at Matthew Simmons's house and would stay there now, because Jerry was gone.

He couldn't help feeling a little excited though, and he realized it was because the old gears had started to work again inside him. For whatever it was worth, tonight he was a *news*man again, not a filler of scrapbooks but a genuine, by-damn man of the press.

Just ahead, posted in the front yard and barely visible despite the light from the homes on the street, was a white wooden sign proclaiming in neat black letters: "Cheryl A. Stanton, D.O. Osteopathic Medicine."

Medicine. Damned drawers full of medicine.

He stopped.

Matthew Simmons had gotten his first job on a newspaper in Chicago right out of high school. The job guaranteed him $25 a week, a permanent supercharge of adrenalin, and a shake in his hands that started after the first month. They put him on the big city police beat.

In taxis, on foot, and sometimes by bicycle, he had charged around the city, trying to beat the cops to the scene, badgering the homicide squad for the details that made a good story: caliber of the gun, length of the knife blade. He wrote about shotgun killings in the slums and about husbands and wives shot to death with polite, silver-colored little automatics in the rich neighborhoods. He had felt sick from the start, and his stomach burned unceasingly.

They moved him off the beat side, finally, and made him a copy editor, and then assistant city editor. For a while, he kept the medicine in his desk drawer out of sight. Before long he simply left it on his desk within handy reach and watched the liquid level in the dark amber bottle drop as the day went on. His stomach still burned.

On his thirty-first birthday, at twelve minutes before deadline on the final home edition, with one inch of the white, milky gunk showing at the bottom of the bottle, Matthew Simmons calmly and deliberately dropped his pencil into the wastebasket. He pushed the papers on his desktop away from him, stood up, and said, "I will not spend another minute of my life doing this." And he walked out.

Eventually he had come to Tanapah—and to the *Herald*—where the big news tended to be who had supper where last night, even with the rumblings of war coming from overseas. Eventually, there was nothing left of the medicine on Matthew Simmons's desktop but a series of ring stains where the bottle had been.

Standing in front of the doctor's sign, he flinched at the voice inside him: *Bullshit, Simmons. Bullshit to feeling noble.*

A town that kept its head was noble. A town that took care of its people was noble. And if there was one way that one man might have a right to feel noble by himself, it was by taking care of the town.

The town didn't need a seventy-one-year-old news chaser running around, hollering out the awful truth about Jerry Meyers. It needed to be told that, yes, something very bad had happened; but just as much, it needed to be told that things were going to be all right.

He took and released a deep breath, then moved ahead at his regular, slower gait up the walk to the front steps of the two-story white frame house, brushing past the lilac bushes just coming into bloom.

Still, what Tanapah needed to know was one thing. What Matthew Simmons needed to know was something else. He didn't feel so good anymore, but he still felt the fires. He had a job to do.

Taped over the doorbell was a note: "Patient asleep. Please knock quietly." Simmons rapped twice against the glassed part of the door and waited.

In a moment, he was looking down and smiling broadly at the little girl who opened the door. "Why hello, Annie," he said. "Say, that's a pretty dress you're wearing."

She tugged at the hem of the dress, a blue flowered print with white lace around the neck. "My mommy made it," she said.

"I'll just bet she did. And is your mommy here?"

From inside the house, he heard footsteps coming toward the doorway and a woman's voice saying, "Who is it, Annie? Oh . . ." Cheryl appeared in the doorway. "Hello, Mr. Simmons."

"Good evening, Cheryl." He nodded to her pleasantly, thinking, *Lord, to be younger.*

"Come in." She swung the door open. "Please. What can I do for you?"

"Well-l-l . . ." Stepping inside, Simmons pulled a peppermint candy wrapped in cellophane from his coat pocket and handed it to the little girl. She glanced at her mother before taking it.

"Say thank you," Cheryl said.

She did and skipped off down the hallway. Simmons's eyes followed the child and noted that on one side of the hall a door was open, revealing a white-walled room with glass-fronted cabinets and a doctor's table in the center.

"Well, I could bore you with stories of all the aches and wheezes that go with getting to be an old coot," he said. "And one of these days, maybe I will."

She laughed. "How many times have I heard that? But today's not the day?"

He shook his head, holding to a tight eye contact with her. "I talked to Herb Jeffries earlier today, Cheryl. He said your patient ought to be coming around about now. I stopped by to chat with him." He reached into his coat pocket again. "Candy?" he offered.

She took the candy but didn't unwrap it. "He needs a lot of rest at this point, Mr. Simmons," she said. "I think he's been questioned enough for one day."

"Questioned?" His bushy white eyebrows went up like skyrockets. "Cheryl, I knew that boy from when he used to sneak into my backyard and steal green apples, and there never was a better woman than his Aunt Lucy, God rest her. I just wanted to see how he was getting along."

The first hints of a smile played at the corners of Cheryl Stanton's mouth. "Tell me something, Matthew Simmons," she said lightly. "Did this foxy grandpa routine always work for you?"

"Nope," he replied. "Not until I got old enough to be a grandpa."

"Well . . ." She glanced down the hallway. "He *is* awake, and I know he'd be glad to see you. But I meant what I said about his needing rest. Don't stay long, and don't say anything to upset him. Doctor's orders."

T he door opened halfway, and Cheryl looked in. "Mick," she said, "you've got a visitor, if you feel up to it."

He didn't. The pain killer was wearing off, and lying there, he was feeling his body come awake a piece at a time. Feeling had returned to his head first. It throbbed and hammered at him. His eyes opened and felt too big to fit the sockets, squeezed and jammed in, bulging. His back was still thick and numb.

She looked at him expectantly.

"Sure," he said.

She disappeared from the doorway, and Mick heard her whisper something in a warning tone. Then she stepped back into the room holding the door open, and said, "It's Matthew Simmons, Mick. You remember?"

The man standing behind her was as familiar a landmark to Mick as the Tanapah water tower. His hair was swept back, silver and thinning, the color complemented by a white mustache. His back was straight as a gun barrel. His face, when he grinned at Mick, became an explosion of lines and creases that hadn't seemed to be there before, radiating mostly from the corners of his eyes.

Matthew Simmons, Mick thought, seemed always to have been old, and yet never to age.

"I remember," Mick's voice came out sounding weaker than

he would have thought possible, "but I wouldn't have thought you would remember me, Mr. Simmons."

Simmons crossed the room to the foot of the bed, then moved to the side where he found a chair and sat facing Mick.

"I recall a certain young boy—mind you, I'm not naming names, Mick—who cut a big chunk out of the cake his aunt was going to enter in the county fair. And she won anyway." Mick saw the old man shift in his seat to glance back at Cheryl, who remained standing in the doorway. When he turned back to Mick, his voice was almost a whisper.

"I want to help you, boy," he said. "Now, I'll tell you quick and straight. The sheriff's got you pegged for killing Jerry Meyers. But as a homicide investigator, ol' Herb knows a lot about parking meters, that's what I'd say. So you tell me one thing, Mick. Has he got it right?"

Mick felt his throat shut. His teeth clenched and his back began slicing at him. *No!* He shook his head.

No! No! No! No!

Cheryl was across the room in a series of fast steps, reaching Mick's bedside and holding his head still between the cool, smooth palms of her hands. She turned sharply to look needle points at Simmons, who had moved out of the way.

"I *told* you . . ." she began, but he cut her off, his voice suddenly gone cold and almost threatening.

"The cuts on his back—what did that to him?"

Cheryl was caught off guard, as if bitten by a friendly old dog. "Why, I don't know."

"Smooth cuts, deep cuts, like a knife? Wide cuts, jagged cuts, spaced cuts, like being raked or being clawed? *Which?*"

"Jag-jagged, hard to sew."

"Like being gouged across the back by a man's fingernails? Say, two men fighting?"

"No," she said. "No. Worse than that." She straightened to face him. "Now that's enough."

Simmons's right arm locked straight out, pointing at Mick. "You can help me get to the truth of it, or you can see that man landed in one hell of a lot of trouble."

"This is the sheriff's business and mine, Mr. Simmons. Not yours."

Mick lay with his eyes closed, the voices swirling around him, seemingly coming at him from both sides and the ceiling all at once.

Simmons's voice boomed, "You said jagged cuts, deep. Now what does that mean? I'd say it means the possibility of a third man—or God knows what else—out there."

Cheryl's reply was determinedly low. "I told you, I don't know. He could have slipped, fallen on something, I don't know—"

"Then *look*, dammit. Think about it. *Somebody's* got to." Simmons's voice paused, dropped back to a normal tone. "Mick?" he said. "Mick, I'm sorry for the fuss here. I'll be back later. We'll get this straightened out, don't you worry about it."

Mick opened his eyes, forcing himself to sit up halfway. "The apple tree," he said, "in front of my aunt's house. Is it still there?"

Simmons hesitated slightly before answering from the doorway, "Was this morning."

Mick let himself fall back again. "Then there's something that's still all right, something real," he muttered.

P ausing outside on the front porch, Simmons said, "I didn't mean to stir things up quite so much, Cheryl, but I did mean it when I said, I'd be back."

"I know," she said. "It's your job, I guess." Her eyes were red-rimmed and shimmery wet.

Simmons shook his head slowly. "No, my job is making sure everybody knows about the 4-H meetings and making sure not to leave the bananas out of the banana pie recipe. Until now anyway."

He turned and headed back down the steps and out into the walk. His stomach burned.

6

It was late, well after midnight. Count Downe, after telling his last joke and selling his last tube of acne cream, had packed it off into the night, leaving behind an empty spotlight, a snowy blank television screen. Mike and Dwight were up in Mike's room, each sitting on one of the twin beds. A pile of monster magazines lay between them on the floor, next to the open box of fat pretzels and the half-empty quart of uncapped Dr. Pepper. Occasionally, ice cubes clinked in their glasses as they turned the magazine pages, absorbed in the photographs and the text.

"I sure think that was one of my favorites," said Mike, and a big pretzel went *craaack!* between his teeth, showering crumbs onto his pajama bottoms. "That was a great part when Karloff came out from under that sheet, all glowy and weird-lookin'—man!"

Dwight nodded not looking up. "Yeah. It was a good one, all right."

There was silence for a few moments. The magazines rustled in their laps.

Mike continued, "I think next to Frankenstein's monster, that's the best role Karloff ever had." He said "Karloff" in the same tones he would've said "Santa Claus" a few years earlier.

Dwight didn't comment. He was looking at a full-page picture of the "Creature from the Black Lagoon," a still from one of the movies. In its arms, cradled gently almost, was a blonde woman in a long white nightgown, her arms hanging limply from her sides, trailing like the gown. Even unconscious, she was beautiful.

Dwight looked at the caption. "Blacky LaGoon carries off Leigh Snowden in U-I's *The Creature Walks Among Us* (1956). Let's hope she doesn't get too *carried away!*"

He studied the picture without really studying it. A late-night breeze rustled the Spider-Man curtains that Mike's mom had made; the warm, humid air signaled the end of spring and the onset of summer.

Dwight felt a creeping restlessness start to work its way into his bones. He couldn't pinpoint it, really, this vague dissatisfaction, but as he stared at the magazine photograph he started to feel as if perhaps he was in the wrong place, sitting up here in this room reading monster magazines, that maybe he should be somewhere else out in the night, somewhere where dark, sweaty bodies pushed against his and the smell of something mysterious hung in the air, where rough voices bumped each other in the dark. He was sitting at a table in that dark, he and Mary Alice, and they were talking low and holding hands across the damp tabletop.

He shifted his shoulders and took a drink of Dr. Pepper. Part of him, most of him before, belonged to the monsters, kept the monsters' secrets safe from the rest of the world. An invisible bond. They slouched and crawled and shambled across the TV screen, their stories broken into neat fifteen-minute chunks by record offers and soft drink ads and the pun-filled jokes of a lonely Count, and he watched it all, keeping their secrets safe, fearing them, loving them.

A part of him belonged to the monsters. But he wasn't looking at the monster now. Instead, he was quietly, almost subconsciously, tracing the dangling leg of the girl as she hung, almost in repose, from the creature's arms in the photo. Dwight followed the curve of her ankle up the inside of the soft, bare leg to the lower edge of the gown, where the merest outline showed through.

Part of him belonged to the monster; but now another part, a part of him that was gaining every day, belonged to the girl. There was no turning back. There were other secrets to keep.

He began to think about Mary Alice's legs.

"Wonder when the movie *The Worm Eaters* is gonna come out? Says here they're makin' it, and this is almost a year old."

Dwight looked up, distracted. Sudden anger flashed in him. Mike was so *dumb*! What did he want to be so *dumb* for? He started to say something, but words wouldn't come. When he looked back down at the magazine, his fingertip was resting gently on the curve of the woman's breast in the photograph. He moved it quickly and flipped the page.

Mike had stopped reading and was staring across the room at him. "Somethin' the matter with you?" he asked.

Dwight stared back, dumbly, the muscles working in his jaws. He wanted to laugh, he wanted to cry, he wanted to jump up and fling the magazine against the wall and throw open the window and yell.

He didn't know why. He fought, trying to keep it under control. He felt embarrassed again, a red, hot embarrassment, like at school with Danny Lane and Mary Alice. *Watchin' your dumb monsters again?*

"I went by the fence today," he said suddenly.

"Huh?"

"I went by that picket fence by that old spooky house. I went by it, *right* by it."

"*That* one?" asked Mike, open-mouthed and incredulous.

Dwight nodded. In spite of himself, a grin split his face. It was a mean grin, a superior grin, a grin that made Dwight feel scary and satanic, like he would enjoy seeing torture and death for real.

"Did not," said Mike, in a voice that indicated he was trying to throw it off, trying to restore the balance that had existed in the room scant moments ago and now threatened to swirl out the window and into the dead night.

"Yes, I did." Dwight's voice was oily, persuasive. "And there wasn't no damn monster there, either." A power was welling up in him, the power of the strong over the weak, the carnivore over its prey, a power so easy to abuse.

"You promise?"

"Yeah." He said it like he'd heard the juvenile delinquent say it in *Little Shop of Horrors*.

"Swear?"

"Yeah. I swear."

"God's word on the Bible?" That was it, the supreme question, the final stopping point for lies.

"God's word on the Bible," said Dwight. "I went by it. In the dark."

"On the same sidewalk in front of it?"

"God's word on the Bible," Dwight repeated. "On the sidewalk in front of it."

Mike leaned against the wall, taken aback. Watching him, Dwight remembered not very long ago one Saturday evening, when they had hidden behind some shrubs across the street and thrown rocks at the house, sticking their heads up just long enough to chunk a rock, and then dropping back down to see if anything would happen. After the ninth or tenth rock, the old screen door had creaked open, tentatively, and they had both crouched in fear as a vague figure appeared in the dark doorway, something where the hand should be glinting in the rays of the dying sun. Later, after they had run off and gotten back to the safety of Mike's home, they both swore that it was a knife they had seen in the hand, a knife with a long, sharp, curved blade.

They hadn't told anyone else.

Mike decided on a new tack. "How come you walked by it tonight, when you never would before?"

"Dunno. Just wanted to."

"Then how come you didn't tell me when you first got here?"

Dwight shrugged elaborately, beginning very much to enjoy lording it over the kid, because that was how he thought of Mike now, as a kid, a little kid who watched horror movies on TV and wasn't interested in girls. "Didn't think it was worth tellin'. Just an old house and an old fence, that's all." He put the magazine aside gently on the bed and grinned again, a grin that felt good, felt bad, a grin that was out of control, that could do great harm and change things forever and there was nothing he could do about it. "That bull about a monster—that's just for *kids.*" The grin had overtaken his face, had control of everything now. He stared hard at Mike, hating himself and glorying in it. "Kids like *you!*"

Mike stared back, open-mouthed. Dwight snorted derisively and looked past Mike, toward the open window and the dumb Spider-Man curtains. A dark, weighty stillness hung suspended in the air between the two of them, a void that had been crossed and could never be recrossed.

"I'm *not* a kid," said Mike, after a moment.

Dwight snorted again. "Yeah, you are."

"Not."

That grin, the dark evil grin. It felt as if it would never leave Dwight's face, that it would be fixed forever, tugging, slicing through the muscles in his cheeks, working his lips back across his teeth until he looked like a snarling dog. "Bet *you* wouldn't go there by yourself."

"I would too." Stinging hot tears of betrayal threatened in Mike's eyes. "I would too."

"Well then . . . let's see you."

"I'll do it tomorrow. First thing when we get up. You can watch me. I'm not scared."

"Yes, you are," Dwight said. "Because *you* think there's something behind there. That's the difference." He stopped a moment, thinking, and the grin cut wider into his face. "The difference is, I know there's not."

"Bull," Mike said uncomfortably. He sniffled and turned his head.

The silence forced itself back between them. A part of Dwight wanted to forget it, forget all that had happened, to go back to leafing through magazines and talking about monsters and being friends again. Another part of him, a deep part that ran through him like an uncontrollable current, knew that there was no way anything could ever be the same anymore. Anything.

"I know something *you're* afraid of," said Mike suddenly. The voice was defiant, but it was a child's voice.

Dwight glanced back at him.

"I know what *you're* afraid of, something you won't do."

At that moment, Dwight felt completely, unshakably safe. There was nothing that could threaten him, nothing at all, especially nothing that a kid like Mike could think up.

"Oh yeah?" he said.

"Yeah." The words began to tumble out. "Remember when you were up here a couple weeks ago and you told me about hanging your arm off the bed when you go to sleep? Huh? You remember that, Dwight?"

The grin was still there, but it had faded a little. "Sure," he returned.

"You said that if you put your arm off the bed in the middle of the night that rats or something worse would come up and chew off your fingers, and you made me close the closet door before we went to bed."

Dwight shot a glance at the open closet at the end of the room, where Mike's monster magazines and comic books and old boxes of other stuff were stacked. It was a deep closet, deep and dark. But Dwight could handle it. He turned back to Mike and said, "Yeah? So what?"

"Well, you're scared about that. You're scared that if you hang your arm off that something will come out and get you in the night."

Dwight snorted.

"You *are!*" Mike continued. "You're scared!" He paused for a moment. "Heck," he said, none too convincingly, "I'm not scared of anything like that, but you are. I've slept with my arm off the bed lots of times."

Dwight had felt a little uncertain for a moment, as if Mike had reached down into him and found a tiny secret nerve and pressed it with his finger. But he forced himself not to think about it, not to think about the things in the night that could come up from under the bed or out of the closet and eat on your fingers or worse, and then, almost immediately, he found that he didn't have to force the thoughts out at all. They were gone. Child's fears.

"That was a couple weeks ago," he said, and it was perfectly clear to him why he shouldn't be scared anymore.

"You're still scared."

Dwight made an elaborate show of taking a sip of his Dr. Pepper, not saying a word.

"You *are*."

Dwight sucked an ice cube up into his mouth and spit it back out in the glass. "Naw. But maybe *you* are."

"Yeah? We'll just see," said Mike quickly, suddenly standing up. He leaned into Dwight's face. "How about if we turn off the light right now, and go to sleep, and I'll leave my arm off the bed? I'm not afraid."

"How will I know if you've got your arm off the bed?"

"Turn on the light anytime you want," said Mike. "You'll see it."

The grin had returned to Dwight again, a hovering, living thing. He looked back up into Mike's eyes. "Okay," he said. "I don't think you can do it. I think you're scared to, but I dare you to hang your arm off the bed tonight. All night."

Mike met his stare. Dwight saw the grin try to flicker across his face, too, but it wasn't there for him, and he couldn't make it work. "And I dare *you*," he said. They shook hands, Mike solemnly, Dwight grinning that awful grin, and then Mike went over and got into his bed.

"Look Dwight," he said, and slowly extended his arm down, until it rested against the wood of the bed frame, the fingers almost brushing the floor. He raised up, switched off the lamp above his bed, and lay down again in the same position.

Dwight nodded and turned off his light. It was silly, the whole thing was a silly crappy child's game and for a moment he thought about not even putting his arm out over the bed, not playing the dumb game at all, because there were other things to think about, grown-up things, important things, things a lot more mysterious than whether you could dangle your arm off a bed or not.

He sighed and lay back in the bed, taking off his pants.

Slowly, his arm slid down the cool sheets and his fingers touched the floor and unfurled. He felt too tired to smile anymore, and the expression left as quickly as if a mask had been lifted, leaving his face blank and empty.

———————

Mike lay in the weighty stillness of the night, occasionally fidgeting. His left arm felt heavy and useless, hanging below him, fingers barely scraping the floor. The tufts of the carpet rested against his knuckles like the stiff bristles of a brush.

And he thought, *You dangle your arm off the bed and there are things in the night, waiting for you to go to sleep.*

His arm jerked a little, settled back.

They're under the bed, big round yellow eyes watching your hand. And they slide silently, like fat furry snakes, until there are lots of them there, the yellow eyes blinking as they line up. In front of them is . . . your hand. Your hand, dangling there in front of them like a worm on a hook, and pretty soon there's lots of them, all watching, crawling around under your bed, and then one of them slithers toward you, and the mouth opens—

A noise! Mike listened. His eyes popped open, and he stared straight ahead, but the darkness of the room was a fog he couldn't penetrate. He forced his eyes closed again, listening hard. The rustling noise was gone.

The wind, he thought. *The wind. The wind.*

There was no breeze in the silent room.

Mike tried to force the thoughts out, to fight the sudden salty taste that had come up in his throat. He thought about Dwight, but then thoughts of Dwight led back around to the monster behind the fence and the people in the old house

behind the fence, and that led back around to the things under
his bed.

Little dark furry things. Things with eyes and claws and
teeth that showed dirty white.

He thought about pulling up his arm, quietly, ever so
quietly, so Dwight couldn't hear, and resting it beside him
under the cool sheet, safe, away from harm, tucked in, safe and
warm.

Now he thought he heard the floor creak, barely under his
bed. The weight. The weight of things gathering, sliding and
crawling and creeping in, silently, lining up, staring at his hand
and then at each other. He listened hard, harder than he had
ever listened to anything before. It seemed as if his whole body
was tensed and attuned to that vague dark space under him,
where the box springs hung like stalactites from the ceiling of a
cave. A cave of monsters.

Outside the bedroom, there was no sound. No sound at all.

Tiny, icy pinpricks began tingling the ends of his fingers.
He wanted to pull his arm up, wanted it more than anything in
the world. But it was all imagination, all his imagination, and
what if Dwight reached up and turned on the light and saw
that he had gotten scared—

What was that? All of him, his body, his energy, his soul
was concentrated on the tingling fingertips. He thought he felt
something brush slightly, ever so slightly, against his hand. His
heart rolled over and pounded dully, like a freshly killed
animal.

That was it. Time for things to be over . . .

No!

Maybe Dwight would find out and maybe he wouldn't. But
Mike would know. That was the thing. Mike would know he
had let himself be scared of something that wasn't . . . probably
wasn't . . . there, just like a little kid, when all he would have to

do to know for sure would be . . . look . . . over the edge . . . of the bed.

Look and see. And go to sleep, then.

Again: something touched his fingers, something furry, but not warm and soft like a furry thing was supposed to be, but scratchy and cold.

Look. Look, and you'll see it's just nothing.

Mike remembered one night when he really *was* a little kid, and he had awakened and seen the head of a wolf, rising up and watching him from the foot of the bed. Black tongue rolling out between its teeth, the wolf had licked its lips—and then it had grinned at him, impossibly, because everybody knows a wolf can't grin, but this one had. And it had frozen Mike, literally frozen him. He'd tried to move, and he couldn't —and to close his eyes, most of all to close his eyes, and he couldn't.

The wolf had come closer, lifting itself over the end of the bed . . . until Mike's leg had jerked, and the bed covers shifted, and then he could see that there was no wolf at all, just the rumpled wad of a quilt. He could see that.

Look, then!

But this was different. It was scary, but there was no magic in it. Mike was scared like he would be scared of a mean dog or scared of falling off a ladder.

He turned his head against the pillow, so he could look down. Very slowly. *You have to be slow and careful. If you move fast, they'll just run off, and you won't ever know if they were there or not.*

The pillow rustled against his ear. Over in the other bed, across the vast floor, Dwight stirred a little. Mike swallowed, and his throat clicked like the latch of an old door.

He looked.

And they looked back at him.

Eyes. Eyes like marbles, green and glittering, attached to nothing, scattered on the floor around his hand.

I should be scared more than this, Mike thought, amazed at himself. *I should be scared like crazy.*

But he wasn't. He was scared, but not like the wolf had scared him. And more than that, the really amazing thing was that he was thinking like somebody in a comic book. He was thinking in clear words you could draw a line around that looked like a cloud, floating over his head at the end of a row of little bubbles.

And he was being answered:

I always knew you were there.

WE ALWAYS WERE.

You can't really hurt me.

IS THAT WHAT YOU THINK?

You can scare me, but that's all.

WE CAN DO MORE THAN YOU EVER IMAGINED.

I'll turn the light on. I'll call my dad . . .

The eyes on the floor began to shift, to pool, to flow together, changing color to a swirling crimson, and taking shape again. Now, four. Now, two. Just two.

His hand—seized. Hard. Hard and down, he was yanked, and something snapped at his shoulder, and he was off the bed, falling in a crazy slow motion, looking back to see Dwight still asleep, and the words that weren't his in his mind, those words telling him . . . telling him . . .

WHAT SHALL I DO WITH YOU? WHAT WOULD YOU LIKE? DID YOU KNOW WHAT WAS UNDER YOUR BED?

A scream. A long, low, horrid animal scream, and it was all over Dwight, enveloping him, and he bolted up in bed and reached wildly for the lamp, the scream piercing him to the bone. The lamp shattered on the floor just as the scream swelled up again, mixed with a bubbling and cracking, and a noise like the rushing wind. Dwight's hand slammed against the wall switch and the light came on.

Mike. On the floor. His body twisted. Screaming, his arm stuck under the bed.

Dwight flattened against the wall. On the floor, Mike lurched, and then his head went under. His body lurched again. Again. His feet flailed and kicked.

Dwight tried to go through the wall, tearing at it with bloodied fingernails, screaming against the sucking noise that had already stopped, had stopped long ago. And he was there, yelling words that made no sense when Mike's dad burst through the door in his underwear, his eyes wild.

A big, strong back—a dad's back—the muscles heaving and straining. The back of his head bobbing as the mattress flew up and curled double, sliding down the wall. The grating of the box springs as they slid away. Mike's mom at the door, her face white. And under the bed, Mike, in the dust and candy wrappers, a tiny rag doll Mike.

And the closet door. Shut.

By itself.

7

Mick Winters lay in the bed, its sheets and blanket and springs now familiar to him, made familiar by his weight and the heat of his body. He knew the bed intimately, subconsciously; it felt a part of him, like he had been born there and had lived and would die there, enveloped by it.

Since Matthew Simmon's visit some hours earlier, sleep had woven in and out of Mick; a sleep that was like a dark and very deep well, a straight vertical shaft dug out of the ground under him and filled with a dry fluid that both supported him and forced him down. He would close his eyes and the dry heavy liquid would seep into his brain, filling it, weighting him down into the shaft. Then, like a feather tossed from the top of a tall building into night's darkness, he would begin to settle down, slowly and heavily, until it felt as if he would sink completely to the bottom.

That was usually when the thoughts started, little exploding synapses of light in the darkness.

Jerry. Snap. *Simmons.* Snap. *The sheriff.* Snap.

What am I doing here?

Snap. Snap. Snap. And the light would force him back up, pushing him up the shaft, dropping him back into his bed with a dull, sickening thud, reality washing over him like a wave of stinging acid. Then the slow process would begin again as he lay, the fluid seeping in, the sinking . . .

The sedative was wearing off. Mick could feel it. It was time to be well again and get up out of this damned bed and *do* something. He forced the heaviness from his mind, made it recede, replacing it with a sense of new purpose, like that of a person who realizes, after a long convalescence, that an old and familiar part of his life is over.

It was time, Mick decided, for a fresh start.

He forced his eyes open. Even the dark room looked different now, clearer, as if he had been watching a black and white movie that had suddenly changed to Technicolor. A new smell was in his nostrils. He was coming back.

Slowly, Mick struggled upright. The pain in his back was as familiar to him as the bed, part of the same package, but it wasn't enough to keep him down. He wanted to get on his feet, to walk to the wall switch and flood the room with light, to throw open the windows and breathe the midnight air of freedom.

He had to *do* something!

Mick unflexed his arm and reached out slowly, sliding it toward the table lamp beside him. He started turning his body as he reached, his head clearing as it turned, muscles all over his body stirring and coming to life. His hand bumped against something soft, and there was a sharp intake of air.

The light beside his bed flickered on. His head completed its turn and he saw Cheryl there, in a chair beside the table, beside his head.

"Oh," she said. "It was you." She laughed a little at the statement, a laughter that was thick with interrupted sleep.

Mick worked his mouth. "Yeah. Yeah, it's me. I'm making a break." He placed his hand beside his thigh on the bed, and pressed, lifting himself up further.

"The hell you are," Cheryl said almost absently as she looked at her watch.

"I'm serious, Cheryl. I'm getting out of here."

"Mick," she began, taking her eyes off the watch and looking at him, "You're not going anywhere. You're pumped up with painkiller—"

"I don't feel it anymore."

"—and I put more stitches in your back than Betsy Ross put in the flag. You've been in shock, you're bruised and battered, and you might have amnesia. Or even aphasia." She started pushing him back down gently, a token effort with no real force in it, but Mick resisted.

"What's aphasia?"

"Well . . . it's an inability to comprehend things."

"What kind of things?"

She smiled, a smile Mick saw as evasive. "Like human speech. Like my human speech, telling you to lie down and take it easy for—"

"Dammit!" Mick shouted, and the force of it tore at his vocal cords. He paused and swallowed, his throat a ribbon of flame. "Dammit," he said again, much more softly. "I can't just lie here, Cheryl. Don't you understand? Matthew Simmons says that the law—what's his name?—"

"Herb Jeffries." Cheryl had taken her hands away from him.

"Herb Jeffries thinks I killed Jerry. You saw yourself how worked up the old man was about it. You keep me in here any longer and the boys're going to be outside the house with torches and ropes."

Cheryl seemed to regard him with new eyes. "And what do you think you can do about it?" she asked. "You haven't suddenly remembered anything about Jerry, have you?"

Mick thought, a little unspoken fear creeping into him. Things were bad enough without turning Cheryl against him. She was all he had. The dull, sour ache of Jerry's memory, what had happened to Jerry, glowered at him from a dark corner of his brain, lurking like a ragged coyote, ready to spring.

"I'm sorry," he said. For what he wasn't sure, but he thought it good to say it anyway. "I just feel helpless." He turned away from her, heard her light a cigarette—the scratch of the match head, the sizzle of the flame, her deep inhalation.

"You . . . you don't believe I killed him, do you?" Mick's voice sliced through the silence.

"What do you think?"

"I think you don't want to believe it." Mick looked at her and their eyes met briefly.

Cheryl started to say something, stopped, and started again, the words set free slowly from her lips. "I don't want to believe that people beat their children with battery cables, or that people starve to death, or that there's a war going on somewhere right now."

"But evidence points to it, right?" Mick said. "That is, if I get your drift."

She exhaled smoke. "I don't know," she said softly, looking off in the far corner of the room where there was no black or white, only gray. "I don't know, I don't know, I don't know."

In the ensuing silence, Mick felt his voice trying to take shape, and failing. But he had to keep on. He had to talk. He told himself, over and over, *after all, it's Cheryl. You know Cheryl. Talk to her.*

He found his voice.

"Cheryl," he said softly, "I didn't kill him." She turned back to him, looking into his eyes. He reached up and took one of her hands, almost instinctively. "You know me. You know I wouldn't, couldn't have killed him. He was my friend."

She continued gazing at him. Slowly, her other hand moved until it rested on top of his. She turned a little in her chair, facing him now. "I do know you," she said, her eyes never leaving his face. "Or at least I did."

"We don't change, Cheryl. We get married, and we go out and get jobs, and people get born and die around us. But we don't really change. None of us. Everything's still there . . . hidden maybe, forgotten but still there."

"Everything?" There was a sudden barely perceptible lightness in her voice, and it was a girl's voice, not a woman's, the voice of the girl in Tanapah that called to him from across Aunt Lucy's backyard, summer after golden summer.

He laughed a little. He thought he knew what she meant.

And then Cheryl shifted her eyes away from his, almost guilty, and her hand left the top of his. Her other hand, where Mick held it, suddenly felt slack and professional, once again the hand of a doctor. It was a subtle change, but a change nonetheless.

Cherry reached for her cigarette and took a last drag. "So tell me," she began. "What's old Mick been doing for the last—what? Twenty years?"

"Close enough," Mick said. The spell, the tension was broken. Now it was talk, just talk, like two old friends meeting unexpectedly at a cocktail party, and Mick just didn't have the will left to make it anything different.

"You went to college, right? Oklahoma State? Your aunt used to tell me about you every once in a while."

"Yeah. I wanted to be a writer. Got into business instead. I went into the service for four years, got out, traveled around a little. The usual."

"What are you doing now?"

"I'm in Kansas City with an ad agency. Writing copy. Nothing very exciting." Mick was beginning to edge off, to feel dull and heavy again. Below him, the dark pit of sleep yawned open, its fluid shimmering all around him.

"And you're . . . not married?"

The question surprised him a little, and he cocked his head in her direction, a question on his lips.

"I didn't see a ring," Cheryl said, by way of explanation.

"Oh . . . okay." Mick paused. "I was once. Married, I mean. We were divorced a while back." Mick felt the pressure of her hand inside his. There was a little sweat beginning to form where they touched, a moisture that made the interface of their flesh seem just a little unnatural, a little prolonged.

"I—should I say I'm sorry?"

"No," Mick said quickly. "She was a jerk." A bitterness, bile-sharp on the back of his tongue, rose at the thought of his ex-wife, a girl who had been as beautiful and promising as a gaily wrapped package under a Christmas tree. It had taken Mick about two years to open the package and find out there was nothing inside.

He suddenly remembered something. "You said you had another name. Not Mallis anymore."

"Right. It's Stanton now."

"I haven't seen Mr. Stanton around."

"You're not likely to, either."

"Divorced too?"

"No," she said, lighting a fresh cigarette. "Dead."

Mick let go of her hand then, felt it slip out. He pushed himself up a little more against the bed.

"When?" he asked.

"Six years ago. He was a rancher. I'd just gotten out of med school and we were going to live in the country together and raise animals. And kids. I was going to be a country doctor . . ." She broke off, started again. "But I didn't even get to hang out my shingle. Six months after we were married a drunk kid ran him off a bridge. I sold his ranch and moved back to town. Annie was born a few months later." She studied the glowing tip of her cigarette.

"It's a dumb thing to say, but I'm sorry."

"It's not dumb. It's just all anyone can say. He was a hell of a good guy, Mick."

"He would've had to be."

She smiled slightly. "Thanks." She didn't look at him.

The stillness edged in again between them, a moving wedge that separated Mick from everything around him. He felt as though he could sleep now, that he'd done enough for one day, although he didn't quite know just exactly what it was he'd done.

From another room came the muffed ringing of a phone.

Cheryl's head jerked up. "What—?" She glanced down at her watch. "It's almost two a.m.," she said, rising to her feet and opening the door. "I'll be right back, Mick. Lie back and see if you can relax a little now." And she was gone.

The ringing stopped. Mick eased back down onto the bed and the waiting pillow. It felt cool again, new and clean and inviting. He exhaled and felt himself began to sink. In a moment he heard Cheryl come back into the room, and he opened his eyes.

She was wearing a harried expression, and there was an air of urgency around her, an air of mobility, of being snapped into action.

"Mick," she said, "I have to go now."

"What is it?"

"Kid on the other side of town. Accident. Do you need something to make you sleep?"

He thought for a moment, feeling the pain in his back, but not too long because the urgency she gave the room worked on him, too. "No. No, I don't think so."

"All right. I'll check on you when I get back. Just try to relax. Sleep if you can." She was out before Mick even realized she was gone. He was left staring at a blank spot in front of the bedroom door.

Mick turned his head and lay flat, settling back again. *Relax,* she had said. He closed his eyes. *You're here in Tanapah, under a doctor's care, safe in bed, and the doctor is Cheryl.*

The sifting down, the settling, began.

Cheryl. A doctor. Tanapah. Here in Tanapah.

Tanapah.

What was he doing in *Tanapah?*

And then, Mick began to remember . . .

Driving into Tanapah, catching a look at the glaring red roof of the new Dairy Queen, thinking for a second that he'd taken a wrong turn . . .

8

There wasn't any Dairy Queen in Tanapah. Kendall's Drug and Fountain was the place for ice cream, a nickel a cone, and if you smiled at him real big and showed a couple of teeth missing in the front, good old Mr. Kendall would grin back and throw on a handful of chocolate sprinkles.

But that was twenty-two years ago.

The Dairy Queen was a patch, covering the hole left alongside the highway where the Texaco station used to be. Every Fourth of July there would be a fireworks stand set up next to the Texaco, and you could hear the cherry bombs booming clear to the far side of Tanapah. People always used to say the place would catch fire and burn to the ground one year, and one year it did. But the fire happened on a Tuesday in November. Mick's Aunt Lucy wrote him all about it.

Aunt Lucy.

The town was thick with memories. For Mick, it was layered with them, like a covering of soft dust, easily stirred. Here, the road went straight where it used to curve, but there, amazingly, was Smitty's Barber Shop, almost as if someone had packed it away when he left and brought it out again just to surprise him. Peeling and yellowed in the corner of the barber shop windows was a sign that read, "Try Wildroot Cream Oil, Charlie."

Mick caught himself singing the old radio jingle, "Try Wildroot Cream Oil . . . Charr-rr-rlie," and remembered how he had come out of Smitty's shop with the wind feeling strangely cool around his ears, and his hair slicked back and smelling exotically sweet. And how he had run all the way back to Aunt Lucy's house so she could smell it too.

Why Mickie, you smell like a real, grown-up man.

There was the old Mertz Variety Store, known to one and all in Tanapah as "the dime store," where Mick would ceremoniously acknowledge the start of each new summer by choosing a new squirt gun. Once, he sneaked up on Aunt Lucy when she was working in the garden and ambushed her with a gurgling little pistol made of clear green plastic, and she turned the garden hose on him.

That's what's missing, that's what's wrong with living in an apartment. Nobody has a garden hose. Nobody knows how it feels to aim the hose straight up and feel the spray coming down again, or how the water tastes—cold and bubbly, and flavored lightly of rubber, and the taste of it mingled with the scents of flowers in Aunt Lucy's garden.

There was the Chieftain Theater, where Roy Rogers or Lash LaRue would clean up the Wild West every Saturday afternoon in a hail of popcorn boxes; and the Elmer T. Gulick Elementary School, a red brick hulk of a place, always empty and brooding. Always, Mick had come to Tanapah after school was out, and left before it started again.

Now, he felt suddenly edgy as he drove past the old school. He heard a metallic creaking sound from the playground and knew if he glanced out the side window, he would see a bunch of kids playing on the swing. Playing "bail-out," probably. The idea was to swing up as high as you could, and then, at the very top where the swing chains started to go slack, to jump off the seat, arching into the air like Commando Cody, bracing your legs, and coming down heels first into the gravel.

Mick identified the edginess. He heard the kids laughing; and, at the same time, heard a tiny, nervous warning from the back of his mind that said: *Don't look. Don't look. You might be one of them.*

A block past the school, on the corner, was the stump of an elm tree. Mick slowed as he approached it, saddened. Each summer for three summers he had tried to climb that tree, and each summer for three summers it had defeated him. The trunk was too thick to put his arms around, and the first branch was a good ten feet off the ground. They called it the Giant. And now, it was just a whitened and cracked old stump, strangely small, and beaten at last.

Mick pulled against the curb and stopped. A left turn past the elm stump would take him to Aunt Lucy's house.

You come and see me, Mickie. You come and see me again. Don't let this be the last time.

But it had been twenty-two years ago. Two college degrees ago. One marriage ago. Now, the old promise was a weight in his throat: "I'll be back. I promise, I'll be back."

Mick had taken the old road into Tanapah. But thanks to the new interstate that shot past town to the east—straight, smooth, and uncaring—there was a new motel called the Plains Inn. It had a Master Charge sticker in the front window of the lobby. It had color TV and a little water-heater gadget on the wall for making instant coffee. It had a blue-water pool occupied by a couple of teenaged girls wearing bikinis, who probably couldn't have said where they were except that it was at least a day's drive from where they were going.

Mick checked into the Plains Inn because it was the one place in Tanapah that didn't hold memories and didn't care who he was or what he promised.

The desk clerk gave him a throwaway smile. The Coke machine took his forty cents and gave him nothing. He fell asleep watching Johnny Carson, whose face had a greenish tint on the TV screen.

He marveled, in the last moments before sleep, that Johnny Carson could follow him so easily from Kansas City to Tanapah.

You come and see me, Mickie.

"I will, I will, Aunt Lucy. Sometime. But it's such a long ways, and I'm always so busy."

I n the morning, he stopped at the motel's restaurant for toast and two cups of black coffee, lingering over the second cup until it had almost turned cold.

Down the row of orange vinyl-covered stools that lined the counter, he recognized Charlie Pruitt. Charlie used to make egg deliveries house-to-house. He looked almost the same now —same half-lidded eyes, and that same smile, the smile that seemed to take great secret delight in absolutely nothing. Only now, his hair was speckled black and gray.

Some of the other kids would try to make Charlie trip and spill his egg basket, and would jeer at him, "Dummy! Dummy!" But Mick always called him Mr. Pruitt because Aunt Lucy said he should. Charlie always called him Mister Michael.

Now, Charlie Pruitt looked directly at him, smiled dumbly, and turned away without the slightest glimmer of recognition.

Mick paid for his coffee and toast and left for the office of Lawyer Morton.

"Y our aunt was a wonderful woman, Mick. Shame you couldn't have been here for the funeral."

Lawyer Morton—everybody called him that, and Mick had never known his real first name—unwrapped an unwieldy cigar. He was a heavy man in a big chair behind a heavy desk, surrounded by walls packed with thick books.

"It was . . . impossible at the time," Mick said. He felt suddenly embarrassed and ashamed, and realized it wasn't the lawyer's fault. Inwardly, he bitterly cursed his own selfishness, his own inertia, that had kept him in Kansas City as his aunt was being lowered into the ground in Tanapah.

"Fine ceremony," Morton said. "Whole town turned out." He rolled the cigar from one side of his mouth to the other. "What sort of business you in now, Mick?"

"Writing. I'm in advertising . . . an ad consultant, you might say."

A puzzled scowl crinkled the lawyer's face. "I might. If I knew what the hell it was."

"I write advertisements. Maybe you saw the one for . . . let's see . . . how about Mama Spinoza's Frozen Pizza: A Wheel of a Deal. I wrote that."

Mickie! Oh, Mickie, what a beautiful poem! You wrote this for me? Why, this is the nicest thing I ever read.

The lawyer snorted, shaking his head. "Stuff tastes like shit, pardon the expression," he said.

Mick shrugged, trying to make it comical. "I don't make the pizza, I just write the ads." Then a thought clouded his mind. "But it's . . . there're a lot of deadlines. I wanted to be here."

Morton pulled open his front desk drawer, fumbled for a moment, and brought out a jingling cluster of keys looped on a chain along with a white cardboard tag. "Here go," he said, and handed the keys to Mick. "Big one opens the front door—but you probably already know that."

I swear, Mickie, I don't know what all these keys are for. But they were Jack's, and they all meant something to him. I don't ever want to lose anything that was his.

"You'll find the place is in darn good shape for being as old as it is," said the lawyer. "Your aunt wasn't one to let things run down. Couple of people already been asking if it's for sale. City people."

"What if I did want to sell it?"

The lawyer turned his head and spat a brown speck of tobacco toward the open window. "Money?" he answered. "Hard to say. It's nothing fancy, but we got here what the city folks call 'charm,' if you follow. The front porch swing, the honeysuckle up the side of the door . . . and the apple tree. That especially."

Mick fingered the keys. "I don't know what I'd ever do with the place."

"Well. . ." Morton leaned back, his chair creaking in protest. "Stop by the office and let me know what you decide. All Lucy ever told me was, when the time came for you to get the house, and no matter how much of a kick the rest of the family put up. She said you'd know why."

The "why" came with a pause afterward and a raising of the lawyer's thin white eyebrows that made it a question.

Mick shook his head no. "Maybe I'll find out," he said.

The black key slid into the front door lock, making a scraping sound as Mick turned it. Then the door opened with a dull click, startling him with its familiarity. Cold against his hand, the oblong-shaped smooth brass doorknob felt oddly small.

Mickie Winters! You come in this house and give your old aunt a nice big hug!

Inside, the first thing he saw was himself—a gold-framed picture of five-year-old Mickie Winters under the apple tree in that first summer he had come to visit Aunt Lucy. It was on the table with the lamp that had bright grapes painted on the shade and a base made to look like a grape cluster.

Mick crossed the room, stepping over the woven throw rug Aunt Lucy never liked anybody but special company to walk on.

He picked up the picture, the picture of him in the Mertz Variety Store frame. He was wearing his red corduroy jacket with a little Howdy Doody sewn on the pocket, his favorite jacket at the time because it felt like it was made out of a cowboy's rope.

He remembered the day the picture had been taken, and how afterward Aunt Lucy had sent him down into the fruit cellar to bring back a jar of apple jelly. "Like a big man," she had said.

Into the cellar . . .

He moved on through the parlor, the sewing room, the three bedrooms upstairs. It all proved exactly what he knew he was going to find: nothing changed, nothing moved, nothing of much notice added since he was a boy.

Certainly, the window in the bedroom that had been his looked out in the same direction as before, through the branches of the same cottonwood tree, out and across the backyard.

To the cellar.

Drawing back the yellowed, rose-patterned curtains, he saw it out there, the grassy blanket of the lawn rising into a loaf-shaped lump with a red, weathered door closed on one end.

Mick Winters saw himself again, five years old, opening that door and hearing the hinges squeak, and taking the first step down—and afterwards, running in tears to Aunt Lucy. He remembered Aunt Lucy holding him, telling him, "You've got to be a big boy now. There's nothing down there except maybe a little field mouse, and he's saying, 'Hey, Mickie. Bring me some cheese next time, okay?'"

She took on a high squeaky voice for the mouse, and Mick giggled and forgot about the cellar for a little while, but he never went near it again except when she told him to go get a jar of canned pickles or peaches. Even then, he would put off going until midday, when the light from the sun would reach down to the very bottom of the cement floor of the cellar.

The day came, though, when he could stand it no longer.

"Aunt Lucy," he said, coming into the sewing room where she was ironing, "I think there's a monster in the fruit cellar."

She set the iron upright at the end of the board and motioned for him to come help her fold the sheet, which was never to touch the floor even though the floor was spotless.

"You've seen a monster in there, have you Mickie? What did it look like?"

Holding the two edges of the sheet even, he said: "I didn't really see it, I just know it's there. It's hiding. It's somewhere. It scares me."

She took the sheet from him, folded it over a couple more times, and put it on top of a stack. "Well, now," she said, taking a pillowcase out of the laundry basket and smoothing it onto the ironing board, "what's its name?"

"Name?"

"It can't be much of a fruit cellar monster without a proper name, would you say? Let's call it . . ." She paused, and Mickie held his breath. "Call it *Goofus*. You go down there and tell it you named it Goofus and see if it still seems as scary to you.

So he did.

And that was the first time he saw Goofus.

M ick pulled the curtain shut. *Check the house over. Get it sold. And get out of here.*

The memories were like a spilled button box. New ones, old ones, big ones, little ones, pretty ones . . .

Button box. Nobody he ever knew but Aunt Lucy had a button box.

He thought all at once about spilling the buttons, and about the deadlines coming up on the July Fourth sale ads, and about telling Sharon—pretty Sharon—all about this room, but that was when he trusted her not to save up things he told her and sharpen them, somehow, into weapons against him.

And he thought: *I don't need this. I don't want to be here.*

But the room held him like a hook sunk deep inside him.

He was in the room where he had stayed those three summers when school was out and before his mom remarried, when she was working too long and too hard to take care of him. Now, he knew that those times were the worst of her life. But for him, they were three of the world's finest summers. They were green seasons of skipping flat rocks across a farm pond rippling with bluegills in the shallow water, of jam sandwiches wrapped in wax paper, and of being just old enough to know that not everybody had it so good.

But the cellar . . .

He knew Goofus was down in the cellar always, waiting like the spiders at the back of the shelves, whether Mickie Winters came to see him or not.

"**D**id you tell him his new name?" Aunt Lucy asked. She looked up as Mick stepped quietly back into the house and its warm, comforting aroma of roasting chicken. He looked back at her, determined not this time—not ever again—to let her see him cry.

"Yeah," he said.

"Well?" She bent and kissed him on the forehead. "What did he have to say about that?"

Mickie tried to smile at her, but the muscles that made his face work felt like wet sand. "He didn't say anything."

"I didn't think he would," she said. "Now, you go wash your hands and get ready for supper."

Mickie didn't really lie.

But in the cellar, back in the far, dark corner, where the shaft of sunlight never touched, and where it was too black for shadows . . . back there . . . it moved.

It moved with the feel of a cold hard wind in a place where the air was still. It moved with the pain of a wounded thing gathering strength. It moved with a purpose, like a snake toward a mouse.

It moved, and then it was gone.

But it didn't say anything.

Mick opened the door to the room across from his that had

been Aunt Lucy's. He saw, there above the bed, the oval wooden frame stained dark from the years, and in it the only glimpse he'd ever had of Uncle Jack. It was their wedding picture. Aunt Lucy's hair was raven black and arranged in girlish ringlets, although her face bore a look of unaccustomed solemnity.

Mick grinned, imagining the trial the photographer must have had convincing her that this of all days—with Jack at her side, having waxed the tips of his mustache until he could have threaded them through a needle—was a day to be grim.

The hair was in ringlets then, but ringlets for no one but Big Jack Beaumont, and it had been combed back and fastened with an amber-colored plastic comb for as long as Mick had known her.

It was fastened in just that way in the second week of his second summer, when she told him, "Mickie, I've got a surprise for you. Come on, it's in the cellar."

He had nearly forgotten the cellar. It had been almost a year since he had last seen it. And he was, of course, not five years old anymore but almost seven, and more afraid of fast-breaking ground balls than of ghosts in the dark.

Mickie had even gone out of his way once to walk past the red cellar door, daring Goofus.

The door was open. He could see inside, but nothing except the apple barrels near the bottom of the stairs. Some dim, distant part of his mind wanted to tell him the apples weren't really apples at all—they were red, beating hearts—but he wouldn't listen.

He told himself that before the summer was done, he would go down the cellar steps and face those tricks of light and shadow that took advantage of little boys and prove them out for what they were.

But—not today.

"No, not now, Aunty Lucy," he said, surprising them both by the sharpness in his voice.

"Why, Mickie. That doesn't sound like you." There was a little hurt, reprimanding tone in her words.

He scuffed the toe of his canvas shoe against the polished hardwood of the living room floor. "I mean . . .I mean, this is such a neat day, Aunt Lucy . . . it doesn't need anything else."

Winking at him, she shook her head. "Don't you say it couldn't be any better, Mickie, until after you smell a good peach pie in the oven." She started toward the back of the house, and he knew she was going out the back door and into the cellar. "The surprise," she said, "is the peaches I canned for you last fall. Come on."

And Mickie was afraid all over again, just as much as when he'd stood shaking that day at the bottom of the cellar stairs, but more—because Aunt Lucy didn't know what was down there.

"No. Don't!" he called.

In answer, he heard the screen door at the back squeak open and whap shut. Mickie ran through the house, down the green-painted hallway, past the phone nook and into the kitchen. He reached the back door only in time to see the top of her head disappear down the cellar steps.

"Aunt Lucy! Aunt Lucy!" His feet tore through the summer grass, and it stained the white shoe tips green as he followed her. Until, without thinking, he had come all the way after her to that very step at the bottom of the cellar where he'd stood before.

The air was dank and stale, laced through with the sweet smell of apples. Sunlight was stifled here. The shelves were velvety with dust, and streamered with cobwebs.

"No, not cherries—peaches." Aunt Lucy was talking to herself. She glanced back at Mickie. "And not just any jar of peaches, mind you. Only the best." She picked a jar off the shelf and made a show of looking it over as if it were filled with a kind of fool's gold only she could tell from the real thing.

Mickie's eyes scanned the cellar again, finding nothing new, just jars and dust and cobwebs, and he felt a load of foolishness being heaped onto the fright he was still carrying. He started to say, "Can I help . . ."

But then, that change again.

Just like before, it happened—but faster. There was a shifting in the corner behind Aunt Lucy, a movement that Mickie sensed in the pit of his stomach and by the tingling at the back of his neck, and then . . . he saw.

The air itself seemed to be coming together to become something hard and heavy. In the corner, there was a blackness pooling, and rising up the side of the cellar wall.

Aunt Lucy, her back still turned to the corner, reached toward a jar on one of the shelves. "Oh, I think this may be the one, Mickie," she said.

The black mass grew until it brushed the top of the cellar. It had no definable shape. Mickie tried to scream, but the sound came out as nothing but a rush of air; and he tried to run—he didn't know whether toward Aunt Lucy or away from her and out the door—but the only way his body reacted was that his hand came up to his face, knuckles jamming in his mouth.

His mind was a whirlpool of images he'd never imagined before. The thing had no shape—but in his mind, he saw the back cellar wall become a black, gaping mouth edged with long teeth. He saw the wall crack and bleed. He saw a black dog, bigger than him and with leathery wings like a bat, walking toward him on its hind legs, and swinging a heavy chain at him. He saw the cellar walls and floor and ceiling matted with crawling flies.

He saw long, spidery hands. Reaching out. Toward Aunt Lucy.

"Yes!" she said. "This is the one, Mickie. You see"—she held the jar up—"I wrote your name on the label, to be sure and save it for you."

The fingers came together around her neck, locked and tightened.

"Why, Mickie," she said, turning. "Your face . . . What's the matter?"

She rushed toward him. Nothing was holding her, after all, and Mickie's face split into a grin that felt like it might take the top of his head off. His voice settled into his throat again. "N-nothing," he said. "Just Goofus. Silly ol' Goofus. You remember."

She handed the jar to him. "You know something?" she said. "You're right. This *is* a spooky old place. Let's us two ghosts get out of here, okay?"

And it *was* okay. It was a trick his mind was playing in the dark, a little boy trick that he'd left in the cellar a year ago, and that was all.

"You know, though . . ." She hesitated. "I think I'll take an extra jar and make a pie for you to take to Mrs. Burton down the way. She hasn't been feeling very well."

She turned back to the shelf. She turned back into the reach of those long, bodiless fingers that had hovered there, waiting for her. They splayed across the sides of her face as she peered into the row of old jars.

No! Mickie ordered himself. *No! You won't fool me again. I know what you are. I can make you go away. I don't believe in you.*

The fingers clawed for a grip against her cheekbones.

She didn't seem to know.

See? I told you so.

The fingers slid up into her silvery, pulled-back hair, around the plastic clasp where some of the strands were loose.

They rose, and shuddered, and disappeared above her head. And as they did, a wisp of her hair rose with them, until it was standing straight out.

Aunt Lucy swatted the back of her head and said, "My sakes, Mickie. What was that?"

The memory broke and scattered, replaced by a soothing one. His back against hard, straight wood. The voices singing "Rock of Ages" all around him. Church.

Mick stood in Aunt Lucy's room in front of her dressing table with its delicately embroidered doilies. In his hand was the opened bottle of a perfume that smelled like lilacs. Her favorite. It was the one she always saved for Sunday mornings. To him, it smelled not so much of flowers as of the still, hot air inside the First Baptist Church, and the feeling of trying to sit still in the wooden pew that was third from the front. It was five pennies tied into the corner of his handkerchief to be unwrapped and dropped into the collection plate.

Mick capped the bottle and set it back on the tabletop.

Once again he was back in a house that hadn't changed and that wouldn't let him change, either. It made him feel warm and protected, scared and little, all at the same time.

It was that feeling, he knew, that had kept himself away from the funeral; it had nothing to do with agency deadlines that couldn't be missed.

Being little. Being scared.

But now, it was time for the last stop on the tour. Time to put old ghosts to rest. Stepping into the carpeted hallway, Mick shut the door to Aunt Lucy's room behind him. He took the stairs down to the parlor, his hand gliding along the white-painted bannister. The middle step creaked the way it always did. It said *Hi!*

At the bottom, he stopped.

Nobody bothered with fruit cellars anymore. There wasn't any reason for going down *there* again. The cellar wouldn't have anything to do with selling the house or settling the estate.

Even Aunt Lucy had quit using it.

She had pointed out the board nailed across the cellar door in his third and last summer in Tanapah.

"Some of the little children from next door were playing around here," she said, "and I was afraid they might go down there and hurt themselves." She bent and pulled a dandelion. "Besides"—and Mickie could tell she was talking more to herself than to him—"I've got plenty of room on the kitchen shelves and a new icebox to boot."

But the next thing she had said was straight to him: "Don't you ever go down there, Mickie. Not for anything. You hear me?"

Now, feeling his heart quicken, he answered the voice in his memory. "I'm sorry, Aunt Lucy, but I've got to."

Eight-year-old Mickie had been too long growing up. It was time.

His shadow chased ahead of him across the backyard, tall and unafraid, and the screen door whipped shut behind him.

Mick stood looking at the grass-covered lump of the cellar the way he had twenty-two years ago, wondering how it could be that Aunt Lucy hadn't seen the thing that appeared to him down there.

But then, he also used to wonder how it was she didn't know about the little elves that were always playing hide-and-seek around the house. Sometimes, he could almost see one duck around the corner or behind the big green sofa in the parlor, but never quite.

He stood in front of the cellar door.

Don't you ever go down there, Mickie. You hear me?

The paint was cracked and peeling, and the board wasn't there anymore. In its place was a heavy silver padlock fixed with metal plates and six big screws driven tightly into the wood.

Pulled from his pocket, the keys rattled in his hand. He sorted through them. There was no key to fit the padlock.

His lungs welcomed the first deep breath he'd taken since coming to the old house. Somewhere down the street, there was a radio playing. It was Waylon Jennings singing "Amanda." It was a beer joint song, not meant to be heard while standing, shivering, on a hot spring evening outside a forgotten old cellar, but in a dark place full of strangers.

Mick turned. He walked away from the cellar, back toward the house, leaving his shadow behind to deal with the locked door.

And then, the image came to hm—immensely unwanted—of Uncle Jack's carpentry box that Aunt Lucy always kept under the kitchen sink. Although the tools had never been of much use to her, she never threw away anything that was Uncle Jack's.

Yes. The wooden box was still there. It held a hammer and crescent wrench, several screwdrivers, a measuring tape and piece of blue chalk—and a hacksaw. Against his hopes, the blade of the saw was strong and not rusted, and there was an extra blade in the bottom of the box.

Sawing would be the fast way.

Do it. Get it over with.

Walking in slow steps back to the cellar door, Mick carried the saw like something dead and heavy.

Do it, he told himself. And the saw blade whispered back to him as it cut against the metal of the padlock hasp, *do it. Do it. Do it.* The metal filings sparkled as they sifted down.

As he worked the blade back and forth, Mick made a promise to his Aunt Lucy that he would go to the hardware store the first thing in the morning and buy a new lock. He would put it on and throw the key away, so that no little boy from next door would wander into the cellar and hurt himself.

The weight of the lock made it swing suddenly toward him when the hasp separated, and he jumped back.

There was no sound from within.

Mick dropped the saw. He reached slowly forward, lifted the lock away, and let it fall. It struck the concrete at the base of the cellar door with a sharp metallic clack that seemed to fill the air and echo like a gunshot.

He flipped the lock plate open, realizing for the first time that putting it on would have been too much of a job for Aunt Lucy. She must have called somebody from McCleary's Hardware downtown to help her.

He gripped the black metal handle on the right side of the door.

Now!

The door scraped open toward him.

Immediately, the smothering, soft smell of rotted fruit rushed out to envelop him. He bent forward into the open door to see . . . the apple barrels still in the same place, but empty now; the shelves beyond full of untouched jars of peaches and cherries.

Mick stood in the open doorway as the sun behind him sank behind a cloud, dimming his sight of the shelves.

"Okay," he said, and his voice came back at him from the pit of the cellar as a hollow echo. "Okay, I did it."

The cellar was impassive.

"But enough's enough. You hear me, Goofus? I'm not

coming down." His breath was so short that the words came in spurts. "So if you're down there, here's your chance to show yourself once and for all. You hear me?"

The echo of his voice was the only answer.

"Okay. I'm going to go home now and be scared of the right things, Goofus—car payments and getting fired from my job, and not you. You hear me?" Mick glanced around suddenly, hoping the people next door hadn't seen him acting out his little ritual of manhood, but the shades were all drawn.

"That does it, then . . ." he said.

He started to close the door, but it scraped on something and stuck.

A kick sent the door jerking forward, and a wedge-shaped splinter of wood popped out from underneath it. The door had swung out, he saw now, trailing chips and splinters. Bits of wood were scattered down the stairs into the darkness. Bits of wood that came from . . .

Mick yanked the door open so that it crunched against the concrete of the cellar entranceway, and he could see the other side, where the wood was gouged and scored in long, jagged trenches, and stained with dried rivulets of black blood.

"Oh no! Oh, Lord!"

From the bottom of the cellar came the smashing, shattering sound of a jar hitting the floor, and then—*That noise!*

It started up, sounding far away, then nearer, then farther way, a high-pitched, whistling noise, almost a whine, and on top of it, a guttural groan, like a huge thing awakening.

Mick stood at the top of the steps, his face and body frozen, listening to the noise, listening to it growing louder, whistling, whistling—

Run! Get out! His mind screamed at him, a terrified scream that had the same pitch as the noise from the cellar. But he seemed to be mesmerized. His brain sent out signals; his body wouldn't respond.

The whistling noise got louder. Mick's body began to tremble, his eyes peering down into the cellar, seeing nothing. And then, a glimpse, just a glimpse, of . . . something.

A whistling. A whistling that changed pitch up and down, like something coming nearer and then farther away almost at the same time. That's what it had sounded like.

But now, safely encased in the steel shell of his Buick, with the air conditioner blowing maximum cold against him, Mick felt more foolish than anything else.

So a jar had fallen off. He had worked himself up about the cellar, convinced himself that there was something down there, and his mind had supplied the rest. One jar that had probably been teetering on the edge of one of those old slumped wooden shelves for years, and the jarring of the door when he slammed it back had been enough to make it drop. Or maybe the wind. Or something.

He must have looked like Lou Costello, slamming the door and jabbing over and over to get the sawed hasp of the lock fixed in place again. Running like hell, he reflected, his mind making up noises.

The wood chips?

Tomorrow. Tomorrow, in the calm and the morning, he would see that there had to be some reason for the wood chips. Some ordinary reason. Entirely sane.

And as for tonight.

The motel had a lounge. He knew without having set foot in the place that there would be soft blue lights playing over the ceiling, and Frank Sinatra on the juke, or maybe a man at the piano playing soft, innocuous music. People would look at him when he came in. If he sat by himself at the bar, the bartender might knowingly point across the room to a woman who had come in alone, too.

He didn't want that.

He wanted Waylon and "Amanda." He wanted smoke and racket, and a roomful of people who didn't care whether he came or went. And beer. He wanted the feeling of his head lifting off, while the rest of him was weighted down and sloshing. And he wouldn't have minded a good fight, either. He wouldn't have minded losing.

The neon sign in front of Scot's Tap was partly burned out so that it read: "cot's T p." It was a small, boxy concrete building that looked like it might have been a gas station at one time. Now, as the sun went down, it was ringed with pickup trucks like squat old frogs around the only puddle in town.

Stepping inside Scot's, Mick knew it was everything he wanted. Two beers later, he looked across the room and saw a face from twenty-two years ago. It was a face still splattered with freckles, but longer and more angular now, attached to a tall, lean body that wore faded jeans and a red-and-white checked shirt.

The other man's face registered stunned surprise for a second, then broke into a grin. He waved at Mick, who returned the grin and called to him.

"Hello, Jerry," he said.

9

Mick Winters wasn't sleepy anymore.

He sat up in bed, sweat evaporating from his face and under his arms into the thick, womb-like darkness where he sat, the pain pounding in his back, an insistent reminder of another darkness.

Like the darkness he and Jerry had plunged into, tires rolling on gravel roads past the whispering sunflowers, challenging the night, the memories. And losing.

Mick reached over, switched on the light. It brought the room around him into focus, a soft focus like in the movies, fuzzy around the edges.

For the first time since the . . . accident, Mick knew he was thinking clearly, recreating all that he had seen and felt and touched. Not only the images of that awful night, but before, long before. He felt as if he was just on the verge of something, some revelation, something that could explain what had happened to him and Jerry, and everything could be okay again.

He pushed back the sheet and slid his legs off the bed, felt his feet touch the carpet, and stood, holding onto the bedpost for support. Taking a deep breath, he moved his hand away from the bed.

"Okay," he said, wavering a little but standing. "Okay, Mr. Mick Winters." The hoarse words fell into the silence and were sucked up.

Mick waited there for a long time, or at least it seemed like a long time to him as he sucked in air and blinked away the little pinpointed dots that swam around in front of him, in front of his eyes, just out of reach. He breathed deeply but slowly, as if a huge gulp of air might upset his balance and send him reeling back onto the bed.

Power was coming back to him, the power to move and walk and to do the things normal people did. He stood and waited for its return. Everything around him seemed just a bit otherworldly: the light by the bed was just a trifle too sharp, his feet were a little too heavy, and his skin had a funny tingling feeling to it, as if the still air around him tickled wherever it met his flesh.

He took one step, a heavy, leaden step toward the foot of the bed. And another. His mind jerked and lurched inside his head, part of it reminding him that his back had begun a painful protest, another stronger part groping about for something that might give meaning to his actions.

My pants, he thought. *I'm looking for my pants.* He'd find his pants, that was the first thing, find his pants and put them on, and then he would be able to do other things.

Mick mumbled to himself, realizing how silly he would sound to someone else. "Wonder where those pants are . . . got to be around here somewhere . . . I'll find them, and then I'll go on out to the kitchen and make some coffee . . . no, maybe I'll have a real breakfast . . ." He liked hearing his own voice; it reassured him.

He bent down, raising the bedspread edge and peering underneath. The pain in his back hit him hard then, and he straightened, grimacing. He stood there for a moment, one hand on the foot of the bed, until the wave of pain passed.

Bacon, maybe. I wonder if Cheryl has any bacon?

He hobbled to the bedroom closet and looked in. Women's winter clothes, sweaters and wool dresses and coats. Nothing there.

Mick had run out of places to look. He glanced down at the crisp, white hospital gown that hit him at about mid-knee and decided that would have to do. As he slowly made his way back toward the bedroom door, he remembered that Cheryl was his doctor. His doctor. That would mean that somewhere back down the line she had taken off his clothes and put that gown on him—she had seen him absolutely stark naked—and the thought of it ran a silly schoolboy thrill through his body. He almost laughed out loud. He hadn't just returned to Tanapah, he had returned to his adolescence too, back to the time when he'd never been kissed by anyone his own age and his biggest, most secret sexual thrill lay between the garish covers of smuggled-in men's magazines with names like *Nugget* and *Knave*. He thought for a moment about the pink, pneumatic-chested magazine nudes, and super-imposed over them was a visual image of Cheryl's long, tapering fingerings unbuttoning his pants, peeling them down . . .

He forced his mind away from the images. Maybe later, later he would think about that, about Cheryl as a woman and a beautiful one at that, but right now there were more urgent matters, things he had to do for himself.

He stood for a moment trying to decide just what it was he had to do.

Bacon. Bacon and eggs. A good breakfast and then . . .
Then?

He shuffled to the bedroom door, wondering if he should just go back to bed and forget the whole thing until the fog in his head and the pain in his back passed—and he could think more clearly about the trouble he was in. But his legs took him out the doorway and into the hall.

It seemed cooler, less stuffy than the bedroom. Mick took a deep breath, continued down the hallway until he got to the stairs, and went down them with difficultly, holding onto the bannister with both hands. There was a light burning somewhere, and as he got closer he saw that it was in the kitchen, the hooded bulb above the stove illuminating softly the outlines of appliances and cabinets.

Mick went to the window, feeling vaguely guilty, and finding the wall switch, he sent the light flooding through the kitchen. Then he went to work. He took eggs from the refrigerator, and bacon, and he found bread in one of the drawers beside the sink. He worked slowly, and all his movements seemed exaggerated, especially the ones involving bending. And all the time he was working, little alarms were going off in his brain, little uneasy riggings, that he couldn't put words to.

Mick found a frying pan and lined up strips of bacon in it, turned the gas burner on low, and listened as the fat started to sizzle.

Everything seemed so familiar, yet so remote. Mick told himself that part of it was the painkiller which put things in a different kind of focus, and that another part of it was his time spent in bed, a time of uneasy limbo, of drug-induced calm that left a psychic hangover, of waiting, of remembering.

But there was a part missing, a part he couldn't name. *Sure,* he thought, *Jerry. And before that, the cellar.*

And something else: a feeling that things didn't stop with

the cellar, or with Jerry, and that they might find out what happened to Jerry but that maybe they—and he—would never really know, not all of it.

This knowledge began to press in on him. The very air of the kitchen seemed filled with it.

It's not over.

Mick shuddered, biting his lip. He felt cold and unwelcome and—scared. Most of all, scared.

A car pulled up outside. Mick glanced up at the clock over the kitchen table and saw that it read 3:38.

Cheryl.

Mick squeezed his hands together, trying to stop shaking. If she came in and saw him there, in the middle of the floor shaking, she'd put him back to bed and dope him up again, and he didn't want that.

The door opened and Cheryl came in, her doctor's bag suspended from one hand. She glanced around quickly at the lights, and then her eyes met Mick's.

Stop shaking, dammit!

"Mick—?" The doctor's bag plopped onto the floor.

"I'm—I'm okay, Cheryl."

She looked over at the stove where the bacon sizzled on top and back to Mick, as if she were afraid to take a step toward him.

His body began to calm.

"I'd sure like to know what the hell you're doing out of bed," Cheryl said.

Mick eased down into a chair, exhaling, the trembling dying away. "I wanted some breakfast. Guess I was a little too weak."

"I *guess.*"

He looked up after a moment, grinning a little. "Mind turning the bacon for me?" he asked.

Cheryl looked at him a couple of seconds longer and then, shaking her head slowly, walked to the stove. "I suppose you want a couple of eggs, too."

"Well, yeah. But this isn't the way it's supposed to work." He watched her as she broke the eggs into the pan with the bacon and plugged in the coffee pot. "I was going to have it ready when you got here. I thought we could have breakfast together . . . and . . . I don't know, *talk* about things, I guess."

She looked around. "What sort of things?"

It was then that Mick noticed the blue tinge of the flesh just under her eyes and the way her eyelids sagged a little. Her pupils flickered at him, and he saw the tiny red webbing in sharp relief against the whites of her eyes.

"I don't know," Mick replied. He spread his palms. "I guess I don't know much this morning."

"That makes two of us," Cheryl muttered.

"I beg your pardon?"

She turned to him again. "Nothing." And then, "Dammit. There's too much grease in this pan." Mick watched her as she buried herself in the kitchen until the bacon and eggs were done, the toast popped up and buttered, and the coffee percolating. Then she got out two plates from a cabinet, loaded them with food, and took them to the table.

Mick's muscles still had a weak, kittenish feel to them, and he wasn't really all that hungry anymore, but he forced himself to go to work on the breakfast. They ate silently, sitting on opposite sides of the table.

Finally, Mick put his fork down. "I guess I wasn't as hungry as I thought," he said sheepishly.

A smile flickered across her face.

"I'm sorry, Cheryl. Hell, I just felt like I had to do something."

"I understand. But you really shouldn't be up." She pushed aside her plate and lit a cigarette.

Something in her manner, the way she moved, made Mick feel suddenly odd, and the little alarms in his mind began ringing again. He said gently, "Are you okay? I mean, you look done in."

"Do I?"

He nodded.

"Well . . ." The word trailed off with the smoke from her cigarette. Mick waited. "I—I don't know, Mick. Something strange—strange things are happening . . ."

"Tonight?"

"Uh-huh."

"What happened?"

Cheryl moved as if to take a drink of her coffee but set the cup back down untouched. "I don't know, Mick, I just don't know. The call was . . . About a boy. On the other side of town. I may have told you that when I left."

"Yeah, you did."

"When I got there, he was dead." Her voice suddenly took on a different tone, one of urgency and confusion, and the words tumbled out. "This is a very small town, Mick. A small town with not very many surprises, and I like that. I like going into houses and reassuring people and prescribing things that I'm pretty sure will work. People thank me and things go like before. Here, people are pretty predictable, and the things that happen to them are, too. The kids get the usual childhood diseases, the adults get colds and the flu, occasionally something more severe but not very often, and when it's time, people that are old enough die." She paused. "Do you understand what I'm trying to say to you?"

"I think so."

"I don't like mysteries. Hell, I don't even like to *read*

mysteries. I like solutions. I do what a garage mechanic or a plumber does. I take things that seem hard to other people and make sense out of them, get things running right again. Or that's what I used to do."

"The boy—"

"Suffocated." She stubbed out her cigarette and lit another.

Mick waited for her to continue. When she didn't, he said, "That's no mystery, is it? I mean—"

"Mick"—her voice raised a little—"he was lying underneath a bed. He shouldn't have suffocated. There was plenty of room for him to breathe under there, but he died anyway."

Mick cast around in his mind. "Was there anyone else—"

"Another boy, a friend. Spending the night. He was hysterical when I arrived, and I couldn't get much out of him. Maybe later." She took a sip of coffee. "But he said something about a dare, and something about things that came out and pulled his friend under the bed."

A dare!

"Like Jerry!" Mick said suddenly.

"What?"

And suddenly Mick was flooded with a hopeless, unreasonable kind of anger. He lashed out at Cheryl. "You want me to talk about Jerry, right? It's the same thing, isn't it! *Isn't it,* Cheryl?"

"Mick." She rose slowly. "What in the world are you talking—"

"I want *out* of here, Cheryl. I've got to get things taken care of!" The anger was beyond him now, out of his control, and he was powerless to stop it. "Thank you for all you've done. Please show me where my clothes are and—"

Cheryl grabbed him suddenly by both shoulders. "Mick. Stop it!"

"I said I want—"

"Stop it!"

There was a heavy, thick quiet as their eyes locked. Mick, aware only of her eyes, now angry slits, and the labored sound of his own breathing, knew that, suddenly and inexplicably, he had run out of things to say.

A door suddenly opened down the hall. They turned to see Annie in a long white nightgown framed in the entryway to the kitchen. She stood there, just outside the circle of light, blinking, staring quietly at Mick and Cheryl.

Cheryl went back to her daughter's side. "Go on back to sleep, hon," she said, stroking her child's hair. "It's not time to get up yet."

"I heard voices, Mommy."

"I know. Mr. Winters and I were just talking."

"It was too loud," said Annie. "You waked me up."

Cheryl gently turned the little girl back down the hall. "I know," she said again. "We'll be quieter." She kissed her on the forehead and guided her toward her room.

Mick watched them walk away from him, the little girl turning once to look over her shoulder at him. He felt awkward and guilty and deflated. When they disappeared into Annie's room, he sighed and sat back down, his head light and swirling. He just wanted things—everything—to be all right, and it seemed as if nothing really was—from the relentless pain in his back and the throbbing in his head, to his sudden outburst at Cheryl, to his unshakeable feeling that everything was wrong, all wrong, all around him. Nothing felt good and right and ordered.

He was an alien, a stranger. He felt like a kid who had come back after being away a long time only to find that his parents and his friends didn't like him anymore, didn't care what happened to him, didn't talk while he was around.

Cheryl came back in quietly and sat down. Before she

could say anything, Mick leaned across the table, stretching an arm toward her.

"I'm sorry, Cheryl. I don't want to have to keep saying I'm sorry to you, but there it is. I am sorry."

"It's okay," she returned. "You're just trying to do things before you're ready. And I understand why you want to be up and around. When the time comes, I'll do everything I can to help you."

"I know, you're doing that now."

Cheryl drank some of her coffee and then put the cup down and stared into it. "I shouldn't be doing this," she said. "Practically four in the morning and I'm sitting here getting wired up on caffeine."

"'Physician, heal thyself.'"

"I know." She shook her head from side to side slowly, as if it required great effort. "I'm just—I don't know. Puzzled is too mild a word, I'm afraid. It's something deeper than that. It's just—"

"I know," Mick said quietly. "First Jerry and now this, right? Two deaths, back to back, that you can't explain."

"That's right, Mick," Cheryl sighed.

Something started at the back of his mind, then, forming words out of the vapors. He was suddenly chilled. "You know," he said, "that's very . . . odd."

"What is?"

"That's something I used to be afraid of."

"What is?"

"Being pulled under the bed. Didn't anyone tell you about that when you were a kid?"

"No, I don't think so."

"If you . . . if you hang your arm off the edge of the bed, something will come out . . . from under the bed, or, I don't know, maybe from out of the closet, but it'll come out and grab your fingers while you're sleeping." He leaned toward Cheryl, the chill subsiding. "Sure you never heard that?"

"No. If I had, I probably would've heard it from you." She smiled a little. "You were the one that always told me those kinds of things."

The words came faster now, as if of their own accord, as if Mick were only the vehicle for their transmission. "And Jerry was afraid of the culvert, of something in the culvert, and maybe those kids—or the one, anyway, that you were . . . called about, was afraid of what was under his bed, and the kids dared each other, and Jerry and I—" He broke off and looked away from Cheryl, feeling stupid.

"Mick? What are you getting at?"

"Hell," he said bitterly. "Nothing. I'm just grabbing at things because I—I just don't understand what's going on. If you can put words on things, then you can understand them. That's what I do for a living, Cheryl." His voice got quiet. "I put words on things so other people can understand. I can't put words on what happened to Jerry, and that's what scares me."

He felt the gentle pressure of her fingers on his arm, but he didn't turn around. His mind was feeling druggy and misty again.

"Mick?" Her voice came from behind him.

He shook his head slowly. In the darkness of his mind the mist parted, and clearly, there before him, was the door. The cellar door.

Want a name? Goofus. There's a name.

"Mick?"

Her voice penetrated his mind, and the mists closed in on him again. He turned slowly to her.

"Look," she said. "We've had an awful lot to deal with in the past two days, both of us. Whatever it is, whatever all this . . . bullshit is, we need to sleep and talk about it tomorrow.

Okay?" Her voice was soothing and gentle, her eyes saying, yes, yes, that's what you need to do. Believe it. I'm the doctor.

He stared at her, feeling helpless again and hating it. Back in their youth, in the three summers of his boyhood, she had been the one, he remembered, the oh-so-rational little girl who had told him there was no such thing as a monster or a werewolf or a vampire, she had told Mack in that serious little-girl voice of hers that *she* wasn't scared of the dark, or funeral homes, or even graveyards.

And over and over again—under Aunt Lucy's apple tree, or on the merry-go-round at the park, or in the tall, cool weeds in the alley behind the vacant lot—she had drilled it into his head:

There's nothing in the cellar, Mick. Nothing. It's all your imagination.

Cheryl walked across the kitchen floor to her bag, fumbled around in it for a moment, and came back, placing a couple of pills in front of Mick on the table.

"Here," she said. "I'll get you some water, and I want you to take these."

He looked over at her.

"To make you sleep."

Mick felt himself smile. "First you serve me coffee, then you give me something to put me out. Upper, downer. You're a regular Dr. Feelgood, aren't you?"

She went to the sink and ran some water in a glass. "I was Elvis's doctor. But don't let it get out, okay?" She was smiling, too.

When she put the water in front of him, Mick said, "You know, it's funny Cheryl."

"What? That I was Elvis's doctor?"

He waved a hand at her. "No. I'm serious now."

"I've been serious for too long. Let me be silly for a minute, Mick."

"Okay. But what I'm going to say is true. When I spent those summers with Aunt Lucy, you were the one who took charge, always strong, never afraid. Now me, I had all my little fears, a kids' little fears, about closets and old houses and empty playgrounds at night. But not you." He looked into her eyes, and reaching out for her hand, found it. "And now, all these years later, I come back to Tanapah and find out that it's still true. Cheryl Mallis is still trying to take care of me. Cheryl Mallis is still the goddamn candle in the darkness."

She smiled at him, squeezing his hand. "No. But I sure wish I was sometimes, Mick. It would make things one hell of a lot easier."

He took her other hand and held it, pulling her face to his. As she came to him, her eyes widened a little, then closed as he kissed her. They stood up, still holding hands, Mick's face close to hers, Mick marveling to himself about how she could smell so good at four a.m. after a long day.

"I'm not so sure we should have done that," she whispered.

"Don't you know? These are the 1980s, Cheryl. People go to bed on the first date now."

Her voice was gentle as she looked at him. "Maybe they do. I don't."

Mick squeezed both her hands again quickly, and let them drop, warmth coursing through his body as he looked at her. "Me, neither. Maybe that's our problem."

"I've got a few problems Mick, but that's not one of them." She reached down and picked up the glass of water and pills from the table. "Now take these and don't let me catch you wandering around until I say it's okay."

He took the pills, washed them down with the water. "Okay, Doc."

When he set the glass back down, she came to him, hugged

him, and kissed his cheek. "Now get lost," she said, pointing a finger upstairs.

Mick climbed the stairs slowly, looking back a couple of times to see her standing in the same position, making sure he did as she said. He ambled down the hallway and got into bed. As the medicine took effect, the last thing he remembered to do was make sure his arm wasn't hanging over the edge.

10

Tanapah slept like a cat with one eye open, restless and edgy.

Lights were on late into the night in windows that habitually were dark after ten. Radios were tuned to unfamiliar stations that kept broadcasting to the night people of cities having nothing to do with Tanapah. Old and forgotten books were picked up and opened again.

Nobody could have said why.

Damned coffee.

Cheryl Stanton lay in bed, sleep eluding her. Suddenly, she heard a faint moan and cry come from Annie's room next door. Pushing back the bed covers, she was on her feet, reaching for a house robe. The cry came again.

"Annie?"

The robe was forgotten in her rush to the child's bedside.

Annie was sprawled on the bed, tossing and flailing her

arms at the moonlight that fell through the open window into a bluish-white rectangle across the bed. Her eyes were clenched shut.

"Annie!" Cheryl caught her in a tight hug. "Wake up, honey. Come on."

Annie quivered and sobbed. Cheryl reached to the nightstand and switched on the lamp. "You were dreaming, just dreaming honey. That's all," she said.

"M-momma?" The little girl's eyes opened hazily. Cheryl picked her up and rocked her gently.

"Everything's all right now, Annie," she said. But her own heart thudded in such terror that she could feel the rush of blood pulsing at her temples and in her fingertips. *Children die in the night.*

Cheryl looked at Annie's bed with its white-painted headboard and pink-and-white checked spread. She imagined that bed overturned, the mattress thrown against the wall. And on the floor . . .

"I love you, Mommy," Annie said.

Taking a deep breath, Cheryl forced herself to be calm and reassuring. *She mustn't ever know. Not ever.* "I love you too, Annie," she said. "What were you dreaming about?"

Annie's brow crinkled in puzzlement. "I forgot."

"Well, it's time to get to sleep again, young lady. You've been up entirely too much tonight." She put Annie back in bed and tucked the covers in around her. "And here's Christy," she said, slipping the little rag doll in beside her.

She kissed Annie on the forehead and clicked the light off.

"The part I 'member," Annie said from the darkness, "was all dark, 'cause it was deep underwater. It was awful."

Cheryl paused in the doorway. "You just remember that you're safe at home in your own bed," she said. *No. Don't think about it.* "Goodnight, Annie." She closed the door gently.

Now, I believe everyone in this house is taken care of, thought Cheryl. *Except me.* What was it Mick has said. *"Physician, heal thyself."*

Cheryl decided that as long as she was up, she would check on Mick, just to assure herself that everything was all right in the Stanton house. Then, maybe she could go to sleep.

She padded up the stairs, clicked on the hall light, and cracked open Mick's door.

The light from the hallway filtered through the room where Mick lay sleeping peacefully. By his bed, the curtains were pulled away from the window, and Cheryl saw a reflection of herself in the glass, a ghost image surrounded by darkness and the lace curtains that waved a little in the breeze. Mick too was reflected, and the way the light and reflections played made it appear that she was standing next to him, right next to his bed. Cheryl turned one way and then another, watching herself in the glass.

Her nightgown was thin, a floral print cut low at the chest, and she knew she looked good in it. Momentarily captivated by their ethereal reflections in the window, she bent slightly in the hallway, and in the glass it looked like she was bending over Mick, her breasts swaying, touching his chest, gently, sensuously—*No!*

Cheryl straightened, feeling foolish. She looked into her dark reflection across the room, narrowing her eyes.

Not again. I'm not going to let it happen again.

But there was an ache in her, a dull hollow ache. She stood there a moment more, and then she crept into the room and looked down at Mick. He was sleeping, deeply and peacefully. Crossing to the window, she reached down and opened it a little more to let some of the breeze in. She was careful not to look into the glass, at herself, at Mick. Together.

She glanced out the window. "I'll be darned," she whispered to herself. "Wonder what the Redmillers are doing up this time of night?" The little house across the way was flooded with light.

Thinking about the Redmillers diverted her, and some of the ache went away then. She crossed the room and closed the door behind her, never looking back at Mick or at the dull, murky reflections of the two of them, little qualities of light, playing along the glass in the hour of not quite dawn.

Otis Redmiller stood at the stove stirring a pot of hot chocolate. He waived a while, turned the fire off, and went to the cupboard for a mug, only to see his wife Hattie standing in the doorway.

"You're up early," she commented

He nodded. "Or pretty damn late. Depends on how you look at it." He carried his mug to the stove. "Couldn't sleep," he grumbled. "Thought I'd get up and read a little."

"You don't have the sense you were born with," she said.

He poured two mugs full, and they sat there in the kitchen —Otis with his gray stubble of a morning beard, and Hattie with her hair curled and netted.

In the silence, the house creaked. And creaked again. They looked at each other.

"Sometimes I think it's trying to talk to me," Otis said.

The screen door to the kitchen, loose on its hinges, rattled as a wind rose and fell, and there was a faint whistling sound coming from the attic.

Hattie took a sip of hot chocolate. She stirred in a spoonful of sugar and tried it again. "Well, I wouldn't worry about that, old man," she said, "Until you start trying to talk back."

Otis didn't laugh.

But the house did, in soft creaks and whispers.

H erb Jeffries sat reading a thick, blue-jacketed book called *Modern Forensic Medicine*. Stretching, he put the book down at the base of the floor lamp, suddenly realizing he had locked onto a single paragraph and had been reading and rereading the same thing.

The book struck something on the floor that made a jingling noise.

Jeffries reached over the thick padded arm of the overstuffed rocker, felt around until his fingers closed on the baby ball. It was a bright yellow ball with a bell inside. He held the ball, turning it slowly, and thought about what it would be like not to be able to touch or hear even such a simple thing.

Cadaver. It was a word that didn't belong in a man's thoughts at home in his own chair. It was a word like a dull black beetle in his mind.

Postmortem. Necrosis. Autopsy.

His wife and the twins were asleep just steps away, but they might as well have been in a different world. Increasingly, he had begun to keep a distance from them, as if his thoughts, like a disease, might be contagious.

In the darkest hours of this restless night, he would unpin the sheriff's badge from the right pocket of his crisply pressed beige shirt and sit touching the points of the star. It had always been just another thing to carry, like the car keys. But now, the badge felt colder and heavier in his hand, demanding that he be cold and strong in return.

A couple of hours earlier, he had taken the plastic pearl handles off his .38-caliber polished chrome revolver and put back the original black grips.

He still felt like a big kid playing cowboy.

Stepping in as sheriff had seemed the natural, if not the only, job for him. His dad had held the office for thirty years; in Grover County, folks said the title of sheriff didn't sound right without the Jeffries name attached to it.

Tom Jeffries, though, had been a brawny-shouldered hulk of a man who cleaned up the last-known ring of cattle rustlers in the Tanapah area by landing three of them in the hospital with a tire iron. To his son, he had left a county in which crime took the form of a stolen car battery now and then, a Coke machine pried open, or a kid shooting at cats with a pellet gun.

What would *he* have done about a man being mutilated out in the country?

The baby ball jingled.

Maybe nothing, Jeffries thought. Maybe *he* would have felt lost and blind, too. *But he wouldn't have been scared. He wouldn't have been so damned scared.*

Ginny Adams stopped suddenly in the darkened hallway.

Unable to sleep, she had come downstairs toward the kitchen for a glass of milk. She had come quietly and without turning the lights on, to keep from waking her parents.

They wouldn't understand another one of her "episodes"— the way her mother had put it.

She had come most of all because of the phone in the kitchen: a white phone on the wall. *Bob* would talk to her. He would listen and try to understand. He wouldn't care how late it was, or early. He wouldn't say something was wrong with her.

Talk to me, Ginny. Tell me. I love you. Those had been his words. Exactly.

She should have told him . . . then. She *had* to tell somebody. And, over the phone, if there was a cloud of disbelief in his eyes, she wouldn't have to see it.

Over the phone, if his words faltered, she could change the subject. *Do you miss school, Bobby?* He wouldn't see the tightening of hurt and betrayal register in her face.

She had come downstairs from her bedroom imagining the click of the receiver as she lifted it. The whirring of the phone dial. The ringing. His voice.

But now, she stopped in the hallway short of the kitchen.

She stopped, and, incredibly, her first thought was a brittle but almost calm one.

It isn't fair.

Then the fear grew from an icy shard at the back of her neck, until it forced a tremble in her knees. She begged herself for the control to hold her breath and back away. Silently. Very silently.

The rules had changed.

She couldn't go into the kitchen at night.

She backed to the stairway and touched the bannister. It felt slick and cool against the wetness of her palm. It was something to trust.

Her eyes strained toward the blackened rectangle of the kitchen doorway. There was no sound, no movement. But he was there.

She could feel him watching her. She felt the burn of his eyes on her, stripping her, not just of nylon and lace but of blood and bone. And life.

There! From the back corner of the kitchen—the glint of a knife blade.

He was waiting.

He must have known that she would sense him there. So, why? Except to let her know that, now, he could get in.

A new rule.

Ginny backed up the stairway, keeping her hand on the bannister. The stairs seemed to shake with the pounding of her heart.

She wanted to scream—but if she screamed, he would laugh at her and be gone into echoes before the lights snapped on. In his place would be empty chair in the corner, or a towel hanging from a hook on the wall. And she would be left explaining that she'd had a bad . . . dream . . . again.

She was halfway up the stairs now.

Ginny, at first, had prayed against insanity. Then, for it.

Insanity was curable.

She *had* to tell it. *Somebody* had to listen to her and then explain to her, very calmly and reassuringly, how to make it go away.

Bobby.

She hesitated, standing still and gripping the bannister so tightly that her fingers felt numb.

Spook games. They were such deliciously scary things to play as a little girl, and all the better, all the scarier, because they were secret.

Little rules. *Ghosts can't come into the laundry room.* Little discoveries. *Ghosts don't like it if you sneeze.* Little safe spots.

The bannister.

Ghosts can't see you if you're holding onto the bannister.

Ginny loosened her grip.

Go to the phone, she told herself. Go call. Nothing will happen to you; nothing can. Go to the phone, and the game will be over.

Trembling, she took the first step down. The second came easier. The third . . .

From the kitchen came a shuffling sound, moving toward her.

She stopped, transfixed with horror, tasting the salt of a tiny drop of perspiration as it slid into the corner of her mouth.

A game. It was a still a game but now with grown-up rules that made it harder to play. There were sounds. There were appearances.

Another step down.

He had been coming closer, always closer since . . . that night . . . in the country, when he had risen up from the pit of a half-forgotten nightmare and she had seen him through the car window.

But, as before, when she was a child, there had been rules, and safe spots.

He can't get me unless I go outside and across the street after dark. That was the first rule, but then it changed, and it was: *He can't get me unless I go out after dark.*

Unless I go out.

Unless I go in the basement without the light on.

Unless I go into the basement.

Now the new rule should have been, *unless I go into the kitchen in the dark;* but he was changing it.

He was coming out.

Ginny leaned slightly over the bannister until she could see the kitchen doorway, and the head emerging from it, the yellow-white skin glowing dimly against the darkness.

It's not real! It's not real! It's not real!

Her hand slapped the wall, reaching up, searching for the light switch.

He grinned at her. His mouth bent impossibly far upward, his lips stretched like parchment over his teeth.

Slowly, he lifted the knife. Slowly, he drew the blade across the back of his free hand, and the blood ran, trailing in rivulets over his long, still fingers

Ghosts can't see you if you're holding onto the bannister.

Ginny held, only dimly aware of the pulsing and cold tingling in her arms, and the ache in her hands.

She held on for life.

He raised the cut hand in front of his face, twisting and bending it at the wrist, as if he were watching it die. The blood ran down his arm in such silence, Ginny could hear the thick drops of it hitting the tiled kitchen floor.

And when his hand was stained a full, glistening darkness, he reached . . . toward . . . her.

Tanapah slept. It slept like a cat with one eye open, wakeful and wary, casting sidewise glances into the shadows.

Nobody could have said why. Almost nobody.

When sleep came, it came like the rippling of water. Soft and soothing at first, then cold.

Cold and inescapable.

11

Mick awoke to an insistent sound that meshed into the dream image of a great bronze bell. He sat up too quickly, his head reeling.

Had a *day* gone by? A whole *day*?

He remembered things in bits and pieces. Cheryl's face over his bed, telling him he needed rest. A tray with pills and a glass of water. Day blending into evening blending into night, all interchangeable. And now?

The doorbell rang again.

Words, he remembered, cutting through the haze of the past twenty-four hours. Words from Cheryl. Doctor's words: *Delayed reaction. Fatigue. Mental exhaustion.*

"Cheryl?" he called. There was no answer. The stillness made him suddenly aware of the clock ticking on the nightstand beside him.

10:23

Again: the bell.

In his confusion, Mick stood, feeling the effects of a

painkiller hangover, his mouth dry, his body stiff and unnatural. Shuffling into the hallway, he heard the bell ring again.

The house seemed flooded with light as he made his way down the stairs. *A whole day. Gone.* He called out for Cheryl one more time, heard nothing in reply, and then said to the door: "Be right there."

Passing the big hallway mirror, he stopped just short of the door and looked at himself, wondering if he should be answering the door at all. He smoothed his unruly hair with his hand and studied the whiskey roughness of his face. And the hospital gown. But he had spoken, and whoever was ringing the bell might have heard him, and it was too late to try to hide.

He opened the door to a young woman in black. The stark dress hung loose over her shoulders, giving it the look of something that didn't belong to her but that had to be worn. She was slender, almost childlike in body, but there were fine lines about her mouth and eyes. Mick's scrutiny stopped short at her eyes, which were reddened, swollen, and very wet. His breath caught.

"Are you . . .Mr. Winters?" she asked.

Mick nodded, feeling tension build in the pit of his stomach.

But for her fingers tugging and twisting at the corners of a white lace handkerchief, she could have been a statue of cold stone. "I'm Marcia Meyers," she said. "I'm Jerry's . . . no, I can't say wife anymore, can I? Jerry's widow."

Mick wanted to run, or to hold her. Nothing between those two extremes seemed to fit. He gestured awkwardly, "Please come in. I was just going to make some coffee."

"No," she said. "I just wanted to . . . see you, because . . . maybe you could tell me . . ."

Tears welled in her eyes, and her voice broke like crystal at the word "Why?"

"I don't know." Mick forced a calmness into his answer. "I can understand why you would blame me, Mrs. Meyers. I blame myself. But I didn't . . ." *Kill him. I didn't kill him. I can't even say it.*

She turned away from him, talking as if she were talking to a third person. Or to a ghost. "The sheriff . . . said he . . .doesn't know what happened to . . . Jerry. Not for sure. I'm not making accusations. All I know about you is that Jerry liked you because he talked about you sometimes."

"I liked Jerry, too. The summers I spent here . . . he was like my kid brother." Mick paused. "He called me one time—got my number from Aunt Lucy, I guess—and asked me . . . about you. It was when he was trying to get up the nerve to ask you to marry him."

She smiled wanly. "And what did you say?"

"I was the voice of caution. He told me to go jump and said thanks for helping him make up his mind."

A warm breeze carried the scent of the lilac bushes from the front walk. "It's good to smell the outdoors again," he said, and then became flustered, realizing how inappropriate his remark must have sounded.

She turned away again. "It was a fine service," she said. "Just about the whole town turned out. I'm . . . sorry you couldn't have been there."

Black dress. The house left empty. He should have known —*should have*—but *no,* he had been too centered on thinking about himself. There was nothing to say. His face flushed and burned, lit by shame and self-anger.

"Jerry . . . they took him . . . to Tulsa. To the medical exam-iner," she said. "I didn't ask, and I don't want to know . . . what they did to him. But they sent him back, and we . . . buried him."

She backed away, taking small, frail steps. "You said I could blame you, Mr. Winters," she said. "I wish it was that easy. I think I came here wanting to blame you and hate you. But all I know is, I miss him . . . so much. All I feel is alone."

Mick stood in the doorway after she'd left. He tapped at the potted fern that hung from a macramé rope to the side of the door. Suddenly, he ripped the pot loose and smashed it to little pieces against the porch. Then he went through the house until he found his suitcase, the one from the motel that had his shaving kit and toothbrush and clothes in it, clothes that he could wear and not feel ashamed.

T*he Tanapah Herald* building was marked with a neon sign that had stopped working years ago. Set into the sign was a clock that, to anyone's memory, had never run. The name of the paper was lettered again in big, chipped, gold letters on the plate window in front, with smaller letters underneath that could be made out to read "Printing and Office Supplies."

The front door was propped open with a box of adding machine tape.

Mick stopped outside the door to catch his breath. From Cheryl's house he had walked about six blocks to the downtown area. It left him in a cold sweat and feeling shaky. It left him feeling good, too—like winning a hard game of tennis, but better, since it wasn't a game.

Mick took a deep breath and drew himself straight. He listened a moment to the clattering of a typewriter from inside the *Herald* office. There was a confident rhythm to the sound, not fast but steady, and even before he went in, Mick could envision from his boyhood days in Tanapah the way Matthew Simmons would be sitting there. No grand piano was ever

approached with more bearing and style than Matthew
Simmons's old Royal Standard.

The floor was concrete, painted green. A crack in the
concrete led from the doorway to the counter, where a poster
reading "Give the United Way" was taped to the back of an old
brass cash register. The side of the counter consisted of a
section of gray metal shelves filled with office provisions;
directly behind it, a desk was occupied by a middle-aged
woman wearing a veiled hat and a dark, floral-print dress. A
pair of white gloves was draped neatly over the edge of a letter
basket at the corner of the desk.

She looked like she'd meant to go to church, Mick thought,
and for a moment things got turned around in his head again
about what day it was. He had slept through Sunday,
hadn't he?

*It was a fine service. Just about the whole town
turned out.*

"Can I help you?" she asked, glancing up at him. Mick felt
suddenly glad that he had at least been able to shave and comb
his hair.

He looked beyond her. The desk in the back corner was
exactly as he remembered it: an L-shaped affair made of
plywood and topped with linoleum, its surface littered with
papers on top of papers which gave the vague impression of
being stacked in order. It was a desk that might have brought
ten dollars at a flea market sale, but the man behind it gave it
the aura of polished oak.

"Sir . . ." the woman began.

"No, thank you," Mick said. "I just stopped in to see Mr.
Simmons."

"Well, he's awfully busy today," the woman answered. She
said something else afterward, but Mick's attention snapped to
the back of the room. Simmons startled him by calling out to

him without appearing to have looked up or missed a beat on the typewriter.

"I said come on over, Mick." The old man hit a row of X's across a word he didn't like. "Have a seat. I'll be with you in a minute."

Mick nodded, edging around the corner. The woman scowled at him. "Mr. Simmons," she said in a low accusing voice, "is working much too hard. Much too—"

Simmons heard her. "This is a newspaper, Mrs. Grier," he said drily. "We don't get the news by telling people to go away."

She sniffed as if greatly affronted and began shuffling papers. It was a practiced reaction to a small drama that, Mick sensed, was played out over and over.

He crossed to Simmons's desk, which faced a single chair upholstered in cracked red vinyl. He sat down as Simmons jerked the paper out of the typewriter, scanned the sheet, and made a couple of corrections, writing in hard strokes with a thick black pencil.

Simmons thumped his fist against the wall behind him that separated the front office from the press room. The door to the press room swung open as if it were automatically activated by a fist hitting the wall.

A tall, skinny young man wearing a denim work apron raced through the doorway. Wordlessly, he took the sheet Simmons handed him and disappeared into the press room.

Simmons turned to face Mick for the first time. "Good to see you up and around, Mick. Sorry things are so hectic around here."

"He's having the time of his life," Mrs. Grier muttered. Simmons glared at her, and she turned her back on him.

"What can I do for you, Mick?" he asked.

Mick remembered coming into the *Herald* office as a kid. He remembered the warm touch of Aunt Lucy's hand on his shoulder and her voice coming from high up and behind him. "I would like to introduce my nephew, Mickie Winters, to you, Mr. Simmons." And Simmons, shaking Mick's hand in a man-to-man fashion, prompted him, "Well now, Mickie, tell me something about yourself."

Mick had been at a loss for starting then, as he was now. "I . . ."—he pointed to Simmons's typewriter—"I just noticed. You've got an electric."

The old man grinned. "And the press in the back is an offset. Doesn't have the old roar when it starts up. It sort of sputs and growls." He thumbed an antacid tablet loose from a half-gone roll on the desktop.

"I need to talk to you," Mick said. "I don't know where to start, and maybe this isn't the time. But I didn't know until too late that Jerry's funeral was today."

Simmons shook his head. "It's over," he said. "You couldn't have changed anything by being there."

"But I *should* have been." Mick realized with a sudden embarrassment that he had shouted. Mrs. Grier had cocked her head toward the back corner. He began again. "It wasn't Cheryl's . . . Dr. Stanton's fault," he said. "She thinks she's protecting me and keeping me in for my own good, but there's so much I don't know."

The phone rang on Simmons's desk, and he caught it on the first ring. He frowned as he listened. "No word? Nothing?" He paused and crunched a second tablet. "Well, Herb, did you think about giving Don's cousin a call up near Lake Hennessy? My guess is that they just changed their mind and went up that way." Another longer pause. "Now take it easy, Herb. Okay? Let me know what you find out."

Simmons noted something on a scratch pad. "It's one thing and then another around here," he said. "This'll be the first time in ten years that I've been able to boot the garden tips columns off the front page."

"I should come to town more often," Mick said. "I stir up some great copy."

His own sarcasm startled him. He couldn't have been more surprised at himself if a knife had dropped out of his shirt sleeve and landed on Simmons's desk. But a bigger surprise was the old man's reaction—a quick look of shame.

"Mick, there's a story that goes around this business," Simmons said, "about a newspaper wire editor back in the sixties. Absolutely devoted to John Kennedy. Well, one day he's left with a twenty-inch hole on the front page and nothing to fill it. And the report comes over the wire machine: John Kennedy shot to death. He says, 'Thank God.'"

Simmons leaned forward. His eyes were the cold steady gray of a winter storm. "Jerry Meyers, and another—one you had nothing to do with—the little Henshaw boy. Tragedies. Unspeakable tragedies. And my job . . . My job is to tell about it. So, I try not to think a lot about people but, instead, about headlines, and how the page is going to fit together. How 'bout some quick coffee?"

Simmons was up and had grabbed his coat from a hook on the wall before Mick could answer.

They walked in silence. Simmons adopted an ambling shuffle that he meant to seem relaxed, but Mick knew it was to keep the pace down. For him, the limping invalid.

A sign announcing "Darlene's Donuts" projected from a brick building in the middle of the block ahead. Suspended from the sign was a wooden donut painted with streaks of purple frosting. It was grotesque and unreal. It fit the mood.

"I heard Jerry's body went to the medical examiner," Mick said.

"That's right." Simmons greeted a farmer they passed on the sidewalk. "I got a copy of the report."

"And?"

Simmons stopped. "You've got a lot of questions, Mick," he said. "You've also got some answers, I think, that you've been keeping back. Now, what would you say to a little round of you spill your beans and I'll spill mine?"

"I'm not trying to keep any secrets, Mr. Simmons. I don't know what I can tell you." Mick looked into the old man's eyes.

"Okay. Let's put this together," Simmons said as they stood facing each other. "Let's start with the bar and find out what you were doing there in the first place."

Mick shrugged. *The sound of a jar smashing. Whistling. Something old coming awake.* "I just wanted a beer."

"*A* beer? I did some checking around the elite clientele of Scot's Tap, Mick. Those that remember you tell me you were doing your best to get stewed that night."

"It was one of those nights. I was upset . . . coming back here. I just wanted the world to turn off for a while."

"Suppose it was one of those nights, and you were back in Kansas City. Where would you go? To a beer dive? I'd have pegged you for a little more class than that."

"I wasn't . . ." *Black blood, and the wood was in splinters.* "I wasn't thinking too straight."

"*Why?* What happened to you? Where had you been?" Simmons's voice pricked him like a needle.

"To the house. It was the house."

"You went to your aunt's place. What happened?"

Oh, lord! And run. Run! "I can't really explain it," Mick said, "Memories. A lot of memories."

"What scared you?"

Mick blanched at the question, looking quickly around the

sidewalk to see if anyone else had heard. The closest pedestrian was a good block away.

Simmons seemed to know everything. He was a white-haired old mystic in gray tweed.

"Mick, you told the sheriff—or sort of told him, from what I gather—that this whole thing started with you and Jerry telling scare stories." Simmons said. "I knew Jerry pretty well. A good man. He worked hard and took care of his family, but he wasn't a dreamer; he didn't have the imagination for it. So, if the two of you were telling scare stories, *you* must have gotten the talk started." He returned a solemn wave to the driver of a passing car. "My question is," he said, "what started *you?*"

Mick stiffened and looked away for a moment, then trained his eyes on Simmons's. "You play a heavy game of spill the beans," he replied. "So far, it's been your turn to ask all the questions. When do I get a chance?"

"Right after this." Simmons stepped close enough to make the arm's length between them uncomfortable. "You said Jerry crawled into the culvert." He motioned to Mick with a palm-up sweep of his hand. "Why?"

"To prove he wasn't scared. I know it sounds stupid—"

"Scared of what?" Simmons made the words burn. "He was claustrophobic? He thought the boogeyman was going to get him? What?"

Mick glanced around again. There was nobody watching them. "He . . . said all the kids used to be scared of a big spider in the culvert."

"Oh?" Simmons drew back, his face tightening. "That's interesting."

A woman came out of the store next to them carrying an armload of packages, and Simmons stepped aside to talk to her.

It was early afternoon, and the downtown was coming alive again, albeit slowly. The stores and offices, closed for Jerry's funeral, were being opened. Tanapah was like any other living thing that had grown old, Mick thought. It had learned to stop and rest when it was hurt.

"Well,"—Simmons came back to Mick and patted his shoulder—"it's my turn to tell, I guess." They started walking again. "You were asking me about the medical examiner's report."

"Yeah." The breeze shifted. The sweet smell of the donut bakery drifted toward them, and Mick's stomach tightened and tilted.

"You must have wondered how come Herb Jeffries, the sheriff, wasn't poking around with more questions yesterday," Simmons said. "It's because of that autopsy report. Herb's a good kid, but he's out of his league and he knows it. And that report—" He made a *tsk* sound, accompanied by a shake of his head. "I think Herb's so mixed up, he's not sure where the sun comes up anymore."

"What was in it?" Mick felt the cold shackles that come with waiting for bad news.

They stopped outside the bakery door, the sign swinging and creaking over their heads.

"Mick," he said. "They had the poor guy listed as dead of 'major trauma,' which seemed to cover everything from a torn jugular vein—his throat ripped open—to being full of . . . insect venom."

Mick took his coffee and sat at a table toward the back of the small shop. Simmons was talking to a portly man in a splotched-white apron standing behind the donut counter. ". . . awful," Mick heard the man say. "It's just not fair."

Simmons joined him a few minutes later. "The town's as upset as it's ever been," he said. "It feels like the war years all over again."

"Herb—you were talking to a Herb on the phone. Back at the office." Mick looked at him squarely. "Jeffries?"

Simmons seemed mildly surprised. "Good observation," he said. "But you slipped in another question on me. It was my turn." Mick didn't respond, and Simmons lowered his eyes and stirred his coffee. His voice dropped. "Yeah," he said. "On top of everything else, Herb's got a couple of ol' boys missing. Jim Curtis and Don Whitaker. Maybe you knew Don."

Mick could almost form a face around the name, a child's face, but it wouldn't come together. He shook his head, not really caring.

"They left to go fishing yesterday afternoon at the coal pit. You remember it? Out east of town. Didn't come back."

Now something did form. A feeling. An old chill. It fell into Mick's awareness like an old thing knocked off a distant, dark shelf, where it had been put to be forgotten.

"The coal pit?" he asked.

Now, Mickie, don't you go around that coal pit. There's a big old heebie-jeebie that lives way down deep in the water, and he has a big, long tongue. And he eats little boys.

"I was always scared to go out to the coal pit," Mick said. "My aunt told me there was a big—"

"Heebie-jeebie." Simmons finished the sentence and punctuated it with a quick, humorless grin. "That heebie-jeebie story has been keeping kids away from the coal pit for as long as I can remember," he said. "Good thing, too. You couldn't ask for a likelier place for a kid to drown."

Mick finished his coffee. It had already gone lukewarm, like his resolve. But he braced himself and started.

"Mr. Simmons, I don't know what this means. Maybe—

probably—nothing. Jerry was killed trying to prove to himself that he wasn't scared. The little boy—Cheryl told me about him —died under his bed, just like *I* used to be afraid something would drag me under and kill me. And now, the coal pit . . ." Mick stopped, fumbling, unsure of what he wanted to say, what point he wanted to make. He looked at Simmons and saw that the words had fallen into the space between them, as if they had never been said.

Simmons set his cup down with a thick china clink. "I'll tell you what you need to be thinking about, Mick," he said. "That night." He pushed a quarter under the saucer. "Now, the doctor told me there's no way you could have been torn up the way you were and have shoved a man's body all the way into the culvert pipe. The sheriff checked all around the ditch and the culvert. He didn't find anything that two men could have used to take each other to pieces. So, who else—or what else— was out there?"

Simmons stood. He stood looking down at Mick, and Mick knew it was a deliberate little power game.

"It's my turn, Mick," he said, "and that's my question."

T hey walked back to the *Herald* office together.

"I haven't seen the paper," Mick said. "It's funny. I guess I've been a pretty hot item, and I've got no idea what's been said about me."

Simmons unwrapped a new roll of Tums from his coat pocket. "Nothing's been said yet. Paper doesn't come out till tomorrow." He popped one of the tablets into his mouth. "But it won't be as much as you might think. Not in the *Herald*, anyway. It's not like the city papers you're used to seeing, Mick.

The people here don't want all the gory details drummed up just for the fun of it."

"But there must be *something*, something that might make people think—"

"According to the *Herald*, tomorrow's edition, Jerry Meyers met with an accident that's still being investigated. And little Mike Henshaw just died 'unexpectedly.' And Mick Winters—an out-of-town visitor and nephew of the late Mrs. Lucille Beaumont, a life-long Tanapah resident—is recovering from injuries sustained in the same accident as Mr. Meyers." He looked at Mick. "I don't know how much more than that I'll ever think is right to print," he said, "but I plan to know *all* of it. We'll be talking again."

They were in front of the newspaper office now, and Mick knew that Simmons meant for that to be a closing line. The old man had turned toward the door when Mick blurted, "Wait a minute, Mr. Simmons."

Simmons spun his heel, his eyebrows arching.

"The story . . . about what happened to Jerry. I'd like to see it."

Simmons nodded. "You can. It'll be out tomorrow. I'll see that you get a copy."

"But—" Mick hesitated. "I mean, I'd like to see it now."

From inside the office, Mick heard Mrs. Grier's thin voice from her place at the front desk. "Mr. Simmons? Mr. Simmons?"

Simmons waved a hand across the door to silence her, his eyes never leaving Mick's. Finally, he said, "I don't usually do that, Mick. Matter of fact, I never show a story around before it's been printed."

"You're not going to be showing it around, Mr. Simmons. You're just going to be showing it to me." Mick took a step toward Simmons. "It might help . . . jog my memory."

Simmons looked at him a moment longer and then stepped inside, motioning Mick to follow. Mick felt as if he had again achieved some sort of minor victory.

They were met at the door by Mrs. Grier. "Bobby's been driving me crazy," she complained to Simmons. "The headline doesn't fit; the headline doesn't fit. Ever since—"

"I'll take care of it," Simmons replied, walking past her toward the back of the office.

Mick heard the woman mutter, "I don't know anything about these things . . ." Then Simmons was gesturing to him to sit in the cracked vinyl chair by his desk. Mick sat, and Simmons disappeared into the back room, reemerging a few moments later with a sheaf of papers in one hand and a long section of what looked to Mick like yellow tape in the other. He placed everything on his desk, shoving the tape off to one side.

"Computers," he said, nodding at the tape. "Got to use this stuff when you go offset. Me, I don't understand it, and what's more, I don't want to understand it." He handed a couple of the sheets of paper to Mick. "Here's what you want."

"Thanks." Mick took them, sat back, and began to read, hardly noticing that Simmons had gone into the back room again.

The typed headline read: "JERRY MEYERS KILLED IN RURAL MISHAP." And right below it, "Local Teens Save Visitor's Life."

Save. Visitor's . . .

Mick tried to read the account, through the additions and deletions on the copy, but his mind seemed to be filled with smoke rings. Everything was urgent, yet nothing was clear. He couldn't hold himself in place.

Mister? Mister? Can you hear me?

He's dead. Bob! He's—

No. There's a pulse, I feel a pulse. Help me. Don't cry, help me.

In a car. In the back seat. He was stretched out in the back seat, and she was cradling his head, and all he could think was . . .

Blood. I got blood on you. I'm sorry. I'm sorry. I got blood on you, and I made you cry.

Mick wrenched himself back into the present. From behind a door at the back of the office came a steady clattering.

He skimmed the story. The couple who had found him were Bob Wrotham and Virginia Adams. Graduating seniors, out on prom night. The boy was employed at McLeay's Hardware—

"Finding anything?" Simmons was suddenly there, studying him from behind the desk.

Mick looked up. "Yeah. Yeah, I am."

"Are you . . . remembering anything?"

Mick stood up, putting the sheets of paper back on Simmons's desk. "Just about what it says here, Mr. Simmons. About being taken back. By the two kids." A sudden thought flashed through his mind. "The article said they'd just graduated."

"That's right."

"Then you have pictures of them, right? In the paper?"

"Last Thursday. Our special graduation issue," Simmons replied. His eyes narrowed. "Why?"

"You have a copy of that paper?"

"Lots of them. But you haven't answered my question."

Mick stood up, his knuckles pressed against the desktop. He met Simmons's eyes. "I'd like to see what they look like, Mr. Simmons. They saved my life, and I don't even know what they look like."

Simmons motioned toward the front of the room. "Mrs. Grier can give you a copy."

"Thanks," Mick said. "And thanks for letting me see the article."

"You're welcome, Mick. But I meant what I told you outside. I mean to find out *everything*. I'll be talking to you again."

"I expect so," Mick said, and he felt a glimmer of understanding weave between them.

Simmons nodded and went back to work. Mick threaded his way to the front and asked Mrs. Grier for the "graduation issue."

She pulled one out, set it on top of her desk, and held out her palm. "That'll be twenty cents," she said primly.

Mick realized with a shock that he didn't have his billfold. He fidgeted for a moment, and then heard Simmons's voice thunder from the back, "*Give* the man a copy, Mrs. Grier."

The woman pressed her mouth into a thin, tight line, but she handed him the paper. Mick looked back and his eyes found Simmons's. A quick hard smile flickered across the old man's face, before Mick turned to walk out into the sunlight.

He walked a block and a half to a small park, where there was a wooden bench bearing the peeling remnants of old green paint. It wasn't until he sat down and felt his own weight against the reality of the park bench that he became aware of the remarkable thing he had just done. He had come to the park after twenty-two years, never once doubting that it would still be there exactly the way it used to be: same sandbox made of railroad ties in the middle, same row of tulips along the curb. The goldfish pond had been filled in. That was the only change.

Where are you going, Mickie?

To the park.

That's fine, only don't pick the flowers.

Mick took a deep breath and realized a second surprise. He felt good. Springtime good, in spite of everything.

He rattled open the paper, trying to hold onto that feeling.

It was a thick issue. Page after page of local merchants' display ads: "Summers' Grocery Congratulates Tanapah's Graduating Seniors and Reminds You That for the Best in Fresh Meats, Remember Summers." "Way to Go, Seniors—From the Bank of Tanapah, For All Your Banking Needs." Mick found what he wanted in the middle of the paper, a two-page spread with photographs arranged against a dark background, and names underneath the photos. He scanned the names. Two of the eighteen names representing the sum total of Tanapah's graduating class were the ones he wanted.

He found Virginia Adams first and studied her picture. Curly hair, from the looks of it light brown, wide eyes, and a delicate, pixie smile. Down the row and to the left, Robert Wrotham: light hair of moderate length parted neatly on the left side, square chin and a strong neck. Football. Maybe wrestling.

He looked at that picture, and then back to Virginia Adams' picture. Kids in a row of kids, all dressed up. High school kids. Prom night.

Blood on you. I'm sorry.

Mick suddenly wanted to split in two and boot himself for the little thought he'd given to anybody but the much-suffering Michael E. Winters.

I'm sorry.

He began to piece together the words he might use, but nothing sounded right.

Thank you. Thank you for the fact that I can stand here and say . . . thank you.

He wasn't aware that the sheriff's cruiser had pulled alongside the curb in front of him until the brakes began grinding and whining at the injustice of being used.

When he saw the car, his heart froze. He stood up to get his system going again, aware that his back had started to hurt.

Herb Jeffries unrolled the window on the driver's side and leaned out, resting his chin against his forearm. His face was the color of worry and no sleep. His eyes seemed to cast shadows that pooled into dark stains of weariness.

"'Day, Mr. Winters," the sheriff rumbled. "I'm surprised to see you out and about."

Mick tried to return the smile. "I sort of surprised myself," he said.

"Lot of bad doing's around here," Jeffries said. His voice trailed away into the sound of children playing in the sandbox.

Faintly, Mick heard the muted roar of a jet plane passing over Tanapah. He imagined being so high in the air that Tanapah, Oklahoma, and all its troubles would be nothing more than a speck.

Jeffries broke the silence. "There's something I got to tell you, Mr. Winters. It sounds like somethin' they'd say on some old late show movies, and I wish I didn't have to say it at all. But here it is." He leaned a little farther out the car window. "Don't leave town," he admonished. "Okay?"

As Jeffries put the car in gear and pulled away, Mick could see his eyes in the rearview mirror, watching him. The car's motor knocked.

He folded the paper under his arm and started walking.

He wanted to be up above the clouds. He wanted great engines to take him away.

But the place he had to go was just down the street.

12

M ick crossed the street to McLeay's Hardware. As a child he had regarded it as a giant of a building. Now it looked old and squat, though it still loomed over the rest of Main Street by virtue of a third floor.

There were stories about the third floor, and how Edwin McLeay's wife had caught him up there with the new salesgirl, and half the town claimed to be looking through the window.

Yeah, but what were they doing, Aunt Lucy?

Just never you mind.

Mickie had imagined that whatever Edwin McLeay was doing to the salesgirl was the same as a pirate would do, whatever that was. The sinister mystery was never solved; but, all these years later, Mick still never went to the third floor of a building without feeling that he wouldn't want to be caught there.

His mind cleared, focused on the newspaper picture. *Be sure to get the name right. Wrotham. Bob Wrotham.* Mick pushed open the thick glass door with its hand-lettered card announcing "Paint Sale!" to the smell of wood and oil, cigar smoke and dust.

A man wearing faded denim overalls was talking with his back turned toward the door, his voice . . .

Angry? Mick caught the tone before the words, and it contained a hard edge.

". . . work in Tulsa," the man was saying. "Lots of them apartments goin' up."

Behind the counter, a portly and balding little man was shaking his head as if to object not just to the general idea, but to each word individually.

"You can't do it, Ralph," the little man said. "What about Mrs. Randolph's kitchen cabinets, and that redwood fence at the Moses place? There's work right here."

The man in overalls put his arm around the shoulder of the boy standing close beside him. "There's no more to be said. Me 'n Dwight just stopped in to tell you goodbye, John. You always done right by me."

They turned, man and boy together, and Mick had to look away to keep from staring.

The boy looked the older. His face was sallow, his eyes sunken and lifeless, his mouth an almost invisible line. He was a boy of twelve, maybe thirteen, thought Mick, with shoulders starting to broaden, but he walked with an old man's shuffle. The rubber soles of his tennis shoes made a soft scraping sound against the hardwood floor.

As they passed Mick and reached the door, the boy's head snapped around with a disjointed quickness. His eyes locked on Mick.

"It was my fault," the boy said. "My fault, 'cause I'm bigger than he was, and he just wanted to show off that he wasn't scared. I made him do it."

Mick was chilled at the words of his own guilt coming from the mouth of a boy.

"It got him," the boy said. "It was waiting for him. It was under the bed all the time, and we knew it, but we wouldn't ever say so. It got him, and Mike's dead."

The late-night emergency call. Cheryl's report of the boy who had died, and now *this*. The parts linked together with an appalling precision.

"No," Mick said. "It wasn't your fault. It was—"
Mine.

The thought registered, not as a flash in his mind but a weight, heavy and suffocating. *My* fault. Something about *me*. The catalyst, bringing monsters to life.

"That's enough, boy." A big hand clamped onto the boy's shoulder, urging him toward the door.

"And now . . ." the boy said, "now, it wants me."

The door opened and closed to the sound of a cheerful bell.

"Well, if that doesn't beat everything," said the little man behind the counter.

He squeezed past the cash register, sidestepping a stack of paint cartons, and crossed the floor to peer out the front window.

"I hope you don't want any work done, Mister," the man said, "'cause there goes the only carpenter in town."

Mick followed the man's line of sight to a pickup truck backing into the street. The side of the truck was lettered "Ralph Braden. General Work." The back was loaded with furniture.

Fear. Mick felt ice in his throat as the realization came to him. The carpenter's voice had been hardened not by anger, but fear.

"I need a . . . a padlock," Mick said, "for a cellar door." The image of red wooden doors bowing outward and splintering seized his mind.

The man stood looking out the window until the truck was out of sight. Then, shaking his head in apparent exasperation at Braden's leaving, he led the way to a jumble of locks heaped in a bin between the masking tape and some plastic-handled screwdrivers of assorted sizes.

Mick chose a heavy lock, double-tempered.

"Can't hardly sell it to you," the little man said. "It's only got one key—"

"That doesn't matter."

"All right," said the little man, leading the way back to the counter. "We'll call it three dollars even, then." As the cash register clanged, Mick reached back for his wallet, realized for the second time that day that he didn't have it. He cleared his throat.

"Uh . . . I'm afraid I don't have my wallet." A sudden thought leaped into his mind. "I guess I'll have to borrow it . . . from Bob."

The little man studied him a moment. "Wrotham? Just a minute." He called over his shoulder toward an opened door in the back. Then to Mick: "Tell him it's three dollars even." Mick nodded as the man reached under the counter, produced a feather duster, and used it to attack a row of box fans on the far side of the store.

"Hey, you're up. It's good to see you, Mr. Winters." Bob Wrotham extended his hand across the counter. Mick recognized him immediately from the newspaper. The one change in the face was a barely recognizable attempt at a mustache.

They shook hands. "I'm glad to *be* up, Bob," Mick said. "And . . . I know it's not like you haven't done enough for me, but could you float me three dollars?" He nodded toward the cash register. "I seem to have forgotten my wallet."

"Sure," Bob returned. He took a five-dollar bill out of his pocket, put it in the register, and took out two dollars change.

Mick watched him. "Thanks. I've been trying to think of some way to express my appreciation. If not for you and Virginia, I'd be a goner."

Bob smiled with visible effort, as if he were bending tin. He brushed a shock of blond hair away from his forehead. "Well . . . I'll be sure and tell her," he said vaguely.

"Look. I was wondering if you and Virginia would let me take you out to supper one of these nights. Call it one more big favor. I could use a good steak and a celebration."

Bob looked at the counter. "That would be great, Mr. Winters, except . . . I don't know, but she probably . . . she might not want to. I could ask her."

The smile was tense now—and reluctant. Mick guessed at the signals. "Or . . . I still want to thank Virginia, of course, but maybe you have another friend you'd like to ask, Bob."

"No." Bob's hands balled to fists on the countertop. "Just her. But—I don't know—there's something gone all flaky with her."

"She's not feeling well?"

"No, not that." He shrugged, groping for words, looking uncomfortable. "Look, I don't mean to make you feel bad, Mr. Winters. It's nothing you could help. The thing is, she just hasn't been the same. I guess that night was pretty hard on her."

I got blood on you, and I made you cry— Mick felt the quickening sickness of having broken something he couldn't replace. "Tell me about her. Please, Bob."

Bob glanced across the store toward the portly man with the feather duster. "I don't know what to tell," he said. "She won't go out of the house. She won't even talk to me."

"She must have said why."

"She said . . . she can't go to the phone anymore. There was a bunch of other stuff. She was talking so fast, I couldn't follow her. She said, 'No place is safe but my room.' She hung up on me."

"When was that?" Mick tagged the question directly on Bob's last word. A Matthew Simmons trick.

"I called her on lunch break."

"Safe from what? What was she talking about?"

The store man bustled back to the counter, past the old brass cash register and toward the back room. "We've got shelves to be stocked, Bob," he said, and went through the door.

"Sorry, Mr. Winters, "Bob said. "I've got to . . ."

Thoughts interlocked for Mick, forming a chain that he couldn't break through, not with logic or any answer that made any sense. The image of Jerry Meyers crouched at the mouth of the culvert meshed with the thought of a little boy dying under his own bed, became the dark, stirring water of the coal pit, became the face of a boy with dead eyes, became a pixie-faced girl named Virginia, became a wall that cracked and bled.

Mick's hand shot across the counter, catching Bob by the shirt sleeve. "Listen to me," he said. "I'm asking a lot, and I am not sure of the reasons, but I think she needs help."

Startled, Bob pulled away. "Okay," he said. "Okay. After work, I'll go see her. I planned to any—"

"Not after work, Bob. *Now*. Can you get off?"

"Well . . . no . . ."

"Then tell me how to get there."

Bob answered with a look of numbed puzzlement, changing to apprehension. "Maybe I'd better go with you," he said, and Mick filled in the rest of it. *Because you're nuts, mister. You need watching.* "Let me check with the boss for a minute."

He stepped away, regarding Mick for another long

moment. When he moved, it was in quick steps into the back room.

Paint smells pierced the silence. Mick paced aimlessly, focusing on shelves filled with drill bits and sandpaper. A workshop. It would be nice to have a workshop. In the garage. A house with a garage. A wife . . .

In the corner was a rack of fishing rods. The top shelf of a showcase in front of the rods was filled with spinning reels, not so much on display as just scattered. Fishing. He hadn't been fishing in years. On the shelf below the fishing reels, behind the dust-clouded glass of the showcase . . .

His attention cut short its wandering. Mick knelt for an eye-level look at the ebony revolver, gleaming with dull blue highlights. Its grips were black, and the barrel was pointed toward him. A .38-caliber, he guessed.

Jerry? Jerry, hang on. I'm coming.

No place is safe. Safe from what?

Mick stepped to the side of the showcase. At the back was a sliding door that shut . . . but was not locked. The store was empty.

He slid the door open. His hand closed around the revolver. The touch of it—hard, like a promise.

I'm coming.

Mick looked for a price sticker. He would . . . what? Buy it? He didn't even have his wallet. It was back . . . somewhere. And even if he *could* buy it—how long would it take for that jewel of a news item to get back to the sheriff?

Bob's voice carried from the rear of the store. "Well, thanks. Thanks, Mr. Spivey. I'll see you tomorrow."

Mick felt the weight of the revolver as it dropped into his jacket pocket. He scanned the shelves—*there!*—grabbing a box of cartridges and moving away from the counter.

The cartridges clacked in his pockets, bulging along with

the pistol. He had acted almost without thought, on the impulse of shadows. Thought came too late. *Put it back! Put it back!*

"Let's go, Mr. Winters," Bob said, crossing toward Mick. Bob wore farm boots that thumped on the floor. The little man was behind the cash register again.

Mick picked up, then put down, a boxed bathroom sink faucet, pretending interest. "Good, Bob," he said.

Mick held the door open. But as he did, the man called out. "Hey! You—mister. Wait a minute."

Mick froze. His heart thudded, and the bulge in his pocket seemed suddenly huge.

Spivey bustled toward him, heaving a paper sack. "You forgot your padlock," he said.

B ob pulled to the curb in front of a two-story white frame house with green trim and a screened-in front porch. A graveled driveway led from the street to the open door of an empty garage standing apart from the house.

The car rumbled and coughed for a few seconds after he switched the ignition off, ending with a sneeze that shook the high-school tassel tied to the rear-view mirror.

"Looks like nobody's home," Mick said.

Bob ran his hands back and forth in half circles against the fake fur cover of the steering wheel. "Her folks both work," he said, looking from the house to Mick. "I don't know . . .what to say to her. I mean, maybe she just doesn't want to talk to me."

Mick briefly envisioned a scene at the door with himself playing a divorced Cupid to a couple of squabbling teenagers; yet, the images that had impelled him to be there were stronger than ever. "Let's find out," he said and swung open the car door.

He led the way up the neatly edged front walk. Bob stepped ahead of him at the screen door to the porch.

"You'd be kind of a shock to her, I think, Mr. Winters," he said. "I'll go knock." He stepped up and rapped with his knuckles on the wooden frame. There was no answer. He knocked again, harder, and they waited. The only sound was the sputtering of a lawn mower from down the street, and the whine and buzz of the bees working the flower bed just off the porch.

Mick tried the door. It was locked. "Which room is hers?" he asked.

"Upstairs."

"Call her name. Loud, so she can hear you."

Bob tried a grin that slipped off. "Are you kidding? Look . . . there's nobody home, and we don't belong, hanging around here."

Mick yelled, "Virginia! Bob's here. Virginia!"

Bob turned away. "Oh, jeez!" he said. He moved toward the porch door with the speed of a kid caught stealing crab applies, his boots thudding against the planks of the floor, almost—but not quite—covering the sudden brittle sound of her voice.

"I can't come down . . ."

Bob was back at the door. "Ginny!"

"I can't. I . . . *can't*. Bob!" Her voice floated down from the window, frail and faraway.

Bob looked at Mick in bewilderment. "She's crying!"

"Kick it open." Mick hit the doorknob with the heel of his hand. "Kick it!"

Glass shattered into the parlor.

Mick went first, taking the stairs two at a time.

He had forgotten himself. A wave of pain washed over his back, and his ankle buckled. Dizziness, thick like a syrup, settled over him. He grabbed for the bannister. "Go on," he said.

Bob moved past him. Mick stood holding the bannister, taking deep and slow breaths. And slowly, his head cleared. *So much for the hero.* His ankle throbbed, daring him to take another step. He called the bluff. It hurt, but it worked.

Reaching the top, he followed the low sounds of voices coming from the room at the end of the hallway, until the words began fitting together.

". . . doesn't make sense," Bob was saying. "You mean—what? A *boogeyman?*"

Mick stopped outside the doorway.

"No," came her voice. "No, not like that." A weak voice, edging toward anger. "You think it's funny?"

"You tell me. What am I supposed to think?"

Mick listened as Ginny's voice became part of the chain, became the smell of decay in a dark place, became another voice, Jerry's.

You know what's in there? A spider.

Jerry, what's got into you?

Silence. Mick entered the bedroom. Bob was sitting stiffly on the edge of the bed, his arms around Ginny like he was holding a lacework of ice crystals.

"Ginny . . ." Mick said. She looked up at him, her face registering not the surprise he had expected but a blankness beyond surprise. She looked at him the way people look at each other after a house fire.

Bob's eyes said: Tell me what to do.

Mick spoke. "Ginny, I heard what you were saying just now. About the man." Speaking slowly was the closest he could come to sounding calm. "I need to ask you something important. Don't hold back, Ginny. Don't be afraid. We're on your side."

She stood as if she wanted to rush toward him. "You believe me?"

"Yes. I think you saw . . . something. Maybe just in your mind." *And maybe not,* he wanted to say. He walked to her and held her gently by the shoulders. "Ginny, when was the first time you saw him, or knew about him? How old were you?"

She glanced toward Bob. He was listening in bewilderment, sucking his lip.

Mick shook her lightly. "I think it was a long time ago, Ginny. I think you were five—maybe six. Am I right?"

"How . . ." Again she looked at Bob, then back to Mick, moisture welling in her eyes. "How did you know?"

Bob suddenly threw up in his arms in a slicing motion. "I don't get it," he said. "What are we talking about? A real guy, or some sort of make-believe. I mean, where is he? And if he's not real . . ." His voice dropped away.

"Finish it!" Ginny wheeled on him. "If this isn't for real, then what's the matter with me? I don't know. *I don't know,* Bobby. But you're not helping."

"He's trying, Ginny. We can see you're in trouble. That's real enough." Mick felt a stirring of dark shapes in the back of his mind, oddly counterbalanced by Ginny's room. The walls were light pink, the trim white. A poster of a soaring dove was mounted on the inside of the door.

"The first thing to do is get you out of here," Mick continued. "Pack a suitcase. We'll find you someplace else to stay for a while. Maybe Dr. Stanton—"

The door swung slightly open. Ginny gasped and flinched.

"Aw, Ginny!" Bob tried, but she clung to him and pointed toward the open doorway, her finger trembling. Her voice bore an icy precision.

"He was . . . waiting for me in that hallway," she said. "Until you came. I could *feel* him."

Mick stepped into the hallway. It was empty and quiet, and smelled of flowers from an arrangement of daisies on a table at the end of the hall.

"There's nobody here, Ginny," he said. A trickle of sweat ran a cold path down the back of his neck, trailing down across his stitches.

"Because he's . . . in the basement." Her eyes were wide. "He's hiding in the basement."

"Shit! Then let's go get him!" Bob strode toward the door.

Mick stepped in front of him, blocking him. "No, Bob. We're getting her out of here. That's all."

"Out and away from what? A spook in the basement? Try telling that to her folks, Mr. Winters."

Mick pulled his fingers away from where they rested on the doorframe. The touch of it was suddenly a reminder that he was in the house of a family that didn't know him. And that he'd gotten there by breaking in.

Bob was right.

The only way to show her there was nothing to be afraid of was to go look.

A stairway from the kitchen led to the basement. The door to the stairway, painted a crisp white, was standing slightly ajar. A long linen calendar decorated with hand-sewn sequins was tacked to it.

Mick had left Bob with Ginny. He had promised to look in the basement and come back with assurance that it was safe. And then, they would all wait for Ginny's mom and dad to come home in the next hour or so. They would then try to explain what had been happening to her—and why the front door had been forced.

Mick, alone in the kitchen, thought of how easily he could wait for a few minutes, go upstairs again, and forget the basement. His ankle throbbed and his back hurt. He needed to get back to Cheryl's house.

Through the partially opened door, he could see the darker and deeper shadows at the bottom of the stairs. It was a darkness like the mouth of the culvert, with Jerry crouched in front of it, saying, *"Maybe you should dare me, Mick. That's what I need to get on with this, I bet. A good dare. C'mon."*

I dare you, dareyou, dareyou . . .

He backed away from the door.

But she would know. To Ginny, he had become—what?—a father figure going to make everything all right again. A big brother. The grownup.

He couldn't conceive of a lie that would not melt in her eyes.

Mick pushed the door open.

The darkness, he saw, had been misleading. The basement was dim but not dark. A dozen or so wooden steps led to the bottom. A dizziness seized him again as he took the first step. It left him lightheaded, not in a physical way, but out of pace with reality.

Buzzing!

Mick jerked his hand from the stairway railing. The fly circled his head and was gone. His hand itched, as though from the touch of a . . . mass of flies, matted and crawling along the stair rail. Images reached for him, kept away by the solid fact of the weight in his jacket pocket.

He would have to get rid of the revolver. Having stolen the gun was no part of a ghost story, any more than the broken front door would go away if he just could get his head straight.

In the basement. He'd hide the gun in the basement. He went down.

His sight became accustomed to the yellowed light filtering into the basement from a pair of low windows, revealing a woodworking bench and tools hung on the wall at one side of the room. Closer to the windows was a washer and dryer combination. A copy of *McCall's* magazine had been left on top of the dryer; and, in front of the white-enameled washer, a pile of clothes. Nothing else.

His heart was gearing down again. His back felt cold with sweat.

Turning, Mick surveyed the workbench more closely. Beneath it were stacked a half dozen paint cans. The gun, left behind those cans, might not be discovered for weeks or even months. It was a possibility.

Better yet, there were boxes of magazines jumbled in the far back corner. Or under the stairway . . .

Mick looked past the stairs toward the clothes pile.

He had remembered it as being more loosely scattered. Now, the clothes were tightly packed, almost wadded into a knot on the floor.

He stepped closer.

There were blue jeans and blouses, shirts, towels, pillowcases.

Mick kicked at the pile. It toppled and came apart.

He felt grateful and foolish at the same time. And more than that, he wanted out. The basement seemed suddenly dark again. It became a place where the walls might crack, where the light could go out.

He reached the basement stairway quickly, but not quickly enough to avoid hearing the rustling sound, the sound of fabric being moved against the floor, that came from behind him.

It's not real. It's not real until I look at it.

His pulse thundered against his temples. Mick felt his head turning toward the sound as if it were in the grip of a giant's hand.

The clothes pile was stirring. It was pulling itself together and . . . lifting. Standing. The moving folds and wrinkles formed a face, contorted in agony, formed a mouth that split open in a scream of pain and rage, formed a hand with long pale fingers—and clenched in that hand . . . the wavering gleam of a knife blade.

Dumbstruck, Mick stumbled backward. He hit the floor on his side. The revolver jabbed into him, and his back burned with the tearing of stitches.

The figure stood before him—tall and emancipated, the skin a dead yellow, the head skull-like, the eyes wide and unblinking, the teeth blackened. It was grinning.

It took a slow step toward him.

Mick jammed his hand into this pocket, his fingers closing around the grip of the revolver.

The figure swayed. Its knee buckled backwards, but it remained erect. The teeth clenched; the face tightened in a spasm of anguish.

Mick drew the gun out of his pocket with a rattling sound.

The bullets!

He fumbled for the box, slid it open, his hands shaking. The shells clattered against the floor in a dance of bright metal.

The figure was moving toward him again, feet shuffling at first, then lifting in firm steps. The fingers played against the handle of the knife, its blade—silvery and curved—pointed toward Mick.

Mick pushed with the ball of his thumb against the cylinder of the revolver, trying to make it swing out. The gun was . . . *broken!*

No! No . . . there! His thumb had accidentally caught

against the button he thought was the firing safety; the cylinder fell into loading position.

Scrambling backward, Mick grabbed the handful of shells from the floor. Loaded. Snapped the cylinder shut.

The figure straightened, drawing the knife above its head . . . and lunged.

Because I believed. Oh God!—because I believed! His mind was a white eternity, against which the grinning figure of horror lifted over him, and the knife plunged toward him.

The revolver fired. The recoil shocked his wrist. Lifting himself from the floor, Mick saw the figure reeling backward. A spray of blood mottled the white enamel of the washer-dryer. The figure, its face warped with fury, struggled to its feet. Mick aimed, this time at the head. He jammed his eyes shut and pulled the trigger, and the sound of the gunshot shook and echoed in the basement, thudding against his ears and in the pit of his stomach.

The figure writhed in silence on the floor, arms wrapped over its face. Blood ran between its fingers.

Mick dropped against the stairway. His ears rang.

Rand and rang . . . He dropped the revolver, pressing his hands over his ears, but the ringing grew louder, became a shriek.

A death scream.

The thing on the floor was dissolving in shimmers like heat waves. It was going into the air, becoming part of the air.

It was . . . *inside him!* Screaming inside him—and still alive.

The scream, like a knife in his mind, cut and twisted. He fell from the stairs, rolling, and everything was red, was fury and agony. His mind was giving way. He could feel it, as if it were his hand that had been cut from him.

The footsteps on the stairway came to him dimly, like

echoes. He watched, then saw Bob, transfixed on the stairway. And Ginny, pushing Bob aside, coming down.

Mick felt her skirt whip against his face. He watched, as if through a clouded window of thick glass, watched her pass him . . . and pick up the gun.

Her face, that pretty pixie face, was white and cold. She had become rage and revenge, her hands interlocked on the grip of the revolver she—

Fired.

The thing on the floor twisted, transmuted, became an animal shape—a wolf, a snake, a creature of no name, teeth and scales.

Fired!

The screaming released him. Mick felt himself drifting in a current of cold and deep water.

Fired!

The final silence was shattering. The gun dropped from Ginny's hands, slamming against the concrete of the basement floor. She fell to her knees, her arms around Mick, shaking violently. He felt his own arms wrap around her.

Mick looked, his eyes aching and half-closed, over Ginny's shoulder. He saw, where the thing had been, a chalky pock mark on the floor. Nothing else.

Except . . . by the washer, a pile of clothes. Blue jeans and blouses, shirts, towels, and pillowcases.

Bob stepped dumbly down the stairway. "Holy Christ," he said.

13

The streetlight at the corner shone down in a cold, yellow pool, and Mick Winters waded through it, limping between a broken line of two blocks of stores, cafes, and old brick buildings, all of them unlighted and vacant, empty shells in the darkness.

It was late. Very late. Mick's mind was filled with woolly clouds, gentle strange images that rolled through and turned over and over again. Going to Matthew Simmons's office had been like going to confession for Mick. There, in the dimly lighted back room, with the paper put to bed and the staff gone home, he had spilled his guts to Matthew Simmons. The Father. And the wall that had separated them had been a wall of words, of attitudes, of vague stares and pointed questions and half-formed accusations.

Matthew Simmons, the priest. And the sacramental wine, the bottle of rye whiskey in the top desk drawer, shoved back on top of some forgotten papers.

The wind shifted as Mick walked, bringing a sweet spring wildness to the sluggish air.

It was a part of him now, Mick knew. The thing in the culvert . . . the killer in Ginny's basement . . . the monster under the bed that dragged the little boy, screaming . . . even the cellar.

Yes, Mick thought. *Especially the cellar.*

He was all of these things, and all of these things were him. He carried their weight, a thick heaviness as real as the weight of the revolver in his pocket, the revolver he had given to Matthew Simmons.

And that made Matthew Simmons a part of it, too.

Would Simmons call Herb Jeffries? He tried to consider the question, but it didn't seem to matter anymore. He had sunk his fingers deep into his own being and torn himself open for Simmons, so Simmons could see it too, this horrible thing that glowed deep within him, so Simmons too could be bathed in its unholy light. That was all he could do.

Mick stumbled a little, his toe springing back against the curb, but it was someone else's foot, someone else's body, and he was outside, looking in and grinning with a curious half-smile at the drunk on the deserted street.

He left his body, came back, listened to the sound of his own breathing, checked himself over with detached interest.

The tenseness was still there; hours of drinking and talking and drinking again hadn't completely quieted his body. The shallow pulsing beat in time to the throbbing of his back and his ankle, a symphony of pain. He walked doggedly on, the soles of his shoes making shuffling noises against the concrete. The quivering was a vibrating outer shell that encased him and his deep, odd stillness within. On impulse, he turned around and looked back down Tanapah's dark main street. Only one diffuse light shone feebly out in the darkness from the disordered row of buildings.

It was light in the back room at the *Tanapah Herald* building.

———

T here was about an inch of rye left in the big bottle. Matthew Simmons measured it, pressing a thick thumb and forefinger against the cold amber glass.

He shook his head sadly and poured his smeared shot glass full, just one more time.

———

T *he indigo stillness of the night . . .*

No, thought Mick, *that's not right,* and his feet slowly scraped along the sidewalk. *Power in the verbs, not in the adjectives.*

The indigo of the night . . .

That's better. There's power in the nouns, too. Back from the sidewalk, set in among fruit trees and hedges, lay a white house with a screen door. Moths and thousands of tiny insects lined the screen underneath the porch light. Mick paused in front of it a moment, thinking.

The night's indigo . . .

How long? Lord, how long ago? The memory flooded over him like warm water from a secret spring as he began walking again.

Your poetry has been scheduled for publication in our February issue. Thanks for thinking of us and please feel free to submit more . . .

A poet. Long ago, he had wanted to be a poet, to take all the feelings and thoughts and events that swirled wildly and randomly around him and funnel them down into his fingers, where they could flow out through his pen and onto the paper in neat, ordered lines. It seemed eons ago that he had set his compass on a course, a course good and true and right.

And then he had begun to grow up, and with every change in his body the compass needle was bumped off course. At first, just a degree or two; then college and the service, the needle flickering more and more in other directions. Finally, the real world had intruded too much, and when he set out on his journey, he found that the needle pointed somewhere else entirely, a place where he ended up writing advertising copy for women's shoes and diet cola and franchise restaurants.

The indigo . . .

He gave it up. His course was set for the night. It was Cheryl Stanton's house, and it was right in front of him.

A light came on inside, and it seemed out of place. There were footsteps, and then the front door rattled and there she was.

"Nice of you to drop by," said Cheryl, who stood aside to let him enter. Her yellow flowered cotton nightgown was covered by a white housecoat, wrapped tightly around her and held with one hand.

Mick stumbled past her, blinking against the light.

"Are you drunk?" she asked as Mick sank down onto a couch in the living room and looked at her.

"Yep." His voice was toneless.

"Great," she shot back bitterly. She started to say something else but didn't. She simply stood there, staring at him, the knuckles white where her hand clenched the robe in front. Finally, she asked, "Why?"

"Matthew Simmons."

"Matthew Simmons got you drunk?"

Mick nodded, leaning forward gingerly. "Or I got Matthew Simmons drunk . . . all d'pends on how you want to look at it. His bottle . . . my story."

"What the *hell* are you talking about?" A thin edge of hysteria had crept into her voice, the hysteria of too many questions and not enough answers, of being awakened in the middle of the night when you shouldn't have gone to sleep in the first place, of an unexplained *something* that whispered to you that things were out of control, and there was no turning back. Mick knew dimly how she felt; he had felt the same way after Ginny's house—but that was before Simmons's office, and the bottle, and the talk.

"You need a drink," he said.

She continued to stare at him, and in her eyes, he saw, and remembered.

Mick, there's nothing in that old cellar. Nothing. Just your 'magination.

Years and years ago, the smell of the rosined lumber in the vacant lot where the new house was going up, of the trellised pink roses on Aunt Lucy's front porch, of the faint antiseptic odor of Cheryl's freshly scrubbed face and hands.

Years, so many years ago, a straight, hard ride through time and space and the smell of freshly mown lawns on a summer day—it was in her eyes, all of it.

Mick cleared his throat. "Drink'd do you a world of good."

But it wasn't doing any good, not anymore, and he was remembering other things now, not the Oklahoma afternoons of his youth, but other newer things, adult things that were yet child things and horrible and real, and suddenly he was telling it all to Cheryl, at first in carefully measured sentences, until the rush of words piled up in his throat and he had to let go.

He told her about Jerry. About the thing in the basement. And the cellar . . . even that.

He let the words spill out, as if telling it all one more time could somehow banish the shadows and specters from his mind. But it didn't happen. Telling it brought him no peace, and even as he was telling it he knew that there were ghosts that did not go away in the light—ghosts that would sit in the living room with you, that would sit in your place and look out of your eyes.

Aunt Lucy, would you . . . I mean, if you don't think I'm too old, would you tuck me in bed?

Of course, Mickie. There, now. How's that?

Fine . . . Aunt Lucy?

What is it, dear?

Aunt Lucy, I guess pretty soon I'll be too old to be tucked in. And . . . and then what happens? What happens when you have your own house and you get scared, and you're too old, and you can't be tucked in?

People don't get too old to be tucked into bed, Mickie. Not ever. They just feel like they're too old to ask.

The covers were snug around him. A kiss on the forehead. The light switched off gently.

"Mick?"

Her voice brought him back. He focused on the Cheryl, standing, watching him.

You can't forget.

"I was just . . . thinking," he said. "The first night that you go to bed scared in your house, that's the time when things change, and you're never a kid again."

Grown-up voices. They never sounded quite right. Sometimes, they were low and full of trouble that didn't make sense. Other times, they were bright and friendly, but in a way that seemed to be making fun of her, fun only grown-ups could understand. ("Annie, if you go to growing any faster, we're just going to have to put a brick on your head to slow you down.")

Sometimes they were laughing, laughing about names she didn't know and things she didn't understand.

They *never* sounded "right as rain," which her mother said sometimes about things that had nothing to do with rain at all.

But they never, had never, *never* sounded as bad and as wrong as right now, as she crouched in the hallway just outside the living room door, listening to her mother and Mr. Winters.

Mostly, it was Mr. Winters talking. His voice was whispery in places, and she couldn't make out all the words, but he was saying something about . . . the cellar . . . Aunt Lucy's backyard. *That* cellar. Something . . . down in the dark . . . in the cellar . . . something . . . *awful.*

Annie shivered. She wasn't sure why. When the big people laughed, she would laugh too, so she would feel big right with them, but this time she shivered and felt small.

What could be so bad about a cellar?

She looked to Christy, but the rag doll eyes looked back at her, offering no help.

Annie scowled, remembering a time when she had gone chasing a small black cat that was new to the neighborhood— calling "Midnight!" because she had named it already, even though she hadn't caught it yet—following it from backyard to backyard all the way to Miz Beaumont's house (her mother sometimes called the woman "Aunt Lucy," but Annie had to call her Miz Beaumont because she was a grown-up).

So, Annie had looked around Miz Beaumont's backyard, sure that Midnight was there somewhere, and then she had seen the cellar. Thinking the cat must have run in there, knowing that it couldn't just disappear, she had gone over to the cellar door, only to find it locked with a padlock on it as big as her hand. She had begun to tug on it, rattling it and thumping it against the door, when she had heard the voice.

"Get away! Go home!"

Annie had whirled around at the sound, and there, in the back doorway, she had seen Miz Beaumont, one hand on a cane, her face angry—*yelling* at her.

"Get away, I said!"

At first, Annie had inched away from the door, surprised and hurt, and then she had begun to run, and halfway home she had burst into tears.

That night she heard her mother's voice, low and serious, full of grown-up trouble, and Annie had known it was about her. She had expected to be punished, but instead her mother had taken her over to Hattie Redmiller's house for a little while. When her mother had come back for her, a present had been sticking out the top of the doctor's bag, a pretty one wrapped in paper with flowers on it, and a card. Her mother had read her the card: "'To Annie, From Aunt Lucy Beaumont,'" and she had handed Annie the package, saying, "She said this was hers when she was little, and she wanted you to have it."

And that was how she had gotten Christy.

Now, Annie remembered what her mother had said when she had lifted Christy out of the box, smoothing the rag doll hair. "She said she was sorry, Annie, and she didn't mean to scare you, do you understand? Aunt Lucy Beaumont is sick, and we'll go and see her, both of us, sometime when she gets better. But I don't want you playing in her yard, okay? Not anymore."

And now, there in the living room, her mother was talking that same way again, talking in that same voice to Mr. Winters.

Annie didn't want to hear it.

Playing spy-in-the-night had turned out not to be any fun at all. Annie turned away and started back to bed on tiptoes, stopping only once in the darkened hallway to look behind her.

Midnight was gone, though. Midnight was always gone just as soon as she really tried to look for him. He was there, but he wasn't.

He was a secret.

He was two little eye glints in the darkness behind her, until she looked.

And then, he was nothing.

Matthew Simmons sat at the desk, screwing the top back on the empty liquor bottle with elaborate, precise movements.

Be hell to pay tomorrow, he thought.

I watched it, Mr. Simmons. It . . . writhed there on the floor. It took different shapes . . . a . . . a wolf, a —I don't know . . . it . . .

Why, Mick? Why did it take those shapes?

It was being . . . everything . . . to her. You see? Everything loathsome and horrible and unnameable that she'd ever met in her worst nightmares. Everything that ever had come to her . . . in the dark. Everything that ever had made her wake up trembling in the middle of the night when all the lights were off, and she was alone with her terror.

Why would it do that, Mick?

It . . . was trying to scare her. Us. Away. To go on living.

But you killed it.

She did. Finally.

And you couldn't kill Jerry's spider?

No.

And the Henshaw boy?

No. It was too powerful for him.

The splashing of liquor into glasses and down throats. The glint of the revolver on the desk. A thick stillness.

I know what you think. Then call Herb Jeffries. You've got the gun. Lock me up. I don't care.

No. I don't think I'll do that.

But I—haven't you heard me? I'm the cause. Put me away and all this could stop.

It would be nice, Mick, if we could blame all the world's troubles on one person, wouldn't it? One person to take the whole stinking rap for everything bad. Everything wrong.

But—if it's not me . . . how can you explain it?

I'll look into it, Mick. I'll look into it.

M ick Winters sat with his head in his hands. Across from him, in an overstuffed chair, sat Cheryl. Smoke curled between them, and the hand that had held the robe together now held a cigarette.

"I've got Ginny here," said Cheryl softly. "For observation. Bob brought her in. I talked to her folks, too."

Mick slowly brought his head up, taking in a deep lungful of air. "She's all right," he said.

"Yes."

"It wasn't a question, Cheryl. I knew she was all right. I was there."

Cheryl nodded. "There's a matter of a broken door, and empty shells in the basement, and . . ."

Mick waited.

"She said she saw . . . just what you told me."

"I know that, too." He looked around. "Got anything to drink?"

Cheryl hesitated a moment and then got up. "Yeah," she said resignedly. "Scotch okay?"

Mick nodded and she left the room, returning a moment later with two glasses and a bottle. She poured a drink for each of them, and Mick watched her, the way she moved, the grace in the practiced doctor's hands, the undulation of her woman's body under the thin cotton where the robe fell open in front. For so long, parts of him had felt dead, and it was as if little lights were coming on in those dead parts, one by one, blinking here, extinguishing there, off and on and off again.

They sipped in silence, facing each other like two chess players across a board, each waiting for the other's move. Finally, Cheryl began. "You told all this to Matthew Simmons, too, right?"

"That's right. All of it."

"Even the part about stealing the gun."

"Un-huh. I gave him the gun. He can do whatever he wants with it."

"And?"

Mick shrugged. "I don't know. Herb Jeffries could be knocking at your door any minute now, for all I know."

"But maybe he believed you?"

"Parts. Maybe."

Cheryl took another drink and swished the Scotch around in her glass, studying it. Mick felt awkward in her presence now, as if some secret point had been reached beyond which he could not go without awakening some dark, unspoken force.

He broke the silence. In slow, precise tones, he said: "I—I don't want you to take this wrong, Cheryl. You've been very good to me. Always. But I don't care what you think about this, or what you say about it."

Her head shot up.

"It's not that I don't care about you," Mick continued, "or your opinions, or what you believe. But I know the truth. I know what happened, I know what I saw and what I did and what will forever be with me." He took a long drink. "It's—it's not right. But it is. And I can't care about how right or logical or —or whatever it is anymore." Their eyes locked, and Mick quickly looked away, feeling alone. "It's in all of us, maybe. Something we carry with us, something that never really goes away, from the first time we hear about it, from the first time we realize that there are things our parents can't fight for us, things that our parents don't even know exist, that are too horrible. From then on, it's ours. They're ours, in all of us. Except— maybe you, Cheryl." He gazed at the coffee table, not wanting to look at her eyes. His mind slipped back, and he started to smile.

"Remember?" he asked.

"Remember what, Mick?"

There was a bittersweetness in his voice. "When we used to play together, those three summers."

"Yes."

"And I was so afraid of things. It wasn't so bad during the day, but just let the night come and . . . a million tiny fears. All around me. Fears of things under the bed, and in the closet, and hanging from the trees like fruit, and black, winged things flying around outside the houses—"

A heavy *thump!* jarred the windowpane behind Cheryl. Mick jumped, the glass in his hand tumbling to the carpet.

"No!" he screamed. "*No!*" He ran to the glass and pressed his fingers hard against the pane, staring wildly out into the night. "You go *away*! I'll *make* you go away!" His voice was shrill and suddenly childlike.

Cheryl was at his side in an instant, tugging at him. "Mick! Mick, look at me!"

He turned toward her, breathing hard through clenched teeth. She clutched his shoulders with powerful fingers.

"Shhh. Mick, listen—"

"I have to fight, Cheryl." His breath hissed. "No good to talk—I have to fight. Do you understand? Do you?"

"There's nothing, Mick. Nothing. Not now. Except a patient and a child you might wake up."

Mick turned back toward the window. She was right. There was nothing moving outside, nothing flying through the air. Perhaps there never had been. His body slumped.

Cheryl said, "It went away. It went away because you fought it."

Still looking out into the darkness, he asked quietly, "Is that really what you think?"

She didn't answer.

He turned his head slowly until his eyes were level with hers. There was a softness there, as if all her reserve had been drained away and she was standing naked and vulnerable before him.

"Is that really what you think, Cheryl?" he asked again.

"What you said about . . . this . . . being in all of us. The fear." Her words came slowly and carefully. "It's in me then, too." Her hands quivered on his shoulder. "We're all afraid of something—is that what you said?"

"Yes."

"And it doesn't die? It doesn't go away?"

He nodded, watching her soft eyes.

"I have that kind of a fear. I fear for every soul that lives, every person that I can touch. And sometimes . . . sometimes,

Mick, that fear comes to life when . . . one of my people dies. I do everything I can, and a person dies anyway. Death brings my fear to life. And it's as real as yours. It just happens more often."

Her eyes wavered then, and he reached out and touched her neck with the tip of one finger. The flesh stiffened at his touch, then slowly relaxed. Mick studied her eyes, her face, the golden child's hair that framed the face. His hand slid to her chin and tilted it up.

They kissed gently, and when he pulled his face back her eyes were clear and unnaturally bright.

"I am afraid," she said, her voice steady and calm. "I just don't want to lose anyone else."

He wrapped an arm around her, awkwardly, and she buried her face in the hollow of his neck. His heart tore at his chest, and he felt his throat and nose and the area behind his eyes begin to thicken and fill up.

W hen . . . *after I shot it . . . I thought I felt it enter me, you know? You understand? But then I knew. It didn't really enter me . . . it had been there all the time. Not just in me or Ginny. But all of us. It's in all of us, waiting.*

Mick, I'm a reasonable man . . .

So am I—or I was. But that's what I think, and now you've got it to share. We have to fight it hard, or it gets us. It gets us.

We can . . . beat it, then?

Yes. We can beat it, Mr. Simmons.

Matthew.

Matthew. We beat it today, Matthew. The scraping of a chair on the floor, a wobbly attempt at standing.

You'd better let me take you back to Cheryl's.

No thanks. Walk'll do me good.

There's blood on your back, Mick.

I know. The stitches. A pause at the doorway. *Please. Please think about it. About everything. And thanks.* The familiar creaking of the door opening and closing onto the night.

And more silence, heavy and thick and real.

Mick sat on the bed, on the very edge of the silk spread, as if he were afraid someone might come along at any minute and ask him just what he thought he was doing there. His eyes kept flitting around the room—to the dressing table, the half-open closet, the dark, framed painting of a seascape above the oak dresser—only to return to the bedroom door. Soon that door would open, and she would come in.

He listened, heard her moving around in the bathroom, opening and closing drawers. The little noises soon gave way to a long, polite silence.

It would be all right, he thought. Everything would be all right because it was Cheryl, and Cheryl always had all the answers, and Cheryl would do her damnedest to help you out.

There's nothing in that old cellar, Mick. It's just your 'magination.

Your 'magination.

The door opened and Cheryl came in, wearing the same cotton print nightdress. Yellow, with little flowers on it.

"I'm sorry I took so long," she said, her hand moving in a little tight arc. "It . . . it's been a long time."

Mick nodded as she came to him, sat down beside him. Her hand touched his cheek.

"Are you sure you feel . . ."

"I feel fine," he said. "Finer all the time."

There's nothing in that old cellar, Mick—

Gently and silently, he eased her down onto the bed. Her hair spread out over the palm of his hand, and he lifted it between his fingers, leaning down to kiss it, inhaling its soft perfume.

She looked at him, and in her eyes was a curious, almost frightening cast, one of longing and memory. And fear.

They kissed, and kissed again, and a part of Mick seemed to break away and float upward.

Every moment was stretched out of time, out of place. Mick felt thick and dreamlike, and when he began edging the hem of the cotton nightdress up over her thighs, he felt as if it were someone else touching her, as if he were over it all, watching yet feeling, through some mysterious connection with the man on the bed.

His hands edged across her smooth stomach, and the rustle of cloth mingled with the warm night breeze from the window. A flickering in the glass of the window caught his eye. The reflection of them on the bed, moving gently with each other. He watched the reflection as his hand moved up, onto her breasts, lifting the garment as he went, until she stretched her arms above her head, and he eased away the last of her modesty. It dropped to the carpet with a sound like the fluttering of wings.

Mick slid his hands over her breasts slowly, the suction of her flesh pulling at his fingers. In the glass, their pink shadows played. He looked from the glass to her, and then began to take off his own clothes as she lay watching. The stitches felt like brambles across his back as he slid off his shirt.

In a moment, he lay down beside her, watching her now and not her reflection. She raised herself on an elbow, her breasts casting deep shadows across her flesh, and began to trace slow circles on his chest with a fingertip. His hand slid slowly up the inside of her thigh, and he watched her eyes widen and then relax, and then they were together, pressed into each other, flesh against flesh, warm and hard and soft and loving.

Suddenly, her eyes opened. Her hand lifted from his back, and she held it up above his head.

Mick turned to see the hand. There on the fingertips, was a smear of dark, sticky blood.

"Mick!" she said. "Your stitches. You—pulled them."

He took her hand gently and placed it back between his shoulders. "It's okay, Cheryl," he said quietly, kissing the hollow of her neck.

"No . . ." She murmured. "No . . . it's not . . ."

He forced her hand down against his skin. His lips next to her ear, he whispered: "It'll wait. Please, Cheryl. It'll wait."

She squeezed him even more tightly then, and her back arched off the mattress, pressing into him, a soft and wild trembling running up and down her body.

M atthew Simmons peered into the trash basket by his desk and shuffled some papers on top of the bottle, so it was hidden from view. He knew someone would find it anyway, probably Mrs. Grier, and then the whole *Tanapah Herald* office would have something to talk about—and maybe worry about—for a while.

Hell with it. Alcohol helped, no doubt about it. Helped you talk patiently and rationally about things that had no patience or rationality to them. So what if they found it? There were important things to consider.

Matthew Simmons made a mental note to pick up another fifth of rye at Old Man Morgan's liquor store first thing tomorrow.

His mind drifted. *So many things,* he thought. *So many things you can't answer.*

He sighed, reached for a paper clip, and began turning it over and over between his fingers.

What the kid said . . . Amazing how he thought anyone that he had ever seen as a child was still a child, firmly fixed in his mind as a runny-nosed miniature human being with big eyes and unkempt hair. And the adults . . . they were like Old Man Morgan, full-grown, authoritative. Sometimes it seemed to Simmons that the entire population of Tanapah could be divided into two groups: old men and kids.

What the kid said, about all of us . . .

Matthew Simmons squeezed the paper clip harder. Without any conscious effort, an image formed in his mind, an image cobwebbed and dim, and he realized then that he had been trying hard not to think about it, not to visualize it. The press.

The damned press, like an animal, always hungry. Day by day, he fed it blocks of words, like chunks of meat.

He had never considered being anything else but a newsman, a feeder of the press, the keeper of a beast that never left him, nor ever thanked him . . . that sucked, through him, the marrow of tragedy, mostly, by which the "news" was made.

The big press in Chicago had thundered and shook the building when it was fed. The offset machine in the back of the *Herald* building purred and growled—but was no less demanding. It wanted the very last of him.

Coming for me. Coming for me!

A tiny clicking noise from behind him started Matthew Simmons out of the vision. He looked down at his shaking hand, saw the paper clip bent double under his fingers. He listened again.

Mice. Forget it. Go home.

And he did. The light in the back room went out, and his key scraped against the front door lock. He stood for a moment, inhaling the night air.

But he didn't forget.

14

The morning pried into his consciousness like a crowbar. Mick awoke by painful degrees, his mouth dry, his body aching, the events of the past night seeping thickly back into his brain. Coffee smells came to him and the sound of frying bacon.

Mick touched his fingertips to his head. It felt feverish. A hot weight glowed inside it, the weight of what had been happening to him, and what had happened to him the day before.

Events came back in a rush. Ginny's house. The basement. Simmons. And Cheryl.

He opened his eyes, saw the room that was hers. In a moment he was ignoring the pains in his head and body, was getting out of the bed, dressing and leaving the room, quietly pulling the door shut behind him.

He padded barefooted down the hall and stopped in the doorway to the kitchen. Cheryl and Annie sat together at the table in the dining area. Annie dawdled, head down, over a plate of scrambled eggs that looked untouched. Cheryl talked to her in a voice that was little more than a whisper.

Mick felt like an intruder again, as if he had no right to be there, shouldn't be there. He started to turn away, but Annie spotted him. Before she could lower her head again, Mick saw the tear streaks under her eyes, the widening of the pupils. She muttered something.

Cheryl turned to look at him and he was surprised to see how drawn her face looked, and how surprised, as if he had caught her in the middle of something that was meant to be a secret—at least from him.

"Good morning, Mick" she said, forcing cordiality.

Mick nodded. "Hi, Cheryl. Hello, Annie."

Annie didn't respond.

"Breakfast?" asked Cheryl.

Mick's voice felt thick in his mouth. "That'd be nice." He walked into the room and took a seat at the table.

Something was very wrong. It wasn't just the hangover, or what was happening to Tanapah, or to him. Something else had crept into this house and this room, had seeped into the warm, cheerful kitchen and the warm, cheerful people there, and Mick suddenly feared that once again, it might be him. Something might be wrong with him, something that reached out from him and infected everyone around him. Simmons had said you couldn't blame all the evils in the world on one person, had told Mick it wasn't his fault, but—

"How about some bacon?" asked Cheryl. "We've got bacon, toast, and eggs this morning."

"Sure," he replied, as she got up from the table and went toward the kitchen. He started to say something to Annie, but she seemed to be avoiding looking at him, so he decided against it. "How's Ginny?" he called to Cheryl, louder than he needed to.

"Fine. Still asleep. Bob Wortham's already been in to check on her—on his way to work. Her parents should be here before too long."

He nodded as she came back and put a cup of coffee in front of him. "Good." A vein in his forehead began to throb.

From the kitchen, Cheryl said, "I need to see you after breakfast, to take care of those stitches."

He nodded again and out of the corner of his eye saw Annie raise her head and stare at him. Taking a sip of coffee, he asked nonchalantly, "Anything wrong, Annie?"

She looked down at her plate, dropping her fork on the table. "Mommy," she said plaintively, "can I go outside now?"

Cheryl looked at her, at Mick, and then said in an unnaturally low voice, "Yes. Go outside now. And don't be scared."

S he worked silently, replacing the stitches.

He winced as the needle went in, relaxed as it wormed through the flesh. Just another pain, another jab to his body, joining all the rest of them. He was learning to live with the pain.

"There," said Cheryl. "That ought to do it." The new pain of the needle was already growing old when she stepped back.

He turned around on the doctor's table and watched as she went to the sink and busied herself, her back turned to him. "You're not going to tell me, are you," he said.

"We've been through that. It's nothing."

"Cheryl. It's not nothing. You've been cold all morning. And Annie . . . if I've done something to upset you both, I want to know. I think I have a right to know."

Her body tensed and she turned to face him. "You have a right?" Her eyes blazed.

"Yeah, I think so."

"You have a right to run off downtown—against my orders —stay out all day and most of the night, break into people's houses and hurt yourself, and come back and tell crazy stories to me and before I know it, you . . ." Her face began to tremble.

"Cheryl," he said quickly as he rose, "I didn't . . . force you."

All the tightness seemed to leave her body then, and she leaned against the table, her eyes closed.

"I know. I know, Mick. I'm sorry."

He suddenly wanted more than anything to touch her, to reestablish their closeness and make things right again. Before he knew it, he was off the table and holding her. She clung to him.

She repeated, "I'm so sorry, Mick." The words whispered past the flesh of his neck.

"I'm sorry, too, Cheryl. I must've worried you half-silly." He kissed her cheek and then pulled back, looking into her eyes. "But there's something else, isn't there?"

Cheryl blinked a couple of times and swallowed. "Uh-huh. Anne," she said. "On top of everything else, Annie."

"Annie?"

"She just seemed different this morning. She's not a moody child, Mick. She's a good child, usually happy and cheerful, but not this morning." Cheryl looked at steadily at Mick. "I guess . . . I guess she heard us last night."

He started to say something but couldn't.

"She heard noises coming from our—my room, and she said it made her afraid, and she was scared and wanted me, but she couldn't come in and get me because that was where the noises were coming from." Cheryl shrugged, tore her eyes away, and shook a lock of hair from her forehead. "She told me she felt alone then. Alone and scared. And she heard your voice in the room."

Mick's first impulse had been to joke it away—*we couldn't have been making that much noise*—and take her in his arms and kiss her again. But then a bad feeling washed over him, bitter and remorseful. He had wanted Cheryl, to hold, to become his, that he might touch the reason and the rightness that was the essence of her. And now, he felt like a leper, a carrier of some loathsome disease that got into innocent people and made them suffer.

"I don't know," Cheryl was saying. "Now Annie's scared, too. You, and I, and Ginny Adams—and Bob Wortham, to judge by the way he acted. So much fear, Mick. I've never dealt with so much fear before, and it makes *me* fearful."

Through the window of the clinic, he caught sight of Annie in the backyard. She was sitting at the base of a pecan tree, tugging little clumps of grass out of the ground.

"I think I'll go talk to her," Mick said. He put his shirt on and buttoned the cuffs. "I've been wanting to talk to her anyway."

Cheryl's grip on his arm was intended to stop him, but somehow it became an embrace. "Don't—" she started.

"Make it worse, right?" He kissed her. "I won't." Turning, he walked through the house and pushed open the back door. The air was misty with flower scents from Hattie Redmiller's garden.

He saw Annie look towards him and quickly move to the far side of the tree, where she was hidden except for the blue gingham tips of her shoulders.

She became, in that sudden, simple movement, a wonder to Mick. Not Cheryl's little girl, not just a small person, but a *child*. He could never be part of her world, not really. And yet, he thought, there were ways, there were words, that might reach her. There *had* to be.

He made no attempt to join her, and sat down, his back to

the tree, ignoring the preliminary pain as his back scraped against the bark. "You know, Annie," he said, "I like you. I like you a lot. I was hoping, maybe, that we could be friends."

No answer. Just the sound of grass being tugged out of the ground. Overhead, leaves rustled lazily, stirred by the spring breeze.

Mick looked toward the window and caught Cheryl watching him with an expression of worry that pierced whatever confidence he had felt. She moved aside, leaving the window as blank as his mind as he grasped for the right thing to say.

He exhaled. "You know, I'll tell you what I like, Annie. I wouldn't tell anybody but a friend, but . . . I like grape jam on top of ice cream—even chocolate. I like *Roadrunner* cartoons, and new pencils, and if nobody is watching, I like to make faces at myself in a mirror. And . . . I'd like to know the things *you* like best, Annie."

A wind fan squeaked from a rooftop.

"Okay, then, I'll guess," Mick said. "You're so much like your mother when she was your age . . ." *So very much. So heart-stopping much.* I'll bet you like some of the things she used to like, too. Let's see. How about strawberry Kool-Aid made into ice cubes? Yeah. And coloring books. And jumping into rain puddles. And . . . what else?"

"Christy," she said.

"Who?"

"Christy! You don't know who Christy is. You don't know *anything!*"

There was a motion, a swishing of feet through the grass, and Mick turned. He was alone under the tree, and Annie was running through the rows of flowers across the way, a streamer of blonde hair bobbing through the kaleidoscope of colors.

"Annie!" He was up and running after her, his temples

throbbing with an ache that had been waiting for just enough blood to start.

He ran, and time shimmered around him.

Down the sidewalk, past the whitened stump that had been the Giant. How many times had he run this same way? How many times, with a balsa wood airplane in his hand stretched overhead, as if sparks and blue smoke might shoot from the plastic propeller and carry him off.

He ran across the schoolyard, gravel scattering from the toes of his shoes. Schoolyard gravel. Clear a circle. See? It's a cat's-eye shooter, and it's luck, and it's magic.

He ran over the crack in the sidewalk that looked like a lightning bolt, with a half-inch drop-off that would make your teeth clack if you hit it on roller skates, only now a whole section—whole sections—of sidewalk zigzagged with lightning.

He ran and was finally forced to limp. Annie disappeared around the corner of the house ahead of him. Mick stopped then, stunned by the sight of the apple tree in the front yard and the honeysuckle clinging to a trellis near the front door.

Mickie Winters! You come in this house and get yourself a nice big hug!

Aunt Lucy's voice called warm and bright in his mind. It called from summers past, when the house and its oven smells, its sunlight and home sounds had been part of her. Now the old house was a cold, white shell, devoid of life, empty of welcomes.

Mick remembered his vow to come back to this echoing ghost of a place, to come back and see that there was nothing to the cellar but a dark hole in the ground, a useless hole—unless a storm came along, or unless someone wanted a jar of preserves. He had wanted to confront that cellar and laugh at himself and go home.

But the house stood to warn him. *Home,* it warned, *can be taken away.*

He walked slowly, down the dusty driveway that curved around the house to the garage in back, being careful not to stumble in the ruts. He panted, and his head ached, and his back ached, and his leg ached.

Damn! He thought, taking a deep breath and holding it, standing still for a moment, regaining his equilibrium. He stared at the house, noting the drawn window shades and a cluster of daffodils that pushed up through the weeds, at the mouth of the drainpipe.

When he started again, rounding the corner of the house, his feet moved in a dream motion, an odd, unnerving contrast to the thudding of his heart.

Annie was waiting for him.

She stood there stiffly, a small figure in blue gingham against the peeling red of the cellar door.

"Annie . . . let's go back now," Mick said, approaching her.

"No." She shook her head, and her blonde hair was silver-soft in the sunlight. "I want to see"—she looked toward the cellar—"what's down *there.*"

"Nothing," Mick said. "Nothing's down there."

"That what are you scairt of?"

Don't you ever go down there, Mickie. You hear me?

Mick fabricated something he hoped would look like a smile. "Just . . . come on now, Annie. Come away. Let's go—"

"I *know* you're scairt. I heard you say so. I heard *lots.* You're scairt, but *I'm* not. See!" And turning, she closed her hand around the lock that held the door. The lock Mick had sawn apart. The lock he had failed to replace.

She brought her hand up, lifting the sawn hasp of the lock almost free from the metal plate that was screwed to the door. Her eyes were on him.

A quivering began in the cellar door.

Mick heard—*thought* he heard—a scraping noise, a raspy tearing of wood, bringing with it the images of bits of wood falling, scattering like confetti down the darkened stairs into the maw of the cellar. The vibrations caused a few flakes of chipped and ancient paint to fall from the door.

"*Annie!*" He moved as in a blur, a haze, with no thought in it. As he grabbed her up in his arms, he saw her eyes go wide as moons. Then the mottled red paint of the door meshed with a wisp of cloud and sky and became the thick green of the uncut grass in Aunt Lucy's backyard as they landed with a thud, faces down.

Mick whipped his head around and stared at the cellar door.

He saw the lock still in place. The cellar door glistened and wavered before him, as if it might dissolve, and then he realized he was crying, the tears clouding his vision.

His arms tightened around Annie to assure that she was still there, still real, still safe.

She sniffled, and her tiny body began to jerk against his as she tried to choke back her own sobs. Mick lifted her to her feet and began to brush the grass away from her dress.

Without looking at him, she said, "You hurt me. You hurt. You *hurt!*" And then dissolved in tears.

"No, Annie," he said quietly, holding her by the shoulders. "I don't do hurting. Not to you, and not to your mother. Not ever." He reached up and wiped the moisture from the corners of his eyes. Bending down, he said, "You know what the trouble is with us, Annie? We're scared of each other. You don't need this cellar to make me afraid. I get really scared when I think that maybe you can't trust, that you won't ever trust me."

Annie sniffed, kicking at the grass with a toe of her shoe. The paths of her tears glistened on her face.

"What do you want to do with me, Annie? Do you want to —do you *really* want to shut me away in that cellar? Forever? Is that what you want?"

Her shoe stamped a miniature cellar into the ground. "No. Not f'ever."

"Well, then. Let's get out of here. We'll go back and start over." Kneeling, he held her at arm's length. Her shoulders trembled lightly in his hands. Suddenly, her eyes shifted from his face, darting to look over his shoulder toward the cellar.

"Midnight!" she cried.

Mick twisted around and the stitches pulled in his back. The cellar door remained closed and locked, but at the base of the door sat a cat, watching them.

Its fur was coarse and black and seemed to have no sheen to it, as if the sunlight had been drawn into it, captured and lost.

"Midnight!" Annie breathed again. There was wonder in her voice.

She sidestepped away from Mick, heading for the cat, but he reached out to stop her. "No, Annie," he said.

"But he's *my* kitty!"

The cat cocked its head toward them. Its eyes shone yellow, the pupils mere slits. It had a sequined collar that glittered, sharp little sparks of light.

"Are you *sure*, Annie?" asked Mick. "I've never seen that cat at your house."

"It is too my cat. And I want to take him home." The stamp of her foot was all little girl, but the insistence that went with it reminded Mick of Cheryl.

Mick glanced at the cat. It sat motionless but for the tick-tock switching of its tail. Just a cat, after all. Not everything in the world, in the world he had come back to, was sinister. Cheryl had shown him that.

"Here's what we'll do, Annie. You run home right now, and

I'll bring it, and we'll see what you mother says." Might as well get the cat myself, thought Mick. If I get scratched, I've already had my tetanus shot.

Annie frowned, gauging the worth of his promise. "Midnight," she said tentatively, glancing back and forth between Mick and the cat.

"Go on, now."

She backed off a step, stood testing him for a moment more, and then turned and ran. She stopped once to look back around a corner of the house.

Mick waited, sweating and cold in the warm air, until she had disappeared. All of a sudden, he felt acutely embarrassed and stupid.

Crying in front of her. What's wrong with you.

What better way, he thought, to upset a child. He bet himself that Annie had never seen Cheryl cry and cursed his own weakness.

You must be in pretty damn bad shape, Winters, to throw it off on a little girl.

He turned toward the cat: *I'll make it up to her.*

The first thing he noticed was that its head was oddly flat and triangular. Siamese, maybe . . . and something else. The cat stretched. The mouth opened pink, and its paws flexed, showing rows of tiny, tooth-white nails. Still, it watched him, and he watched it.

Approaching the cat slowly, his hand outstretched, Mick allowed himself only one glance at the lock on the door. It was in place, and the door was silent. Perhaps it had always been.

The cat's eyes never left him.

Bending down, Mick brushed the stiff fur at the back of the cat's neck.

Grab. Grab it now!

His hand cupped gently, stroking. "Midnight?" he said.

Before he felt the pain—the searing of his hand—he saw the smoke. It was gray, a swirling breath of smoke, stirring from the fur of the cat, crawling up between his fingers. Smoke. And the licking of yellow-white fire, the flame of the cat's eyes, the eyes that were fixed on him.

Mick jerked his hand away, jamming his knuckles into his mouth.

The cat burned. Still it sat, never moving. Sparks rose around it, and the ground blackened under it.

It burned, the air thickened.

It burned, leaving nothing but the small white teeth set into a smoke-laden, constricting mass of twisted black, then nothing but smoke.

And then, nothing at all.

Annie was in the schoolyard. She was sitting on a swing set, but she wasn't swinging.

"You didn't go home," Mick said.

"You didn't bring Midnight."

"It . . . wasn't your cat, Annie."

He took her hand, marveling at it. Such a strong little hand. "Come with me," he said, and they walked, kicking gravel.

They walked past the Giant, through Hattie Redmiller's bright giftwrap of a garden.

"Cin'mon toast," Annie said.

Her voice startled Mick like the sudden flutter of a butterfly. "What?" he asked.

"Cin'mon toast. That's what I like. And Momma's blue dress that she wears with white beads."

"Blowing on a dandelion ball," Mick said.

Cheryl was waiting for them. She stood in the doorway as they came into the backyard.

"Sounds like a pretty interesting conversation," she smiled but only a little, a smile accomplished by the tugging of small muscles. It wasn't what Mick had expected and wanted. It wasn't the smile he deserved.

"Matthew Simmons just called," she said as Annie and Mick walked into the house. Her eyes caught his. "For you, Mick. He wouldn't say why."

15

T he phone dial seemed to taunt him, turning slowly, giving him time to think between the numbers. And in that time, the soft, scraping sound of the moving dial became the sound of the clothes scraping across the floor in the shape of a man, the echo of the pistol when he fired, and the sound of scraping—*Jerry!*—in the culvert, and the cat that burned, sizzle of hair on fire, evaporating into—

"*Herald* office. Simmons"

—and Matthew Simmons, the sound of his voice, the weight of his gray eyes in the darkness, as Mick spilled secrets into the night—

"This is the *Herald.* Can I *help* you?" The put-upon edge in his voice snapped Mick back.

"Yeah. Hello . . . Mr. Simmons."

"That you, Mick?"

"Yeah."

Simmons's voice bore just a trace of strain. "Well, I thought you ought to know. Sheriff's getting up a search party to go check the area around the coal pit."

The coal pit.

"The two men that disappeared—" Mick began.

"Jim Curtis and Don Whitaker. They're still missing. But I got to thinking . . . they took Whitaker's car—and that car was his baby. He was so damned proud of that vehicle that he'd never want to leave it out in the rain, even layered an inch thick with polished wax. And the day they went off, there was rain in the forecast."

"That was—what?—two days ago?" Time for Mick had come unstrung, was either stopped dead or going so fast he couldn't hang onto it.

"Right," Simmons said. "So, this morning, I woke up and—Mick, I could've *kicked* myself, it was so obvious. I called Herb Jeffries, told him where to look for the car. And, sure enough, there it was, parked out of sight in a clump of elm trees about a quarter mile south of the coal pit. Parked out of the rain."

"Any sign of the two men?"

"No. Nothing," Simmons said. "They must have been somewhere around the coal pit, though. So, the sheriff started poking around, working his way down to the slope of the pit."

Mick felt it coming. "And what did he find?" He felt the hairs on the back of his neck rise. He listened as Simmons swallowed something. It sounded like coffee, but the grunt that followed suggested medicine.

"Cat tracks," Simmons said. "The size of a saucer and sunk an inch deep into the ground."

"Cat? You mean a cougar?"

"That's all it could be. Nobody's had proof of a cougar being around here for the last twenty years; a few so-called sightings, nothing like this. But . . . there it is."

Mick's heart raced, and the phone became heavy and cold in his hand. "I think I know what you're telling me," he said.

"And sure—*sure!*—I'd rather think it was a cat that got Jerry. But it *wasn't.*"

"Oh? So, you *did* see, after all."

"I didn't say that."

"Then how would you know?"

"Here's a question for *you,* Mr. Simmons. How do you know that those tracks at the coal pit had to be made by a cougar? All you've got to go on is the word of Herb Jeffries, that kid of a sheriff. 'Herb's a good kid,' you told me, 'but he's out of his league.'"

"Mick, dammit, now you're playing *my* game."

"You don't want to believe me. That's the problem. You don't want to believe any part of what I told you last night—or even to try."

"That's not true, Mick. I—"

Mick fought to keep his voice down. "Sure, Mr. Simmons, maybe your damned cat is up there all right. But that doesn't even begin—doesn't even *begin!*—to explain what's been happening."

The silence that followed was broken by Simmons's dry wheeze. Mick couldn't tell whether he was laughing or coughing. "I called you for two reasons, Mick," he said presently. "One, to tell you about the tracks and search party. And second, to see if you'd stick to the story you told me last night, even if I gave you a way out of it."

"The search party," Mick said finally. "I want to go."

"Good. You can meet me in front of the courthouse in an hour."

Cheryl fought him. As Mick went upstairs to change his clothes, she was right behind him, alternately rational, authoritarian, and pleading. But Mick shook her off, and soon she gave up and left him alone.

Thirty minutes later, Mick had walked three blocks on his way to town when he heard a car pulling to a stop beside him. He turned to see a white Buick, with Cheryl behind the wheel. She swung the passenger door open and said quietly, "Get in."

He just looked at her.

"If those men have been hurt, they're going to need me," she said. "Furthermore, I can keep an eye on you, since you've decided not to listen to reason. We can talk on the way."

He got in. "What about Annie? And Ginny?"

"Hattie Redmiller's at my house. She watches Annie a lot when I have to be away. And she knows how to take care of things."

They drove to the front of the old red brick county court-house building, where the usual excitement was the clicking of checkers beneath the shade trees.

Today, though, a swarm of pickup trucks and cars were parked, jammed, and double-parked around the courthouse yard, where a throng of men were milling about, most of them carrying rifles or shotguns. There were a number of boys, too, trying to crowd toward the front of the group, and barking dogs, and a baby crying from someplace in the middle of the bunch, and other people looking out the open windows of the courthouse.

"Look at that," Mick said. "Where did they all *come* from, Cheryl?"

Cheryl shrugged. "I don't know. Everywhere around here," she said, "word travels fast."

Standing on the front steps of the building, Herb Jeffries

was doing his best to take charge. Mick saw Matthew Simmons at the edge of the crowd, surveying the commotion in the company of another man: a burly, bearded man clad in a plaid shirt and faded jeans, who carried a scoped deer rifle held in the bend of his right arm.

Cheryl tapped the horn, once, twice. Simmons turned, saw her, and motioned to the other man, leading the way to Cheryl's car.

"Mick," she said as they approached, looking down at her hands on the steering wheel. "I've never been much at imagining things, you know that. But . . . I've got a bad feeling. I'm scared. For you—and for me."

Mick started to answer, wishing he could do something—hold her, anything—but it was too late. The back door of the car opened.

"'Day, Cheryl," Simmons said as he slid across the back seat. He was followed by the second man. "Let's beat the rush." Simmons gestured out the window where the crowd in front of the courthouse had begun to move toward the parking area.

Cheryl made a U-turn and headed toward Main Street while Simmons made the introductions. "This is Joe-Bob Harper. Joe-Bob's the county extension agent. Bags himself a buck every year or so, too."

Mick leaned across the seat to shake hands. Cheryl said, "Didn't I treat your boy for mono last year?"

"That's a fact, Doc," the man replied.

"I thought so. How's he doing?"

"Just fine. You did a real good job." Harper peered out the window. "I'll tell you somethin'," he muttered. "Any cat out there's gonna be scared clear to Mexico by the time that posse gets through stompin' around."

"What about the men?" Mick asked. "Could a big cat have . . . well . . ."

"That's a stumper, all right," Harper answered. "A cougar'd go after a cow by first choice; a rabbit—a skunk, even—not a man, hardly ever. Figure two hundred pounds or so, and sure, it's plenty big enough to bring a man down. But *two* men?"

He paused for a bite of tobacco. Looking from side to side, he rubbed his hand against the spotless white vinyl of the car seat, shrugged, and dropped the wad back into his shirt pocket. "More likely," he said, stroking his beard, "well, you'd need to have heard it to know what I'm talkin' about: the cry of a mountain cat. Sounds true to hell the same as a woman's scream, all wild and full of pain. Now . . . you put a couple of guys out in the country, get 'em a little spooked, and lay *that* on 'em. They're probably still flyin' off heels to th' wind."

He turned away, looking out the window as the car jounced and wheeled off the highway onto the dirt road that led to the coal pit.

"Might've thought Old Satan had come to get 'em," he said, chewing thoughtfully.

Cheryl parked in the field near the high edge of the abandoned coal pit. A rectangular gouge, the pit was two hundred feet long and filled with seepage from the water table. Its perimeter was rimmed by a sagging wire fence, beyond which water lay dark and deep, rippling ever so slightly.

Rippling. Like loose skin.

Mick caught himself thinking, *There's a big old heebie-jeebie that lives way down deep in the water . . .*

Then: *Because I believed. Oh God!—because I believed;* and the memory of the basement, like a chained thing suddenly came loose, overtook him.

Cheryl's touch on his arm brought him back to the present. "Are you all right? You look pale," she said.

He nodded, fashioning a smile, and clasped her hand.

"You think there's much chance of the cougar still being close by?" Simmons asked Harper.

"Possible." He swung open the car door and stepped out. "Also possible, it could've been a dog. I want a good look at those tracks before everything gets messed up around here." Pulling a handful of shells from his pants pocket, he loaded the rifle. "Be just as well if the rest of you stayed in the car."

"That suits me just fine," Cheryl said.

Harper shouldered the rifle and made his way through the tall grass, over a break in the fence, then down the embankment toward the sloping end of the pit, where he disappeared from view.

At almost the same time, the first of the other cars from town rounded the curve and stopped behind Cheryl's car in a spill of dust. A pickup followed, loaded with people. Mick thought he recognized a few of them from his first night in town: a bunch of potbellies who, he imagined, regularly found some excuse to spend the warm afternoons in Scot's Tap. The first man jumped out of the truck and waved a shotgun over the crushed top of his red polka-dotted farm cap, shouting, "Whooo-eee-e!"

"That's just what I was afraid of," Simmons said. "We'll be lucky if nobody gets shot out here."

The cars kept coming —six, ten, fifteen—and finally, the sheriff's car. A loose knot of men had already started down to the pit level the way Harper had gone.

Six-packs of beer were being broken out of ice chests. Car doors were slamming like cannon fire. Jokes were traded amid the clatter of guns being readied.

"Seems like every time the town needs a talking to, I get the job," Simmons remarked. He climbed out of the car, took a couple of slow steps toward an open space where he could be seen.

"Now just hold on, you men," he ordered. His voice was strong, but he did not shout.

He waited. From the car, Mick and Cheryl watched as the noise stopped and all heads turned.

"First off," Simmons continued in the same tone, "let's remember we're out here because two of your neighbors are missing. I don't have to tell you that something may have happened to them." He paused. "And as for this . . . cougar . . . if it *is* a cougar"—Simmons shifted his sight across the length of the pit—"you all know Joe-Bob Harper's the man to take care of that. So, how about giving him a chance to do his job?"

Mick followed Simmons's line of sight, over the heads of some men who had paused at the edge of the pit to listen to Simmons.

Across the pit, Harper had emerged onto the slope. He knelt, reached out, and traced something on the ground.

"That's where I saw it."

Startled by the sound of Herb Jeffries' low rumble of a voice, Mick turned. The sheriff stood near the car, next to Simmons.

"Awful glad you're out here, Mr. Simmons," Jeffries said.

Across the way, Harper straightened and looked toward the high edge of the pit. In silence, broken only by the singing of a meadowlark, the men clustered around the near edge looked back at him.

"S'pose he tracked down Ol' Satan?" somebody asked, setting off a lot of talk and more laughs. But the laughter seemed quick and brittle to Mick's ears.

"What's this 'Satan' they keep talking about?" Mick asked Cheryl.

She answered with a half-smile. "Oh, you probably remember. That old story about—"

Harper began motioning to the crowd: Stay there. Turning his head quickly from side to side and holding his rifle at ready, he left the slope and disappeared into the brush and tree stand that would put him out of sight again until he neared the top of the pit's high edge.

"He's onto something," Simmons said, glancing back at Mick's open window. Mick nodded and watched.

Minutes passed. The crowd stirred but spoke little. All eyes were trained intently on a clearing of the black oaks that tangled along the embankment, watching for Harper.

The branches moved and crackled.

Jaws tightened; cigarettes dropped. Some of the men took a step back.

"Joe-Bob . . .?" Jeffries' call was punctuated by the *pop!* of his holster unsnapping.

Harper emerged. His face was as hard and as sharp-edged as ice, his eyes dark and narrowed.

"Cat tracks, all right," he said. "Biggest I ever saw." He spat a brown rivulet of tobacco juice. "I'd say we got us one hell of a—"

From behind, it was on him, too fast to be recognized. Too big to be believed. A shadow cast by nothing. A shadow leaving the ground, seeming to hang and take shape in the air, coming down, hard and black, the head flat and triangular, more snake than cat-like, more snake fangs than cat teeth, white teeth, the flash of yellow eyes.

Harper flew forward, knocked aside like a toy, the rifle spinning out of his hands.

There were screams, but to Mick, there was only one, and he answered it. Throwing himself across the seat toward Cheryl, he pulled her toward him and down to the floor of the car, holding her and shielding her.

The car jolted. A man's head was pitched through the glass of the rear side window. And then the firing began.

It was sporadic at first, mingled with outcries and the sound of bodies in crazed motion, and was matched shot for shot by the shudders Mick felt run through Cheryl and through her into him.

"Mick . . . my God, Mick! What *is* it?"

The rifle fire blurred to a roar of strength that rose, crested, and died to the twisting wham of a repeating shotgun.

When it was over, the air bled with silence.

The area beyond Cheryl's car was a battleground, swirling with bluish-gray smoke.

Mick climbed out. He turned at the sound of a sharp, mechanical clicking and noticed Jeffries standing near the edge of the pit. The sheriff's arm was locked straight out, his hand knotted around the grip of a service revolver, pulling the trigger again and again, the hammer hitting on empty rounds.

Mick followed the line of the gun barrel down to the ground, to a scarlet-streaked and glistening clump of flattening weeds. It looked as if something had fallen there, something large. Something that bled.

He looked back at Jeffries who stood, his lips moving but making no sound, the hammer of his revolver clicking against metal. His pants cuffs were stained red, his beige shirt spattered.

Mick started toward him, but Matthew Simmons reached him first.

"Okay, Herb," Simmons said. "It's all right, Herb." The old man talked as he unwrapped Jeffries' fingers from the gun and took it away.

"Better get to your car, Herb," he said, pocketing the revolver. "Call us up some help. Herb, we need some help out here."

Jeffries nodded slowly, turned, and saw Mick.

"It's dead, isn't it?" he asked Mick. His voice rumbled brokenly. "I saw it die, but then . . . but, it *had* to die. I shot its eyes out." He turned to Simmons. "Didn't I, Mr. Simmons?"

"Get hold of yourself, Herb, and get to your radio."

"Yes, sir." Nodding again to himself, Jeffries turned and began to shamble off, back toward where the cars were parked and where splintered knots of people stood, dazed and silent.

Mick crossed to the bloody patch of ground where Simmons stood with a few other men. "Mr. Simmons," he asked, "what—"

"Herb! We got it, didn't we! We got that son-of-a-bitch, didn't we!"

Mick and Simmons turned toward the source of the noise and saw a thin blond man in new overalls standing in front of Jeffries. He carried a rifle in one hand; the other gripped Jeffries' shoulder hard.

"Damned if we didn't get him, Herb!" the man shouted. "We got *Old Satan!*" He grinned wildly into the uncomprehending face of the lawman.

Mick heard Simmons way "Wilbur!"; saw the blond man look around once toward them and then back to Jeffries.

"C'mon, Herb! We got *Old Satan!*"

Simmons took three quick steps toward the two men. "Wilbur, now you just knock off the crap. We've got plenty of trouble out here without you going crazy on us. Leave Herb alone."

The man dropped his hand from Jeffries' shoulder. "Didn't you see it?" he demanded.

"See what?" asked Simmons.

"*Old Satan!* Hell, just like I always pictured him since I was a kid—eight foot long if he was an inch! It was like—like he was flyin' or somethin'. Right into the water. But we got him. Shot the bastard down."

Simmons shook his head slowly. "I didn't see anything, Wilbur."

"Well *they* did." The man waved his hand in a wide arc, indicating the other men. "They wasn't shootin' at *nothing!*" He looked past Simmons to the men behind him. "Tell him, men. Tell him who we shot, so he can go back and write it up in his paper!"

As Simmons turned around to face the men, a memory suddenly electrified Mick, yanking him back through the years and landing him hard on a summer's night, outside his aunt's house. They were playing kick-the-can that night in the back-yard with some of the neighborhood kids, and there was one kid there whom Mick had not seen before or since, a big kid with big ears and close-cropped hair who lived out in the country and was staying in town, spending the night with a friend or cousin who lived in the neighborhood. It had been a firefly night, with running and shouting and hiding in the bushes or around the corner of houses or in trees, skinning up them until the leaves hid you from whoever was it . . . and then, late, after the wind had come up and the fireflies were gone, he and the new kid were caught, having to stay on base until someone came running up to kick the can and set them free. And then—

The wind howled once, like a woman's scream. And the kid's face, suddenly strained and spook-eyed, was illuminated in the dim glow of the porch light as he turned to Mick slowly, and whispered, "*Old Satan.*"

He lived out in the hills away from town, and he still wore the rhinestone collar from when he was with the circus, and whenever a rancher lost a cow, or the dogs went crazy in the night, or you were out fishing too late and it got dark and you could feel the eyes on you, out there in the trees, watching you, it was—

"Satan," Mick said, looking at the pool of blood on the ground. "Old Satan."

The voices around Mick were just that—voices, disembodied voices, mostly unfamiliar except the one that belonged to Simmons. Mick didn't look toward them. He watched for the tangled weeds and blood on the ground, watched it shimmer in the light like a field of rubies.

"I ain't sayin' *what* we saw, Mr. Simmons. But it was somethin'. Somethin' awful big."

Another voice. "I hit it. I know I hit it, whatever it was."

"Don't lie, Charlie! You know what it was! You saw it just like I did, God-damn it! That chain—that collar, sparklin'—"

"*Bullshit!*" Simmons's voice. "You don't see it now, do you? *Do you,* Wilbur?"

There was no reply.

"You want to know about Old Satan, Wilbur? I'll tell you about Old Satan. I was here when it happened, when that circus still overwintered around these parts—and that was forty years ago."

His voice demanded attention, and Mick found himself staring at Simmons and the others.

"Cost a quarter to look at him," Simmons continued. "'Satan the Mighty,' they called him. Folks around here said he looked more like a toothless old barn cat. Wouldn't even be any good as a mouser, they said. Hell, he was a *joke*. So, one night the circus train pulls out, jumps the tracks just outside of town, and the cage breaks open. Escaped—one feeble old panther, never to be seen again, for the likely good reason that he starved to death."

The men were silent, casting quick embarrassed glances at

each other or looking at the ground. Even the blond man, Wilbur, just stared.

"But—"

The word was out of Mick's mouth before he knew it. The eyes that fastened on him seemed to be looking for explanations, for answers, for something that Mick knew he couldn't give. How could he explain it? How could he tell them that it didn't matter whether Old Satan, the first Old Satan, died or not, that as long as he was alive in their memories, then he was real, he was not dead.

"The stories kept up, Mr. Simmons," he said, "about Old Satan. They kept on, and they kept growing. For years. People *believed*."

Simmons's eyes narrowed, and Mick knew that the old man knew what he was getting at, knew he was harkening back to their conversation of the night before. But the voice was cold and precise when Simmons said, "It was just a story."

The men looked silently at him, their eyes boring into him, transferring their fear and confusion and guilt to him, until he had to turn away.

Cheryl came toward him then, her crisp white blouse mottled with red.

"Mr. Harper is dead," she said. "I've got Arnie Billings stretched out in the back of a pickup. He's the worst one otherwise." She paused, wiping her forehead with the back of her hand.

Mick nodded, but then he realized that she was addressing herself more to Simmons than to him.

They didn't know. They didn't know, and he couldn't explain it to them, not to any of them, not even Simmons. Not even Cheryl.

A cloud passed over the sun, throwing a shadow onto the weeds and matted blood at Mick's feet, turning them very dark.

The wind came up, skimming over the blood, and it seemed to sparkle a little, inches away from the toe of his shoe. He watched it.

They don't understand.

Behind him, Cheryl was saying, "Benny Carter—he was a medic, Vietnam—he's with him, now, and he'll ride back there with him, but we've got to get him down to Nowata to the hospital."

They didn't just understand that you had to believe, and when you believed, it was like remembering, and when you remembered—

Cheryl said, "I need someone to drive. It can't wait."

The wind whipped at the blood, flattening the leaves of the weeds. Mick tried to turn away, to say, "I'll go, Cheryl," but he was transfixed by the blood, the blood and the memory of the country kid, both of which wedged a new thought into his mind then—that a new, old fear had just broken loose.

Old Satan.

The wind whistled, and before Mick's eyes, the pool of blood that stuck to the stalks of the weeds and soaked into the grass seemed to begin whirling, to coalesce and shimmer before him, to . . . rise up, swept by the wind, whirling, then growing smaller, deeper, separating into—

Two red eyes.

Two red eyes, dark and deep as eternity's tunnel, throwing him back through time and then passing through him, washing over him, and as he felt the white-hot slap of claws against his leg and began to fall, he seemed to fly through the air, borne by the wind, the wind that had now changed its pitch until it sounded like . . . a woman's scream.

16

A dark rain had come and gone, leaving the countryside wet but not clean, cold but not refreshed.

Mick sat high on the bank looking down into the pit, away from the rain and away from the people.

Once he glanced, behind him, toward the field. It looked like a county fair. Pickups and station wagons and late model cars were parked in uneven rows across the meadow, with more arriving as he watched. Word *had* traveled fast. Now, not only the men of Tanapah, but the women and children as well, clustered around the area, talking in groups beside cars and in the bed of the pickups, beer cans and shotguns glinting in the gray light.

Mick realized that some of the newly arrived must be people just now getting off work. Was it that late?

Bravely, people walked in little groups to the rim of the coal pit and peered into the water, pointing at where the great cat had disappeared, and talking of how the water had churned and gone crimson. Some of them even occasionally tried to climb over the rim and down the banks to the water, only to have Jeffries appear and shoo them away.

Ding-dong, the witch is dead. As if there were no more witches.

Someone else—how long ago? An hour? Two? Maybe three?—had driven the pickup to Nowata, carrying the wounded man and the Vietnam medic.

Mick had simply walked away, over to a spot where the gray shale jutted out of the new grass, and sat down, listening to the sound of thunder on the horizon, smelling the rain in the air, blocking out everyone, everything—even Cheryl, as she bandaged his leg ("You fell, Mick." Fell on *what?*"), and Simmons, who tried to talk with him. Finally, Simmons had said, "Leave him be," and walked away.

He heard Simmons borrowing a car, talking about getting back into Tanapah to put out a newspaper, followed by the revving of an engine, and he had known Simmons had gone.

Simmons—the first one to listen, but not to believe.

And then the rains had come, sending people scurrying back to their cars, sending Cheryl out to talk with him one last time, a pleading tone in her voice. "Please, Mick. Just get up and get in the car."

"No. No thanks, Cheryl. Not now."

Then he was alone in the rain.

Now Mick felt away from it all, above it all. He was only aware of the currents moving through his body, deep and swirling currents that came together at his brain and pushed hard against it. He wanted to open a hole, a pinpoint, onto a dark unused part of his mind and squeeze all those currents into the hole and seal it. Then he wouldn't have to think, wouldn't have to act, again. He felt as if he were losing his mind, sitting there in the field with the people all around him, and he didn't care.

Footsteps crunched behind him. Someone was coming. He sat there and silently prayed that they'd go away, that they'd turn and veer away from him.

They stopped right next to him. The rustle of clothing behind him told Mick that someone was squatting down. That meant more talk, more aggravation. Why couldn't they leave him alone?

"Beer?" asked the deep voice, and a thin, strong hand thrust a sweating metal cylinder in front of him.

Mick took it automatically, nodding once. Herb Jeffries hunkered down in front of him, as Mick popped the top on his beer.

"Clouds still got rain in 'em. Looks like we're gonna get it again."

Mick nodded again, reluctantly turning his gaze to the horizon, where squat black clouds piled on top of each other.

"Hurt much?"

"No," said Mick, glancing down at the crimson-speckled bandage around his calf where the pants had been torn away. He tilted the beer can and took a long swallow.

Jeffries cleared his throat. "You been out here a long time, Mr. Winters. The doc's sorta worried about you . . ." His voice trailed off. When Mick didn't answer, he continued, "I told her I'd come out here and tell you what I told her—might make some difference."

Mick looked directly at him for the first time. "Tell me what, sheriff?" he asked slowly.

Jeffries' eyes flickered. "That you ain't a suspect anymore. You didn't have nothin' to do with what happened . . . out here. And . . ." He reached out a bony hand, touching Mick's shoulder awkwardly. "I'm sorry. For suspectin' you."

"It's your job," Mick said tonelessly.

"I know. But it don't feel right when you're wrong." He

cleared his throat again. "Anyhow, you're free to go. I don't want—" Suddenly, his eyes flashed. "*Hey you!*"

Mick looked up. A few hundred feet in front of him, where the bank dropped down sharply into the water, a man was disappearing.

"Hey!" yelled Jeffries again, getting to his feet.

The man's head poked up, a green-and-white baseball cap covering most of the forehead.

"Payne?" shouted Jeffries, his body arched forward.

"Yeah?" came the voice.

"I said nobody goes down there! You think I was just saying that to hear my gums flap or what?"

The faraway face stared at Jeffries for a few more seconds. Between the two men, clusters of onlookers momentarily stopped what they were doing, watching the confrontation.

It was over in a moment. The baseball cap and the face disappeared, and an arm went up, waving a fist from which the middle finger protruded.

"Dammit, Charlie! Get up here with everyone else!"

But the figure had disappeared from view.

Jeffries swore again and started running across the grass to the rim of the pit, toward the place where the man had been. Mick watched him for a moment, and then his gaze wandered.

You're free to go. That's what Jeffries what had told him. So, why didn't he, then? He wasn't helping there. He had done all he could, with Ginny and with Simmons. He'd tried to tell them, tried to warn them, and nobody had listened, and now he'd had all he could take. What was keeping him there? Who'd stop him? Cheryl?

He scanned the cars, for her. He didn't see her, but he knew she was there, helping. Fighting. *Maybe fighting something I created.* Simmons had told him no, he wasn't responsible, no one could be responsible. Maybe Simmons was wrong.

And maybe Simmons wasn't wrong. But whoever was right, the fact—the horrible, irrefutable fact—was that it was happening. Here.

So, let them look. Let them discover it for themselves, these damned people, let them try to figure out what was going on. And when they found out it was something you couldn't put into words, when the excuses and explanations died on their lips in the awful face of it, he wouldn't be there. He'd be back in Kansas City in his apartment, or out somewhere, lost in the color and noise of the people and things he didn't have to be involved with. He'd be safe.

Mick finished the beer, crushed the can and tossed it aside. He'd put the damned house with the damned cellar up for sale and get someone to send him the papers, and he wouldn't have to see this place, this place with its horrors and its memories and its dark secrets ever again. Write it off and go home and let someone else fight. It was all too much.

Behind him, car doors slammed. In front of him, a few people wandered around the field, near the edge of the pit, looking down and talking. Jeffries hadn't reappeared.

It might just save him, save his sanity. Pick up and go, and don't look back.

Leave. Leave Tanapah and the old memories sucked out of an ancient gravesite and bury them again forever.

Leave Cheryl, because she was a part of it too.

Leave Cheryl? She was everything he had always wanted, always dreamed of—but she and *this* were inextricably bound, intertwined and inseparable. He could not have her without—

A hoarse shout arose from the pit, and the few people standing above it seemed to buckle at the sound. The shout rose above the noise of the crowd behind Mick, soared and sank like a Wagnerian chord.

The voices froze, half-finished casual sentences suspended

forever, and then the crowd was running, running toward the edge of the pit, and Mick ran too, joining the others in their rush.

Below Mick the bank of the coal pit sloped down at a sharp angle for about a hundred yards. Jagged shale blended gradually into limestone and then sandstone before leveling off into rocky soil and weeds at the water's edge.

The crowd filled in around him, and his eyes were their eyes, his ears their ears, and, worst of all, his memories were theirs, a shared and secret knowledge that rippled through them.

The pit.

Mick stared, they all stared, at Herb Jeffries flattened against an outcropping of rock in the bank, his pistol out and pointed at . . . the water.

The man Jeffries had gone after stood open-mouthed near the water's edge, his shotgun hanging slack in front of him. Between the two men, another man's body lay face down on the bank, the arms splayed out at impossible angles, the clothes tattered and heavy with water, soaking.

There's a big old heebie-jeebie—

The water rippled, and Jeffries and the man inched back away from it. Ripples turned to waves, which turned into one great wave out of which something big and dark flew, arching through the air and dropping heavily onto where it rolled and flopped still.

A man.

Lives way down deep in the water—

A couple of people shouted, and the cries were swallowed up in the murmur that ran through the mass of people touching them all and becoming a babbling that was almost inhuman. A hundred yards below them, Jeffries' hand, the one with the pistol, began to shake wildly.

Mick looked down on the sheriff, at the top of his head and the side of his body and the shaking arm.

"Mick?" Cheryl was beside him, but he couldn't look at her, couldn't tear his eyes away. The second body lay on top of the first, one arm curled over it.

"Mick? What is it?" The noise of the crowd almost drowned out the sound of her voice, made it sound confused and thin and faraway.

Has a big long tongue—and he eats little boys!

But the boys were men now, and the girls who had heard it too had grown into women, and they were still in Tanapah, and they remembered.

The smooth surface of the water erupted into turbulence again, and a third body broke the surface as if thrown, legs over arms over waving legs. The noise of the water beneath it was almost like laughter.

17

D eadlines. *Dead . . . lines.*

Matthew Simmons fitted a blank piece of paper into the same typewriter with which, only yesterday, he had listed the winners of the annual end-of-school spelling bee at Gulick Elementary, and with which he would now list the men killed and injured—and those still missing—at the coal pit.

He wrote: *Death, sudden and tragic . . .*

The typewriter keys clacked and echoed in the empty office.

Mrs. Grier, and the guys from the press room, like most of the town, had gone to the pit—to follow, to see, and perhaps to help.

Rain spattered, then curtained the storefront window of the *Herald* building.

Deadlines.

Always, there were deadlines set, as if the fates that shaped and twisted people's lives were supposed to know that the press had to run on time.

In Chicago, the press had run on time because there were payrolls that went into overtime if it didn't, and delivery trucks waiting; there were contracts, and regulations, and a half-century of tradition all melted into a single commandment: *Do it on time.*

In Tanapah, there was Mrs. Whitehall, who called in a fume that was not good for her blood pressure if her Thursday night's paper was ten minutes late. There was Freddie in the back shop, who would catch hell for being home late for supper. There was Simmons himself, who could not envision nor tolerate any other way of running a newspaper except on time, even if he owned the place. Even if meeting his own imposed deadline meant leaving alone from the coal pit—before it was really even necessary, he reminded himself. Even if his stomach hurt.

Tomorrow morning might be soon enough if he rushed it, if he slammed out the copy Wednesday morning, if he whipped everyone in the place into a fever pitch. Then the Thursday edition of the paper might be ready at the usual time; it could go out, into the coin machines and to the stores, around midnight Wednesday night. But he reminded himself, that would be cutting it close. Too close. He wanted to allow himself that margin.

The town would get its paper on time. And the paper—by being there, and by being on time the same time as any other Thursday edition—would stand as a reassurance, his reassurance, to the town. That was the best he could do.

Bullshit!

Simmons paused, his hands arched over the typewriter keyboard. The best he could do was to ask the right questions, was to get the whole story. *That.* Nothing less.

Now the questions came back at him like wasps in his mind, along with the voice of the Winters kid telling him: *You don't want to believe me. That's the problem. You don't want to believe any part of what I told you last night—or even to try. Sure, maybe your damned cat is up there all right. But that doesn't even begin—doesn't even begin—to explain what's been happening!*

Simmons slid open the bottom drawer of his desk. He reached under jumbles of papers and file folders, his fingers closing on a brown envelope. Slowly, he emptied the envelope onto his desktop. The newspaper clippings fell into a pile that he spread across the desk.

From Boston—the story of a thirty-three-year-old office supplies salesman found strangled to death in his own bedroom closet. From Ames, Iowa—the story of a retired Army Colonel found dead and mutilated in the den of his home, his severed arm clenched in the teeth of a lion's head mounted on the wall. And from Fort Worth, Texas—the story of a junior college English teacher who had disappeared after going into the attic of his house to set a squirrel trap.

The Fort Worth story read, "Neighbors said Greg Owens had talked for weeks about noises in the attic. He said the 'squirrels up there' kept him awake nights. A close friend said that Owens didn't want to set a trap because, ever since boyhood, he had been afraid of the 'monsters' he imagined lay in wait in the attic darkness . . ."

Simmons's reading was interrupted by the sound of gears meshing, the sound of metal shifting against the concrete floor of the back shop; it was so subtle, so even that it was almost covered by the noise of the rain outside. He did not let himself look toward the door that led to the back room.

Picking up the clippings again, he dropped them one by one, into the envelope. It was a small collection, one he had put together in one morning's reading of the *Tulsa World* and a half-dozen out-of-state papers he liked to follow.

Put it together . . . and now what?

Put a thousand such stories together . . . and then what?

Maybe it was like learning what a word meant. You learned the meaning of some word, and then all of a sudden you seemed to see it everywhere you looked—until you realized the reason: you had been ignoring it before. Maybe that was it. But maybe not.

The hiss of the rain didn't prevent him from hearing Mick Winters' voice: "All of us."

All of us. Jerry Meyers. Ginny Adams. The little Braden boy. Joe-Bob Harper. *All of us.*

The listing was over, the easy part done. The story of what had happened in—had happened to—the town of Tanapah could not be told by reciting the facts. It cried for explanation.

Simmons's fingers translated his thoughts onto paper. A half-remembered quotation: *Fear was the first thing on earth to make gods—*

From the back shop, a clanking noise made him feel like he'd swallowed a breath of winter.

Explanation.

Old fears are a part of us, all of us . . .

The keyboard fell silent.

The wasps swarmed in his mind.

At the pit. Who would turn such a thing loose? Explain it. Account for it. Name the answer or accept the impossible. And —do it on time.

An old man in an empty office. An old man alone with a town to take care of, and no answers. He had come to the end he feared most.

It was hungry back there, that machine wound with newsprint. Hungry again. He had nothing to give it.

Simmons thought of himself as he had been on the city desk of the *Chicago Star*. He felt the same pain in his gut. He thought of himself standing up and proclaiming, "I will not spend another minute of my life doing this," and walking out.

Packing the car.

Driving. Just driving. Going nowhere.

Then . . . Tanapah.

Life ran in comfortable cycles there. Babies were born and were wanted. Old folks were missed when they died. Crime was a kid stealing a car battery. There were scandals, but they didn't make the newspaper.

Matthew Simmons had come home to a place he had never seen before, where he was wanted, and where he would be missed. And only on rare nights, alone with his work, would he wonder if he had sought out the fitting place for himself or had just gone into hiding.

A particularly mean wasp made him wonder if he could deal with hard news anymore, if he still had the strength for a knife's plunge to lay open the truth.

Outside, the rain slackened to a spattering stillness.

And now . . . he knew. The press. The damned press.

It had lured him and lulled him. It had led him on. It had let him feel needed, given him pride, made the town trust him. It had done all that like a beast with the cunning to play at affections so that it might be served.

What would he write? That the town was under siege by its own fears become flesh and form? That every dark corner might hold some new horror? That there were no answers?

Simmons ripped the paper out of the typewriter and tore the sheet in half. From the back shop came the whine of machinery, of gears and bearings, and the whirring plates of the press.

Simmons took his fresh bottle of rye from his top drawer, where it lay next to the .38-caliber revolver that Mick Winters had given him. He splashed some of the amber liquid into a shot glass, and for the first time—the first time since the noises in back had begun, some days ago—he sat listening, watching the door.

There *were* answers. He *did* have the strength. The truth lay in wait for him on the other side of the door that could as well have been the mouth of a culvert or the darkened crawl-space under a bed.

Slowly, he downed the rye.

Then the scream of twisting metal hurtled through the door at him, accompanied by the sound of a motor pushed to an impossible roar, becoming a devil's voice, taunting him. Daring him. Coming for him.

He stood, and walked to the door, noting the pounding of his heart as a fact, and the copper taste in his mouth. The thick-ness of the air. The renewed hammering of the rain.

He swung open the door.

And the press rose to meet him, lifting itself from its pit in the concrete floor.

Simmons watched it almost calmly, almost coldly, taking note of the details. The legs. The black, metallic scales. Reptil-ian. But the back legs were covered with a coarse black hair.

It lifted itself again, and its claws hit the concrete with a clacking and scraping sound.

The source? Mythology. No! The back legs were from a textbook illustration of the monster Grendel from *Beowulf*. A college English text. Third shelf up, home library. Unsettling somehow. Never liked to look at it. An image half-forgotten, very accurately reproduced.

It moved toward him. The ribbon of a newsprint had ripped loose, had become a tongue that extended, black and writhing. The sides of the machine took on rounded contours, muscles that bunched and extended, but were still metal, not alive.

Simmons gauged his reaction of fear. But beyond that, there was a lack of surprise. Disappointing in a way.

Question: Is *this* it? Oh, come on now. Given seventy-one years of doubts and sleepless nights to draw on, given just the human nightmare of growing old and being alone, is there nothing more fearsome that could be tinkered together for me?

It sank back onto its haunches, spring loaded to leap toward him.

Deadlines.

His life had been pinioned by deadlines, and they had been met, one by one, each on time.

Now, one more. The last one.

He beheld the thing come for him, not in fear but with interest. That it could leap so high . . .

18

They stood like a wall at the edge of the coal pit, the people of Tanapah. They were housewives and storekeepers and school kids . . . held in place for that fragment of time. They were mortared by terror.

Mick watched as Herb Jeffries rose slowly, quavering, to his feet on the bank of the pit. He saw the other man—the one who had gone down the embankment against Jeffries' order—scramble backward and away, shotgun left behind, barrel half in the water.

Jeffries looked up toward the crowd, his face as pale as sand, the bodies of two men laying almost at his feet. The third body had landed a little distance away.

The sheriff's head lowered in jerks like a thing controlled by clockwork. He looked up at the crowd. "This here's . . ." he began, gesturing toward the top body, "Jim Curtis."

The eyes glistened white, staring sightlessly at the people.

Behind Mick a woman sobbed, and people rushed to help her.

Jeffries looked away, then back up at the crowd again, his face a plea. *Somebody. Anybody else. Somebody else can do this.*

But the wall had reshaped itself.

Turning, Jeffries bent stiffly, gripped Curtis's shirt sleeve and tugged at it . . . once . . . twice . . . as if hoping to awaken him. He clasped the dead arm. Water poured from the shirt sleeve and ran through his fingers.

He pulled the top body aside.

The body of the second man was lying face down, and it made a sucking sound as Jeffries pulled at it, rolling it out of the mud. The face, white and swollen, lolled toward him.

"Don . . ." Jeffries' voice choked. "Don Whitaker."

The sheriff dropped to his hands and knees, wrenching away from the dead man, only to be confronted by the twisted shape of the third body.

It lay an arm's length in front of him, on its side, its back toward Mick and the crowd that watched in utter silence from the edge of the pit. The face was against the ground.

Jeffries approached it on his hands and knees.

Mick turned aside, forcing his way through the crowd. *Free to go. Free to go.*

He fixed his sight past the cars to the hilltop beyond, projecting himself to the top of that hill, and from there to the edge of the gray-clouded horizon.

Motion. He would be in motion, and nothing else. Motion in a straight line that never stopped. The town of Tanapah was not *his* town. The people, not his. The nightmare, their own. He was out of it.

He thought he was numbed beyond stopping or turning when the sound of a raw scream in a voice barely recognizable as that of Jeffries, slammed into him.

Yet he *had* turned.

Somehow, *he* was the one climbing over the edge of the pit.

Feeling a hand on his shoulder, he glanced back to see Cheryl. He felt bonded and bound to her.

He felt as if he were part of a dream as he reached for holds in the rain-soaked embankment. He saw hands—*his* hands—grabbing at weeds and outcroppings of rock thick with water and mud.

He half-slid, half-scrambled down the side of the pit, toward the bottom. Suddenly, his foot slipped, and he dropped several feet, hitting the bank with a pain that lanced up through his legs, through his spine, through the dream-mists, and he was at the bottom of the pit where it was *all* real.

He looked around, saw Jeffries stumbling back knee-deep into the water, his arm pointing toward the body of the third man. The sheriff's eyes were wide with terror; his mouth worked at words that had no sound.

Mick approached him slowly, oblivious to all else. He forced himself not to look back at the bodies, the body, forced himself not to look at whatever it was that terrified Jeffries. He didn't even want to imagine. He had seen too much already.

"Come on," said Mick, approaching the edge of the water and extending his hand toward the sheriff. "Let's just get the hell out of here."

Jeffries' eyes flickered toward Mick, then back to the third corpse.

"Come on," Mick said again.

Suddenly, Jeffries shook his head violently. "Me!" he shouted, his stiffened arm still pointing. "*Me!*"

Mick knew without looking. Two men had been missing. Three bodies were thrown from the water. The third was for Jeffries.

A gift from the dark side, just the thing for a back country good ol' boy forced suddenly to dwell on thoughts of dying. The oldest fear.

Mick stepped forward. He caught Jeffries' hand, forcing it down. "No," he said. "Not you. It's not you."

Jeffries looked at Mick squarely for the first time, allowing himself to be led out of the water. "Not?"

"No." Mick held the sheriff's arm and guided him in a wide arc around the bodies. The other man in the pit seemed not to notice them. He stood against the bank, looking straight ahead, looking at nothing.

Mick scanned the wall of the pit, found a place that wasn't too steep, and pulled Jeffries toward it, feeling the eyes of the crowd. He felt a sudden anger.

"Somebody *help* me!" he shouted. "Help me with this man!" With Mick behind him, helping him, Jeffries began to climb up the side of the embankment. The crowd stirred, and hands reached toward the sheriff, waving out into space at the rim of the pit. Mick finally stepped back and watched as the hands lifted Jeffries to safety.

The eyes of the crowd were on him again. Dark eyes, as dark as the rain clouds. He felt himself pierced by those eyes, and by something else—darker and cold beyond reason—watching from behind him. From the water.

Mick turned. The other man had found a place to climb, and he was scrabbling up another side of the pit, his shotgun forgotten behind him.

Mick was alone, alone in the bottom of the pit, alone with three corpses.

He faced the crowd. "The third man," he said loudly, "is nobody. Nobody we know. We're all getting out of here."

He searched the row of faces poised above him, found Jeffries and Bob Wortham. Mrs. Grier from the *Herald* office. The little man from the hardware store. Finally, Cheryl, her eyes staring blankly, the wind lifting the blonde hair around her face. Her look was directed not at him but at the body.

"It's—it's a girl, Mick," she said. "A little girl."

Mick jerked around toward the body. A man's body. But different now. Shorter. Not Jeffries'.

A sudden disjointed chorus of voices rent the air, spilled toward him. Young voices, old voices, men's and women's and teenager's voices:

"A man—"

"—a boy—"

"Why, it's a girl—with blonde hair—"

"My—my *father*—"

"*Jennie!*"

"It's a baby—my *God!—my baby!—*"

A woman burst through the crowd, screaming for her baby. Hands grabbed her, kept her from plunging over the rim.

Mick turned from them slowly. Behind him, the crowd noises swelled, but they were swept from his mind as he stared at the body. The third body.

It was wearing the gray slacks and light checkered sports coat Mick had worn on the day he drove into Tanapah. It was wearing the shoes that had taken him . . . into the cellar.

He walked toward the body in slow motion. His heels sunk like gravediggers' spades into the wet ground

But all the kids go out there, Aunt Lucy.

I don't care. You stay away from that coal pit, Mickie. It's a nasty place. It could hurt a little boy.

He almost reeled from the thick smell of rot. The water lapped with a smacking sound. Mick knelt, gripped the shoulder, and pulled it toward him. It rolled heavily . . . the torso first, then the head, the face blanched and swollen, caked with mud.

His face . . .

His eyes.

His mouth, and the deeper line creased in the left corner.

The slight scar at the bottom of his right cheek.

The one capped tooth in the lower jaw . . .

It had stolen him. It had given back a death mask, a carica-ture molded of horror and decay.

Mick gagged but was not afraid. He only felt rage. *Rage!*

He was white fire. He was blood. He was madness. He was fear without fear, become inhuman.

His hand gripped the stock of the shotgun dropped half in the water.

He stumbled, then stood. He took aim, the white bead at the end of the barrel in line between the dead eyes of the thing that had stolen him. His finger tightened, trembling, against the trigger.

From eternity's distance, he heard people screaming; heard bodies in frenzy. The wall had broken.

Mick glanced to the side. He saw Cheryl and Bob Wortham and others scrambling, sliding, falling down the bank, skidding and rolling and getting up running.

It's a girl, Mick—a little girl!

My baby!

Me—ME!

Each of them. Stolen. Each of them shown the one death they feared most.

Mick knew that the face waiting for Cheryl would be Annie's. *That* for her, *that* for loving. *That* for refusing to fear for herself.

The hell it would!

But even as he meant to pull the trigger, his hand went numb in shock.

The body lifted. It bent at the middle, the torso rising toward him. The eyes—*his* eyes—widened. The mouth—*his*—curled in a grin, spilling black water. It was his face and—*Cheryl's*—and Aunt Lucy's and Jerry Meyer's, and *his* again—

and the arms stretched out, the white hands grasping toward him.

Mick stiffened. The fury he felt was a tight wire strung from his mind to the tip of his finger coiled on the gun's trigger —a wire that snapped as the waxen-faced figure lurched to its feet. Mick felt the jolt of the gun recoil against his shoulder.

Disbelieving, he saw the face explode in front of him like a balloon full of liquid. He pumped a second shell into the chamber.

His sight swept from the remains of the thing on the mud bank, across to the townspeople that had reformed the wall scant steps behind him, a ragged thing now, and up, to those who had stayed at the top of the embankment.

"Bob," he said, "are you with me?"

Bob Wortham stepped forward, shakily gripping a deer rifle. "Y-yes sir, Mr. Winters," he said.

"Cheryl?"

She stepped beside him, her eyes wet and red, her blouse and skirt smeared with mud and blood. She looked at the headless thing in the wet ground of the bank.

"It wasn't Annie, Cheryl. You left Annie back at your house with Hattie Redmiller. It only looked like . . ." Mick struggled for words. There were none to make sense.

She finished it for him. "Looked like Annie," she said. "And looked like . . . you."

He reached his free arm out for her then, and she came to him, her hands wrapping tight around his body. Waves of water built and fell in front of them, matching the thudding inside Mick.

"Herb Jeffries!" Mick called. "Jeffries!"

The sheriff appeared through a parting of the crowd.

"This town needs a man in charge. That's you."

Mick saw some of the faces in the crowd turn toward the

sheriff as he nodded. "Be back in a minute," he said, and disappeared through the wall of people.

Mick's eyes swept the crowd above the pit. He thought, *What am I doing?* But it was swept away by words that came slowly and deliberately from his mouth.

"We're all scared," he said to the crowd, surprised by the boom in his voice. "*All* of us. We've grown up scared of a hundred things we'd never talk about, never think about if we could help it. But look at us now."

The crowd was silent, expectant.

"We're not running. Not now. We're standing together, right here. And together, we've got an old . . . a very old score to settle!"

Jeffries pushed into the open, sliding and then jumping down the embankment, the polished stock of a lever-action Winchester rifle glinting as he held it double-handed over his head.

He reached Mick. "Never shot this thing once," he said. "Kept it oiled, though, just like the old man. I don't think he'd be mindin' a lick if I borrowed it."

Mick turned toward the shifting water of the coal pit. A cold wind swept over the water, whipping his hair. Giving Cheryl an awkward squeeze, he put both hands on the shotgun. His hands felt icy against the stock.

"There's a big old heebie-jeebie . . ." he said, shouldering the gun. "Lives way down deep."

He aimed point blank at the water.

Jeffries aimed. Bob Wortham aimed.

From the side and the embankment there came the clattering of other guns, raised and aimed into the black, churning waves of the pit.

Mick fired, and the water went up in a spout, falling in a slow, silent spray.

Mick felt the rage leave him, sucked from him, drifting away like the water mist. He felt doubt, a sudden, horrible, foolish doubt.

No one else had fired.

They had held off at the last instant, realizing they had been led into an insanity.

He waited for the laughter. But there was none—only a whisper.

"Mick," Cheryl said. "Oh, God, Mick . . . look at it."

The water, where his shot had struck, had not closed over itself. It was ripped back like torn flesh.

The people around him stood dumbstruck. Some began to back away.

Mick chilled at the sight of the water, and at the awful discovery that he had not begun to know the limits of fear; that fear was a mouth ever-widening, hungry to swallow him.

Then, a rifle cracked. Jeffries'.

The next shot was Bob's. "For Ginny," he hissed. "For Ginny, you *goddam*. . ." and he fired again, splattering the surface.

The water rolled back in a shuddering wave toward the center of the pit, building to a tumorous swell in the middle.

From the bank, a barrage of gunfire shredded the base of the swell, tearing open a long, jagged wound; but the water kept bulging and rising, as if some huge thing were coming up, throwing off its cover.

Mick saw eyes in the waves, eyes that flickered in the whitecaps.

A tongue of black water snaked out in a coiling blur from the center of the well, and he leaped aside, grabbing Cheryl, as the tongue fell in a spill of slime over the spot where they had stood.

A gaping maw opened in the shuddering, watery bulge, and

the tongue lashed again, arcing over Mick and Cheryl, slapping the side of the bank with such force that the ground crumbled. A man-shape in blue denim—for Mick, nothing more registered —toppled and fell with broken wet earth, and the black tongue was on him, wrapped snakelike around him. It lifted him screaming, high into the slate-gray sky over the pit and let him go.

They watched. The falling man was a writhing speck of blue. He seemed stuck in the sky, waving his doll-arms at the people who had known him, grown up with him.

He struck water with a distant, soft *smack*, and the waves swallowed him.

On the bank there was panic. People screamed and shoved against each other, pushing to get away.

The wind off the pit had turned oily and thick with decay. Mick reeled as the smell of it pooled in his stomach. The surface of the pit muscled upward, and again the maw split open.

Mick's eyes swept from the pit to Jeffries and Bob Wortham on the shoreline, holding fast, loading and firing, to the commotion of some dozen men trying to scale the muddy side of the embankment, guns dropped and forgotten. Their faces were hollow, their eyes, oddly expressionless in contrast to the grasping and flailing of their bodies, as if the heads had been severed but somehow stayed in place. They were puppets of terror.

The more they screamed, the more they ran, and the more it grew. The thing in the pit. It was feeding on fear, sucking fear from all around it.

Mick could see it, smell it. He could *feel* it growing.

"Get back here!" Mick ran shouting toward the embankment. With one outstretched hand, he caught the belt of a portly man sputtering against the mud wall like a fly against a windowpane. He gave the belt a jerk, and the man toppled backward, sprawling on the ground.

Mick yelled at the downed man, at the others around him. "Don't you *see*? It's *all* of us—all of us scared, such a long time scared! So much to be afraid of, so many old fears—*we did this!*"

He scanned the faces around him. The blankness was shifting to looks of horror and bewilderment, pain and anger. Cold and killing anger. Mick sensed it in the set of a jaw here, the ice-gleam of an eye there. It was like a sword, capable of cutting in any direction.

Cheryl, at Mick's side, cried, "Listen to him. *Listen!*"

"Our fear overloaded, turned to lightning. It struck in the dark. It sparked life out of the shadows. That's good enough for now. That's all we need to know." Mick probed the crowd, locking eyes.

He had them. Maybe not for long, but long enough. He grabbed a rock. "And now, here, we make it stop!"

The rock was heavy in his hand as he hefted it, threw it with a force that made his shoulder snap. It hit with a thudding and cracking sound, rebounding from the surface, leaving an ugly and quavering depression.

"Here!" He slapped another rock into the hand of the man closest to him, a balding, bespectacled little man whose fingers trembled.

"Throw it!"

From the pit, the tongue snaked toward them, trailing a sizzle of black water.

Some of the men broke and ran.

"THROW IT!"

The rock sailed—a small rock, thrown by a little man into the face of terror, thrown spinning toward the pit, then lost in a volley of rocks.

From behind Mick, from the sides of the ridge above him, there was a sudden barrage of rocks and renewed gunfire. Rocks peppered and bounced on the shorelines as the tongue fell twisting and foaming, dissolving into the dirt of the bank, and a new sound went up . . .

Jeering. Cheers.

There was Jeffries, directing the shots of a half-dozen men into the center of the swell, and giving a cowboy whoop as the mass of water suddenly flattened to a roiling frenzy of waves and black foam in the center of the pit.

And Bob Wortham, spitting a wad of gum into the water.

And Cheryl, running to intercept a small boy as he charged toward the water, pointing his finger and yelling, "Bang! Bang!"

The water quieted.

As Mick watched, shotgun hanging simply from one hand, it quieted, caught by a breeze and brought lapping, gently, over the bank, toward the bodies of Jim Curtis and Don Whitaker.

It washed toward the third form, the one that Mick has seen as himself—that *would* have been him, had the thing in the pit caught him alone.

As he knew he would be. The next time.

19

The rain came again, stronger than before.

It came in sheets, blowing and stinging, and the people standing on the rim of the pit began breaking away in small sodden clusters, trudging back to the cars and pickups that squatted like dark animals, waiting.

The rain continued. Finally, only three figures stood on the edge: Jeffries, the rain pouring down off the brim of his hat, splashing onto the barrel of his rifle, Cheryl, and Mick.

They weren't even staring anymore. They were simply looking, gazing down the sloping bank to the water's edge, at the two bodies that now mingled shamelessly with the mud and water and chunks of dripping earth from the bank. Mick couldn't see the third corpse. He wasn't even sure it was there anymore.

A pair of headlights flickered in the pasture behind them, and Jeffries slowly turned.

"Funeral home ambulance," he said. "Soon's they get those bodies loaded, I'm going for a while, anyway." The sheriff wiped water from his eyes.

Cheryl nodded. Automobile engines caught and died away behind them.

"Guess they figure it's all over, all the folks."

Mick, standing next to them, heard Jeffries, felt the beams of light sweeping across his body like moths, but he didn't respond. He kept his eyes on the two figures at the water's edge, as if he expected the half-buried corpses to suddenly get up, shake themselves off, and come dancing toward him like marionettes. The storm and rain had made things very dark, the bodies black and barely perceptible lumps, but he watched them anyway. You couldn't be too careful.

The sheriff's words penetrated his mind. *Guess they figure it's all over.*

Sure, Mick thought. *All over for them. They all believed, and they fought it until they believed it was dead. That's the way most people are. So, they'll go home, and when they talk about it —if they talk about it at all—they'll know it's over for them.*

And so it is. All over for this time, for this place. But all over?

Mick felt his lips curl in a smile, water splashing into the corners.

They didn't understand, didn't have to understand, didn't want to understand. But he did. He finally understood. It was a never-ending fight, a horrible struggle that stretched out past the universe and beyond to infinity. A battle with things you couldn't see, couldn't hear, couldn't touch until they were ready to let you.

A battle with the darkness.

"Mick?" Cheryl's hand was wet on his sleeve. Behind him, he heard the sounds of more engines revving, cars being thrown into gear. He looked at her.

"Let's go." Her voice was soft against the beating of the

rain, her eyes large, framed by her rain-plastered hair. "There's nothing more we can do."

Nothing more? What do you mean, Cheryl, nothing more?

"Mick, are you all right?"

He nodded, said "Sure," and took her arm, turning back toward the field. Barely visible in the rain, the long ambulance with "Hardage Funeral Home" lettered across the side pulled up some yards away from them, its red light revolving in the darkness. Mick wanted to leave. He didn't want to know how many bodies they would end up loading—two or three. Or four.

He looked ahead. The little red dots that mingled with the white ones were taillights, and that meant cars, and that mean people were going home, trailing each other slowly across the field and onto the road. Home.

Suddenly, Mick's foot came down onto an ice chest and his bad leg bucked, spilling him onto the ground to the sound of tearing Styrofoam. Cheryl dropped to one knee beside him, Jeffries grabbing his shoulder. He shrugged them away and pulled himself back up. Mud dripped from his arms and shirtfront.

Cheryl said, "Mick, are you—"

"Fine. I'm fine." He took her arm again, limping a little, and they continued on through the rain.

When they reached her Buick, Mick walked slowly around to the passenger side, holding onto the hood for support, and got in. It was nice and dry inside the car, but the water that soaked his clothes and his body made it wet and uncomfortable. He shut the door, looking through the rain-streaked windshield, and caught glimpses of Cheryl and Jeffries talking, and then the tall man walked away.

Cheryl slid in behind the wheel. The dark rain and the howling wind pressed in at them from all sides. Cheryl reached for the ignition key with a dripping hand, stopped, and leaned back against the seat, tilting her head up. Water ran from her and soaked into the headrest. Looking over at her, Mick saw her hands tight on the steering wheel, the knuckles white and glistening.

"You want me to drive?"

"I'll be okay in a minute." She closed her eyes tightly, sniffled a couple of times, and then reached down and started the car.

When she glanced over at Mick, he saw a thousand unnamable things flickering in her eyes and he reached for her. She dropped against him as if her bones were gone. Her hair was slick against his cheek.

"I'm going to hold up, Mick" she mumbled. "Honest."

"I know," he said, his hand sliding over her hair down to the smooth skin at the base of her neck.

"I've . . . got to. For Annie's sake."

"And for mine," Mick said. Her head came up then, her eyes bored into his. They were wet, whether from tears or rain Mick didn't know.

"You mean that," she said, and it wasn't a question.

Mick pushed the sticky hair back from her forehead. "Sure I do."

"When I saw Annie—or I thought I saw Annie—down there. You took charge. You told me—that thing—wasn't her. And you made me believe it."

Mick nodded.

"I could've—would've fallen apart then, Mick. If not for you."

He kissed her forehead, feeling suddenly very warm and very close to her. "It was my turn to hold up," he said slowly. "That's the secret, or part of it. We have to hold up for each other."

"At different times."

"Yeah." Mick drew back and smiled at her. This was part of it, part of winning, even if the victory was only momentary and partial. "It wouldn't work for both of us to go under at the same time, would it?"

She flipped on the car's headlights and eased the transmission into first gear. Not looking at him she said, "I really do love you," and put her foot on the pedal.

The car crept through the downpour toward Tanapah. Inside it was still.

Cheryl broke the silence. "I'm not letting myself think about Annie, Mick. Talk to me so I won't think about her."

"Annie's fine. I know it."

"You've known these things all along, haven't you?"

"No more than anyone else." Mick searched his mind for something else to say as the car hummed underneath them, tires churning through water. He started to go off into a story about his childhood, back at Aunt Lucy's in the summer, just something to string words together, words that would beat back the sounds of the storm and Cheryl's thoughts of her daughter. But when he thought of Aunt Lucy's, something broke through into his mind, a thought that had been trying to get at him for a long time, and it ate and nibbled its way into his consciousness. There was nothing he could do to stop it this time.

"Can you tell me some—no, never mind," Cheryl said, her eyes on the road. "I don't want to think about it anymore, what all this means or what all this is, or even if it's over—"

"It's never over," Mick said, suddenly and ferociously.

"What do you mean?"

He turned to her. "Remember last night? Remember Ginny, who's still there at your house? And remember what I told you? You said you believed me then, or you acted like it anyway, and you said we could fight it!"

"Yes, but—"

"Don't you *see* Cheryl? We *always* fight! We sometimes fight together, and sometimes we have to fight alone, but we always *have to fight!*"

"I'm . . . I'm not understanding you, Mick."

The car jolted suddenly with the here-and-gone impact of having struck something loose on the road, like hitting a dog. There was a whipping motion of dark leaves against the grille. The head of a sunflower broke loose and came spinning toward the windshield, rebounding with a *crack!* And a shrill whine. Cheryl flinched. She let go of the wheel and the car swerved, toward the roadside, toward a shifting mass of . . .

Mick grabbed the wheel. He spun it toward him, and the car bounced, fishtailing back not the middle of the road. The wheels dropped into the center ruts.

Cheryl swallowed hard. "I think you'd better drive," she said.

"No. Don't stop." Mick held his breath a moment, letting the saw blades leave his voice. "You're doing fine. Just fine."

Before he could stop himself, he had glanced into the rearview mirror, then sharply back at Cheryl. But she hadn't looked back. She hadn't seen.

Thank the Lord, he thought.

The speedometer read almost sixty. Any faster on a rutted, gravel and dirt road, and the car would be hard to control.

He glanced at the mirror again.

Yes, sixty was fast enough. Behind, in the red spill of the taillights, the ones chasing them were fewer and losing distance. They were dropping, crawling back to the roadside.

The car sped on.

"You said *fight*, Mick." Cheryl's hands were cold, clamped onto the steering wheel in the white glow of the dashboard. "Tell me how. Tell me *what*. 'Confused' is such a sorry word for what I feel."

It took him a few moments to reply, and when he did his voice was low and restrained. "You're a doctor," he said. "You've studied medicine, and you know that a long time ago there were no doctors, and people lived in fear of everything, all diseases, and diseases came along and the people got sick and died and there was nothing anyone could do to help."

"Yes."

"And then—I don't know, it's all jumbled up. But . . . even then, people *tried* to fight. They didn't know what they were doing, but they knew they had to fight. And people died anyway, millions of them, but some of them lived, and maybe it was because they fought, or because they prayed, or maybe it was just damned luck. And then . . . well, then, people started learning because they were scared, and started fighting more. They still lost but they continued to fight and they won a little, too. After Hippocrates there was Pasteur and then penicillin and then the Salk vaccine and people went on fighting—and there were some things they weren't scared of anymore because the sources of those fears were run down and tagged and identified. People found stuff that would whip their fears and people *believed* they could be whipped and . . ." The words ran out for him then, as suddenly as they had come. "Hell, I don't know." Through the enveloping storm, Mick saw the lights of Tanapah's Main Street, feeble and dim in the darkness.

"You've just got to fight," he muttered, half to himself. "You've got to fight. There's no way out of it."

Outside the car, the rain whipped against the metal and rubber glass; inside the car, there was silence again. The Main Street of Tanapah was desolate and empty, tiny lights winking out of buildings where nobody lived.

"Wait a minute!" Mick cried, pressing his face against the window.

"What is it?"

He jabbed his finger against the glass. "Slow down! Right here, Cheryl."

The brakes caught on the wet street and the car skidded to a stop. Mick pushed the door open.

Cheryl's voice came from behind him. "Mick! Where are you going?"

The rain pelted him from all sides. He started not to answer her, to run through the street and onto the sidewalk and into the building, but then he turned, holding himself back.

"I need to see Simmons!" he shouted above the noise of the storm.

"Why?"

Mick stuck his head in and lowered his voice. "He needs to know, Cheryl. About the coal pit."

"I'm sure he's already been told, Mick. All those people out there—surely they went by to tell him. Some of them, anyway." When Mick didn't make a move to get in, she added, "Mick, I have to go. I want to see Annie—"

"He's got to hear it from me." He looked at her, resisting the pull of her eyes. "You go see Annie. I'll be all right."

"Mick—" Cheryl's voice was cut off by the slam of his door as he turned away, walking off into the rain toward the single light that burned from the *Tanapah Herald* building, a light that Mick knew meant Matthew Simmons was there.

Cheryl Stanton pressed her forehead against the steering wheel. The rain beat a tattoo on the roof of her car, sounding like all the silence in the world. Loneliness and despair, wet and distilled, cascaded out of the heavens at her.

She tried to think, couldn't. What was the proper course? She was a woman of action—had to be. So what? What?

Her mind kept weaving back to her daughter, Annie, and Annie's face, and the way she looked when she was dressed up for Sunday school, all crisp and proper and right. Her daughter.

The daughter she had thought she had seen, there, flung out of the water, rolling shamelessly on the bank. Dead.

But Mick told her no, and he was right. Mick. Annie. Herself, Cheryl Stanton the doctor, with her black bag and her reassuring smile. Annie's smile.

Dammit! Where *was* he?

Cheryl lifted her head and squinted into the storm toward the *Herald* building. Nothing had changed. The light still burned. No movement in front of it.

It was so hard, so hard to make the choice—the seemingly little insignificant choice about whether to stay or go. To run to Annie and sweep her up in her arms and clasp her to her body and be able to protect her again. If she could.

But Mick. What about him? The engine idled, sending a soft rumbling through the car's interior.

A hard decision. So incredibly hard.

Cheryl cocked her head as if she were trying to listen to something far away. She sat like that for an instant, then threw the gearshift into first and pulled off the street into one of the angled parking slots in front of the *Herald* building. In three steps, she had reached the office door.

She couldn't see much at first. The lights in the front part of the building were off. Her head snapped around, her eyes fastened on the back room, down past the desks and shelves and filing cabinets.

And then she saw them.

The huge black press, half in and half out of the door; beside it, Mick. Under it—

Matthew Simmons!

Cheryl ran, dropping down beside Mick, who didn't look at her. In the half-dark, the old man's eyes were wide and glistening, staring at the ceiling, reflecting the dull glow from the naked light bulb above his face. His lips moved slowly. Mick's hands were under his head, cradling it.

". . . and . . ." Simmons was whispering, ". . . you'll get the damn thing out . . . I . . . don't care if you . . . have to . . . mimeograph   .   .   .   you'll   get   it   out, kid . . . and . . . they'll . . . *know* . . . they'll *know* . . ."

Cheryl quickly surveyed the prone man. One arm lay stretched out at the wrong angle, splayed against the green concrete floor, crushed and bleeding. Beside Mick's knee, a gelatinous pool had formed, sticky against Simmons's tattered white shirt. Cheryl peered underneath the press, saw where it dug into the leg, smashing it against the concrete.

She grabbed Mick and pulled him to his feet. "We've got to move this press!"

"H'lo . . . Cheryl," Simmons said, his cracked lips bending into a smile. Mick turned to her slowly, looking first at her and then back down to Simmons.

"Mick, help me."

His eyes regained their focus and he got to his feet. Together, they shoved hard against the huge press.

It gave way. It gave way as if it were made of aluminum instead of steel and iron, tipping and sliding on one edge, away from Simmons's leg.

Like, Cheryl thought, *like it's hollow. Nothing inside. Spent!*

She dropped to her knees. Simmons lay gasping, his eyes staring upward, filled with tears of pain. But he still smiled.

"Now you just . . . go on . . . Cheryl. I'm all right. But I . . . have to talk. To Mick."

"I'll go get my bag," Cheryl said to Mick as he helped her up. She went out the way she had come in, grabbing at light switches as she went, flooding the room with light behind her. In what seemed like seconds to her, she was back with her doctor's bag. And then her hands were going over Matthew Simmons's body, expertly and delicately, probing and touching and finding answers to questions.

Not as bad as I thought, she said to herself, filling a syringe with Demerol. *He may make it.* She was barely aware that Simmons and Mick were talking, but she picked up the occasional word.

Desk . . .

gun . . .

top drawer . . .

Cheryl sunk the needle into a patch of sagging flesh, saw it wince under her hand and then relax. Suddenly, she heard movement around her and realized that Mick was no longer by her side. And at the same time, with her hands moving in front of her, grabbing bandages and antiseptics and swabs, she thought: *Annie!*

The words that formed around the agony came out in her doctor's voice, quiet and commanding, and her hands never stopped moving.

"Mick," she said. "I want you to make a call for me." No answer. "Mick?" She looked up from the old man then.

Mick sat against the edge of Simmons's desk, a bottle of rye whiskey in his right hand. In the other hand, a revolver dangled loosely. He didn't seem to be looking at anything.

"Mick!" she said more loudly. "Do you hear me?"

His eyes moved, came to a focus on her. "Yeah?" he said dully.

Cheryl rapped out a telephone number. "Call it. It's my house."

Mick looked at her a moment more and then his eyes drifted away. She turned back to Simmons, her ears picking up the sound of Mick's dialing. Midway through, he asked for the number again and she gave it to him.

Simmons's breathing was regular now, the pulse faint but even. Cheryl heard Mick speaking into the phone, and her own pulse quickened. Then she heard his voice, talking to her.

"Cheryl?"

She set Simmon's wrist gently back down on the floor and got up. As she took the receiver from Mick, she said, "I think he'll make it."

Cheryl saw Mick nod, pick up the bottle of rye again, and take a long drink. And then, all her attention turned to the telephone, as she heard her daughter's voice. "Mommy?"

A lump welled up in Cheryl's throat, and she was unable to speak.

"Mommy?"

The wavering in Cheryl's voice was part laughter, part hysteria. "Yes. Yes, dear. I'm here. I'm here. Are you all right?"

"Well of *course* I'm all right. Missus Redmiller and I are playing Old Maid."

Thank you, God, thought Cheryl. *Thank you.*

"You can play too when you come home. Missus Redmiller said you can play it with three. I asked her."

"I'll be there soon, honey. There's been an . . . accident. I have to be there for a little while."

"Oh, *I* know. You always have to be there."

Cheryl's heart felt full and warm. "Okay. Okay, you little thing. You precious little thing. I'll be with you soon, and—and don't be afraid."

There was a pause on the other end, and Annie's voice took on a curious tone. "I'm not afraid, Mommy. There's nothing to be afraid of. Is there?"

"No. No. Of course not. I'll see you real soon." The receiver clicked back into its cradle, and Cheryl turned. "I'm so glad she's all right, everything's all right, I—Mick?"

There was no answer. Cheryl was looking down the

corridor at the front door, half-opened onto the street, the dark
rain spattering on the concrete floor.

———————————

Cheryl's Buick sped through the storm, Mick at the
wheel. By his side, resting on the seat, was the
revolver he had taken from the hardware store, the
revolver he had given Matthew Simmons.

*The gun from Simmons. The car from Cheryl. And whatever
I've got is the final part. The final, missing part. And it's mine.
More than that, it's me, and I'm all of them, and all of them
are me.*

The car flew on.

*Cheryl, with her bag full of medicine and her needles and
her soft butterfly hands . . . Old Simmons—God bless him—he
knows! He poked at it with his mind and his typewriter and the
facts he laid out before him like playing cards, and now he
knows . . . and Herb Jeffries with his rifle, and Ginny, wielding
the pistol I was unable to hold, and firing, and firing, because it
was hers and not mine—*

The street was dark, and rain beat down on the white car,
black and powerful.

*And Aunt Lucy . . . even Aunt Lucy. She may not have been
an educated woman, but she knew what she had to do. She called
the thing "Goofus," so little Mickie wouldn't be afraid, then
when I was gone she slipped down and put a padlock on the
door. She knew it, too, and she fought.*

And that was it. You fought, or you were consumed. There
was no way out of it. You fought subtly, sneaking around so the
kids wouldn't know, or you fought screaming and cursing, or
tight-lipped and defiant. However you did it, you had to do it.
Some people didn't. And maybe that was why there were earth-

quakes, and tornadoes, and traffic accidents, and the threat of nuclear war always, and old people dying in the streets, their throats ripped open by young punks. Because some people believed—but didn't fight.

The old cliché rang through his mind, strong and clear and good: *First of all, you clean up your own backyard.* He slowed, peering at the dark houses along the street. He knew where it was, and he had found it. The rutted ground of the driveway was muddy under his tires. He turned off the lights, killed the ignition, sat breathing heavily in the darkness.

Your own backyard.

Aunt Lucy had willed him the house. Aunt Lucy knew about Goofus. Lawyer Morton's words came back to him: *She said you'd know why.*

Mick reached down and turned on the dome light. He opened the glove compartment and found what he had hoped would be there. A flashlight. The dome light clicked off.

Rain continued to beat against the roof of the car. A gust of wind whipped the drops harder. Mick opened the door and climbed out of the car. His feet hit the ground and it gave a little, soft and mushy.

Fight them.

The pencil beam of the flashlight described an arc, illuminating the screen of the porch and the weathered paint on the side of the house and the apple tree, leaves heavy and beaten by the storm. Mick walked past it all, taking it all in and then forgetting it. Only once, when the light played along the alley behind the house, did he stop, if only for a moment.

The rain had played a strange trick on him. It had made a pattern, a far-away, long-ago pattern, and in between the droplets and behind them he thought he saw Cheryl Mallis, her little-girl smile showing white teeth, her golden hair shining like the sun. And behind her, a hand on her shoulder, Aunt Lucy . . .

She said you'd know.

Then the beam moved and fastened. It illuminated the lump of ground that rose out of the backyard, a big, sodden mound like a crypt where things were buried that people just didn't talk about.

The cellar door was before him now. He moved toward it. The rain made little ghosts around him.

Don't you ever go down there, Mickie. You hear me?

But he didn't hear. He couldn't, wasn't supposed to anymore. Aunt Lucy had been talking to five-year-old Mickie Winters, not to Mick, not anymore.

Don't you ever . . .

And how did she bear it, knowing the horror of the cellar and having no one to tell. By how many years had it shortened her life?

The light played on the hasp, glinting from the broken padlock that held the door shut. Half-cursing, half-crying, Mick ripped the lock aside. He jerked the door back with the toe of his shoe. It flew open, slamming against the earthen side of the cellar. The inside of the door, gouged and splintered, was stained with a glistening darkness.

Old fears. They were endless and everywhere. They were everyone's.

But *this* one—*this* one was his.

Mick took the first step down. The rain beat around him, in his eyes, his mouth, spattering the concrete of the cellar stairs.

He took the second step, ducking his head under the door frame, and felt the rain no longer. The light in his hand seemed no more than a flickering candle; the darkness engulfed him.

Two more steps, and his feet hit the floor, crunching on shattered glass. The air was thick with rot. His knee brushed the apple barrel that, so many years ago, he had imagined was filled with beating hearts. He flashed the light toward it.

Inside the barrel, something moved with a squishing noise.

Mick did not look. He was not surprised.

He swung the light toward the shelves lining the cellar walls, back toward the corner.

The light dimmed and went out, as if a hand had closed around it.

There was a whistling sound. He heard it, it seemed, from a great distance, coming closer, increasing in pitch and fury—the sound of a chain being swung in a widening circle.

Mick knew what it was, as he knew that the other noise—the crackling and rustling—was of wings.

Or it could have been all in his mind, couldn't it? The stain on the door could have been rainwater. The sound in the barrel . . .

It didn't matter. That was the point.

He had something to do.

Mick felt an odd tension pulling the lines of his face. He was smiling. *Yes!*—by damn—grinning. *Grinning!*

"Hello, Goofus," he said.

He raised the revolver and fired, the muzzle flash spattering light in his eyes . . .

And fired again.

And again.

20

here? WHERE?

WHe was on his knees, raking at the cans and bottles under the kitchen sink in Aunt Lucy's house, where the toolbox had been. A container of liquid cleaner spun across the buckled linoleum floor, shattered against the wall, drenching the kitchen in a sudden oil smell of pine.

WHERE?

The smell forced him to slow his breathing, and each breath curdled in the pit of his stomach. He got to his feet, holding a deep breath and closing his eyes, and his head slowly began to clear. And in the darkness, the answer came.

In the hall closet. On the top shelf.

It came to him suddenly, a rush of images coalescing around a mental picture of Aunt Lucy, reaching back onto that shelf, a bittersweet smile on her face. The last act before parting. Each year, just before putting him on the bus for home, she would go to the very back of that shelf and bring out a wrapped and ribboned surprise for him, wiping her hands and fussing, and one year it had been a school box with a Hershey bar in it, another year, a bottle of Wildroot Cream Oil, and . . .

She always reached standing tiptoe, and most often, she jiggled the kerosene lamp that she always kept at the front of the shelf.

Mick yanked at the closet door. Even as it swung open, his hand fastened around the base of the lamp. The door slammed against the wall, the noise echoing against the sound of the rain outside, and Mick slapped at the shelf for the box of kitchen matches he knew would be there.

Crouching in the hallway, he set the lamp on the wood floor, pulled off the glass chimney, and slid open the matchbox. The head snapped soggily off the first match he tried to light. The second one lit with a sizzle, and he held it to the wick with trembling fingers, his other hand adjusting the kerosene flow until the wick began to burn.

He picked it up and ran, his feet thudding along the hallway, where Aunt Lucy had never allowed running. Through the kitchen, out the back door, the screen door wailing at being kicked open into the storm. He ran, one hand cupped over the lantern, the flame hot against his palm. Ahead, the cellar awaited him, and as he neared it a sudden strobe-flash of lightning illuminated it, etching its shape in cold white lines against the darkness.

The rain hit like needle jabs, and a whining noise crossed his ear as a hail stone exploded in glistening fragments against the door frame. Mick never slowed. He plunged through the open door, lamp held out in front of him. Hail began cracking at his heels. Bits of ice skittered down the cellar stairs, dancing in the lamplight.

Fire and ice, fire and ice. And how will the world end? Burning or frozen?

His mind suddenly detached, took him out of the cellar and

the storm, back to his own apartment, the bedroom, the book-case headboard, *The Collected Works of Robert Frost*. And Cheryl. Cheryl in bed with him, close to him. Safe. Safe from the storm beating against the window, and rain and thunder, and hail, and glass breaking. Then he was back in the cellar, without her or anyone else, the lamp casting a wavering glow that brought shadows to life in the corners behind the shelves.

A thick dripping sound, separate from the storm noise, made him jerk back from the shelf rows. Slowly, he lifted the lamp toward the sound.

Shards of glass glinted back to him, the remains of a broken mason jar surrounded by thick wet peach slices. Behind that, another jar stood, its top shattered. The syrup that dripped from the shelf smelled of cloves and cinnamon.

Turning, Mick brought the light close to the back wall of the cellar. He found two marks where the bullets had struck.

One in the shelf, two in the wall. He had fired . . . how many? Only three? It had seemed like more, but he wasn't sure. He looked down, saw the revolver in the center of the concrete floor, just where he had dropped it. Useless now.

Maybe . . . always useless. Now. And then.

He looked up the stairs toward the open door. The night sky was a heavy black, streaked gray with rain, and the air smelled stale. The cellar . . .

Small. So very suddenly and very oddly small.

To Mickie, it had been a cave, a cave with dark and unproved recesses, a place to avoid whenever possible. To Mick, moments ago, it had loomed as the gateway to hell, and he had stood in it, firing a small pistol into the maw of eternity, defiant, terrified.

And now?

He was startled to find himself standing bent to keep from scraping his head on the ceiling. The flickering lamplight revealed nothing more than a cramped and neglected place for keeping canned goods cool and out of the light. Mick leaned back against the wall, the breath easing out of him in a long sigh, struggling for some sort of fix on reality, for something— however small—that he could feel, could know, was undeniably *real*. But *real* was elusive—like being sick and trying to remember exactly the feeling of being well.

The door!

He took a step up, reached, and pulled the door shut, muffling the sound of the rain. The lamp trembled in his hand.

The door . . . was real. He held the lamp closer, and his heart jumped a little as he looked at the dark wood, clawed and gouged, stained with dried blood, one of the boards cracked and bowed.

The proof of another reality.

Mick reached down to the cracked board and pressed the palm of his hand against it. It gave, and he withdrew his hand.

One good punch, he thought. *One good punch would smash through.*

And then, he understood.

It hadn't been the door that had kept Goofus shut up in the cellar.

Goofus had been waiting.

For me! The thought screamed through Mick.

Waiting for me! Knowing I would—I had to—come back! Waiting now—for the door to open!

Outside the door, the lock plate swung shut with a click. Mick heard it, above the spattering of the storm.

The wind, he tried to believe.

Another sound—the padlock, dropping into place.

Mick crouched, looking at the door, at the warped board, the gashes in the wood, fumes from the lamp swirling around him. He realized that he wasn't afraid of being trapped, that the door couldn't hold him if he really wanted out.

Did he really want out?

You bastard, he snarled, starting at the door.

Goofus was . . . out there. Taunting him, manipulating him. Daring him to come out. Now the cellar—not Aunt Lucy's house, not his car, not Kansas City, not being with Cheryl—the cellar was the safe place. The only safe place.

With a scream, he kicked the door with a force that snapped the bottom of the weakened board. He kicked again, the force throwing him off-balance, and as he threw out his hand for support, the lamp dropped, spreading a sheet of liquid flame across the cellar floor. It licked at his feet, and climbed up the walls toward the shelves, engulfing them. Clutching the splintered edge of the board, he ripped it toward him, broke it off, kicked out a second board. Oily smoke boiled up around him.

Mick forced his way through the broken opening, headfirst, into the rain. Snakes' tongues of fire followed him, sparks darting up behind him, sputtering. A bolt of lightning shot yellow-green across the sky. He pulled himself through, cleared the front of the cellar, and ran a few steps, panting, his head upraised, rain falling into this mouth and dripping down his cheeks.

He stopped and looked around. He was standing on the same spot on Aunt Lucy's lawn where Mickie Winters had stood ankle-deep in clover, winding a rubber-band airplane until the rubber was double-knotted; where he had stood, glancing now and then over his shoulder toward the cellar.

The fire roared through the cellar door, charring the wood black.

Mick looked from the cellar up toward the window of the room that had been his. The window glass seemed to be melting in blurs of red and orange, streamered with rain and reflecting the cellar fire. Behind the glass, a movement, a shifting of something dark. And eyes, brighter than the fire lights, bearing down on him.

Look for me.

The intensity of those eyes . . .

Look for me.

. . . did not put the words in his mind. The words were his own.

In the shadows and darkness.

There had to be words to blunt the feeling.

I am the emptiness.

To keep him sane.

In the silence of an empty room. Look for me. In the stillness that comes between the flash of lightning and the sound of thunder. In the quiet behind a closed door. In the feeling of being watched. In the stopping of your heart. Look for me.

The eyes drew back and were gone. The window dimmed to black as the cellar fire faded.

Gone.

Never there. Mick wanted so much to believe it. *The fire's reflection, that's all.*

And the cellar door? *Jammed shut.*

The marks inside the door? The claw marks in the wood? What about those?

Mick turned again toward the cellar. The door was gone now, burned to black and ashen remains, shouldering. Around him, the rain softened to a cool mist, settling over Aunt Lucy's backyard.

Mickie Winters would never play there again.

Mick felt himself being watched by the darkness that massed at the side of the house, as if it were trying to bar the way between him and the people he had come to love.

Cheryl . . . Annie . . .

He laughed just a little at the unexpected loss of at least one fear, that of having a family.

And Matthew Simmons . . .

He supposed Mr. Simmons (*Matt?* No, it would always be Mr. Simmons.) might be able to use some help at the *Herald* from a younger guy who used to have a way with words.

The darkness awaited him.

Look for me.

He hardly noticed the high, wet grass brushing at his feet as he walked away, as he left the remains of the cellar behind him, forming an answer to the call of the darkness.

You, he returned, *you look for me.*

EPILOGUE

"Mud Show"
by Ron Wolfe

Mick Winters eyed his breakfast plate of steak and peppered eggs, haystack of fries and a dollop of ketchup like a red corsage on the chipped white plate.

"Ease your conscience, sir," the carnival man said. "It's not bribery for a good newspaper story. Everybody gets the same."

Mick surveyed the company he shared in the traveling show's mess tent, with its drab canvas sides rolled up to encourage the flutter of a cool little wake-up breeze.

He and the boss shared elbow room at the end of a long folding table. Five such tables filled the tent with a bleary gathering of carnival workers, and they'd all gone to work on identical plates of steak and eggs, nobody looking especially blessed

"I can't pay people what they're worth, not anymore," the

carnival man said. "But I've found if you just give folks a decent breakfast, they'll stay on the job longer than they should. Besides, where else are they going to go?"

Mick couldn't tell which of the baggy and shirtless and hair-rollered might be the ride operators, which the game agents, the funnel-cake sellers. They all looked in degrees like he would have, left to himself. The necktie made his collar itch.

But the carnival man dressed his part from spats to pepper-mint pocket square: red-and-white striped jacket, red bow tie, curled-up mustache the color of sugar, straw topper that he could doff to show the pink line where his hair parted in the middle, a real ding-dong daddy.

"You're saying this year will be the last," Mick said, "is that right?" He timed his question just as the carnival man took a bite, which gave Mick the chance to bring out his reporter's notebook without it being a distraction. The man nodded.

Mick had accepted the invitation of breakfast at the carnival as an unlikely chance to find an actual story in what Mr. Simmons called a "sweet-pea annual." It was Simmons's name for something that came around every year like the rabbit show at the county fair, like the soil conservation banquet, that people expected to see covered as news even though nothing new ever happened.

The summer carnival came and went, came and went, and the *Tanapah Herald* dutifully chronicled each of its many passings with yet another photo of the same Ferris wheel. Mick intended to carry on as editor-reporter, the job he took over from Matthew Simmons.

Mr. Simmons had retired to Arizona, but Mick he still did things the Simmons way—or would have. But this year broke the routine.

The breakfast invitation had come attached to a press

release that read: "KIDD'S CARNIVAL and *Phantasmagoria!* announces final tour."

Kidd was the name, as on the gold engraved tag on the carnival man's lapel, "O.U. Kidd."

Mick noted the tag, and the carnival man caught him looking. "Real name, yes," the man said. "Orwell Uriah Kidd. At your service, kiddo. My parents had quite the sense of humor."

Mick wrote and circled the name twice in his notebook, a reporter's trick to compliment the quote. Nice one, Mr. O.U. Kidd. Let's give out some more like that.

"Talk about names, here's an even better one for you," the carnival man said, leaning back. "Mr. and Mrs. Loving could have named their daughter after Aunt Mildred, but they did not—they named her Candy. Playmate of the Month for January 1979, from right here in Oklahoma, remember?"

"I think so," Mick said, and it was such a lame thing to say to another man, but the husband-dad instinct had been quick to set in. His mind didn't call up the fold-out image that he'd once saved in a dresser drawer, but a picture of the icy reaction that Cheryl would have to it, and how it would feel to see his stepdaughter, Annie, on display.

"Well, then, Mr. Waters — "

"Winters."

"Winters, I correct myself." The carnival man gestured as if reading a circus banner in the sky. "Michael. Edward. Winters."

Mick reached for his coffee to avoid showing surprise, while he wondered just how much the carnival man knew about him —how much about Tanapah. He had lightened his coffee to nearly beige. Anything too black still made him think of dark nights, dark basements.

Tanapah had been national news, all over the wires once the state police were involved. But the town had retreated, had cloaked itself in the trappings of normalcy so completely that it could have fooled Norman Rockwell. "The little town that went crazy" hadn't gone quite crazy enough to hold attention.

"The point is, Mr. Winters," the carnival man said, "you've passed my little test to see how careful I have to be about what I can say to you. It takes at least some small taste for the taboo to appreciate a carnival. I've been testing out newspaper reporters all along this tour, looking for the right one to tell my story. And you? There's something about you. I think we understand each other."

Flies swarmed the open tent, mingled with the smell of grease.

"Try your steak," the carnival man said. "I'll talk ahead to give you a chance. Top-rate sirloin, is it not? But regarding the come-on I sent to your paper, the *Herald*—sadly true, we're closing down. There no more room for a little five-night mud show. People'd rather sit home and watch television. I would, too."

———

Mick left as the first scatter of a crowd arrived to take in the wonders of Kidd's Carnival. His notebook had fattened with bent and wrinkled pages, penned full of carnival jargon, "cake eaters," "gazoonies," and can't-believe-he's-saying-this quotes that nailed the story.

—*"Diogenes knew where to swing his lantern. He never came to the carnival in search of an honest soul. I promise safer rides than most, honest games more times than not. But nobody comes to me for safety and assurance, they come for a good time."*

Kidd's tale was that of boy who loved the carnival, a young man whose first job had been helping people in and out the cars that ran through Mr. Toad's Wild Ride at Disneyland—

and how he finally saved up and bought his own carnival, and how he expanded by picking up the remainders of other shows that went broke.

Mick had been so wanting to string words into a real story, a piece of writing better than Mr. Simmons could have made it, one the Associated Press would transmit to other member papers all around, as far off as Arizona. He looked forward to reciting some of the carnival man's quotes to Cheryl.

—*"Some people want to ride a time machine back to child-hood. We call it a merry-go-round. Some want to show how brave they are, how smart they are, what big-spenders they are. And some just want the giggles."*

—*"Some want to cheat the cheaters, and they win enough to feel like they've won everything. They paid fifty dollars, they got a stuffed toy—slum, we call it—to impress their girlfriends. But they got what they paid for. They all leave with what they came for."*

—*"We satisfy certain dreams, and we will be greatly missed by people who don't even know what's gone."*

H e wrote at Mr. Simmons's desk, only this time it felt like *his* desk, *his* story, *his* way.

The old editor's Royal Standard typewriter was rightfully enshrined under a square glass case on the front counter. Mick's addition to the office was a brand-new Apple IIe, the slickest computer that 1983 had to offer, just waiting for him to give it a real spin.

He used practically every word of his notes, and the story was the best thing he'd ever written. It made him want to go back to the carnival—made him want to bring the family.

They hadn't planned to attend. Cheryl had a load of

medical insurance papers to deal with, and not even Annie was much interested in dizzy rides.

"I don't like it, Mr. Mick-the-dad," Annie said. "It makes scratches in the sky."

"Carnival searchlights."

"Would I have to burp? I don't think burpin's much fun."

But this would be the last time they could see the real thing, what was left of it.

He imagined the carnival man would give them a top-rate greeting.

M ick bought three admission bracelets just as the lights went on, all those strings of bulbs that looked ugly in the sunlight and like Christmas and fireworks at night.

The rides clanked, the Wipeout, the Scrambler, and the air tasted of machine oil and cotton candy. And now, Mick could place the carnival workers he'd seen at breakfast into their job roles, like pieces on a game board. Here the Tilt-a-whirl operator, there the guy selling balloons and glow sticks—the same guy he'd seen drop a spoon.

The carnival man was nowhere in sight. Mick watched for him as he bought Annie a yellow balloon, and a green-glowing bracelet for Annie's doll, Christy.

"Mick! We're trying to save, remember," Cheryl said. "We have expenses coming." No balloon for her.

They joined a crowd of very few strangers, those few probably having come from even smaller towns around Tanapah, and farms beyond the smallest. Just about everyone knew the newspaper editor, and even more knew the town doctor. It was a throng of hand waves and hellos, and some embarrassed looks at having been caught in some act of silliness.

Annie knelt to pick up a gleaming quarter from between her feet, as if her two pink Care Bear shoes had found it. "Mine!" she yipped and held it high with no care that her balloon had flown away.

"You know what that's called, Annie, what you just did?" Mick said, showing off his newly acquired carnival jargon. "That's called 'reading the midway.' People drop all kinds of things, and if you keep watching the ground, there's no telling what you might find."

"We're not gathering dirty things off the ground," Cheryl said, and steered the way to the show's mildest attraction, a shallow tank of little boats that ran in slow circles.

It was too much a little kid ride even for Annie. "Christy c'n go," she said, "I'll watch." But Cheryl had not eased the limits on guarding their girl, had become even more intensely protective.

"We'll be fine here, and you go see the rest of the carnival," Cheryl said. "Bring us back a funnel cake, just one. Don't ride anything that looks dangerous."

The rejection stung, but he'd set himself up for it. Mick knew she hadn't wanted to waste time at the carnival, and she wasn't going to let herself enjoy any part of it. There was a momentary snap of anger—at her? himself?—that he couldn't share this with her.

Some back-burning little part of him wondered if they were in the shakedown stretch of a marriage that happened too quickly, or the start of no marriage at all. Fifteen months married, five weeks she'd been pregnant, no marriage at all.

At least he had convinced her to quit smoking, or rather encouraged her to accept the answer that therapy provided. Her first husband had smoked. Cigarettes symbolized her guilt at not being able to save him and kept him still with her every time she lit up. And now, she could be done with cigarettes, just like that. Because of Mick. Because he loved her.

Is that so? Then love her a little more, why don't you, faithful husband? Love her enough to concede that maybe she was right to worry about the carnival.

Mick saw the sheriff go by in a stiff gait, with his thumbs hooked behind his belt buckle, with suspicious eyes, as if he would leap on any chance to shut down the whole commotion. It wasn't like Herb Jeffries to go hard-nose, and it wasn't like Cheryl to oppose any kind of family outing. Maybe they saw something in the surroundings that he didn't.

He remembered when the carnival set up on Tanapah's Main Street, and then the fairgrounds, and this year—a rented farm field where the trampled ground gave literal meaning to the term, "mud show."

Maybe it was a little too shabby, or maybe just an off night, a mistake. He should let it go.

But then, wouldn't that mean the story was all a mistake, too?—not the breakthrough piece of writing he thought he'd done, nothing but a lie that made him think he was the right man to run the newspaper?

"I want to find the carnival man," Mick said. "He's a character. I think you'd like to meet him before we go."

M ick wandered the grounds, the midway, the food stands, the game tents they called "joints" and saw nothing of the red-and-white-striped O.U. Kidd.

Human and metal shrieks, garish colors, and streaming lights surrounded him, and bad music blared over bad speakers, and the queasy smells of hot dogs and onions that hadn't stayed down.

He came by himself to the edge of the carnival, to the false front that made the scare ride look bigger and more threatening than it was. The front was made of plywood painted black and purple, festooned with comic tombstones ("Here lies he who lies. Who he?"), and skeletons and sketchy ghosts that were depicted in slashes and smears of white paint.

The ride operator was another of the carnies Mick had seen before. He slumped there at the ride booth, head down, a skinny kid who'd sat through breakfast in the same sort of daze.

Closer, Mick saw the kid was playing with something cupped in his hands, and the ride—he couldn't believe it!

The ride was the same one that had scared him so many years before. The ghosts were painted a thin white that allowed the old letters to show through, like ghosts themselves, enough to make out:

BL-ODY –UNNEL O- TER-OR.

The carnival man had collected the bones of other shows, dead shows, including this from the long-gone Freeman Brothers Combined Carnival, another victim of high diesel and low turn-out.

The kid nodded him toward the front car of the empty train that sat waiting. Mick halted, yet found himself alone in the car, the chipped and scratched safety bar already lowered to hold him in. And the ride began.

The car banged through a set of swinging doors, into the dark, the dancing dots of light—into the laughter. The sound was old, scratchy, like dust in his ears, the recorded howls of mad voices.

"Flee! Flee before—"

The recording failed, but Mick finished the line from memory, "before it's too late."

He pitched to the side as the car swung into the path of a screeching skeleton. Boney white arms lifted, and broken white fingers grasped at him. Thrown again, he grasped the bar as the car dodged away, only to confront a cackling witch on a broom suspended in mid-air.

An upright coffin creaked open, and Dracula sprang out with a rush of dank air, his scarlet mouth split open to a snapping fury of yellow fangs.

Mick knew what came next, but it couldn't be, not so long after he'd run from this place, into the rain, secure in his new-found knowledge that dead things don't always stay down.

But everything fell down eventually, even Dave, glowing-orange Dave, the hanged man who had dangled over the tracks from a noose around his neck.

Even Dave—and safe enough, the ride came to that spot, what had to be that spot where the hanged man waited, and Dave had been replaced by a ridiculous bat.

Frankenstein's monster blocked the way out. Sparks crackled from the bolts in his green neck. The monster hunched to the side of the crooked door marked "Exit," ready to lunge.

One crazy voice joined another, another as the ride careened straight toward the door, and Mick realized the loudest of the insane lot was him—his own laughter, held for so long, it welled up at fake scares made of plaster and chicken wire, rubber and fishing line, phony metaphors to banish real fears, building to explosion, screaming his way to freedom.

The car swerved again, colliding into a painted brick wall that turned out to be a gate, and he was out of the ride, back into the kaleidoscope of the carnival.

His eyes watered and stung, but he made out the red-and-white carnival man in the sullen kid's place behind a black panel, some kind of control board. The carnival man waved to him, and the carnival man said something Mick couldn't hear, but the remembered words formed in his head.

"They all leave with what they came for."

Never stopping, never slowing, the caterpillar train of cars plunged Mick through the entry doors again, this time into pitch dark, into a void that felt like falling. And the time machine carried him back.

To feel again Aunt Lucy's embrace, so warm, his face against her apron. To play again, to catch fireflies in a Mason jar, only pretending to be upset when Aunt Lucy made him let the fairy flies go. To play sidewalk games, chalk games, running games, barefoot in the endless sea and time of summer grass.

To find the doors open to the cellar in Aunt Lucy's back-yard, and to wonder what she really knew about the depths of the cellar, maybe more than she ever let on, isn't that possible?

Was it jelly in those sealed-tight jars on the cool, shadowed shelves, or did it look like clotted blood? Did she lock the doors to keep her little nephew safe, or did she lock the doors to keep him from finding out too much about what she kept down there?

What she allowed, invited—what she kept waiting for the right time, the right summer, the right boy.

Goofus. Hear the chain swing wider and wider, Goofus coming out of the shadows, Goofus by another name, a different name that only Aunt Lucy could say.

Mick had no real memory of childhood except with Aunt Lucy. Where had he come from? Anywhere at all? Or had he materialized out of dust motes in the cellar, Aunt Lucy's cellar.

Snips and snails and puppy dog tails. Teeth and blood and waiting to climb into the living light with a terrible hunger to consume the sun, that's what little boys are made of, that's what little boys are made into, isn't that right?

All he had to do was take his rightful place.

The ride would end, and he would take his rightful place.

Mick stepped out of the ride car, hoping his legs would hold him. The carnival was a blur, a world of candy-colored phantoms. The dumb kid had returned to his job as operator. He looked up as Mick shambled past.

The kid's thin face struck a recollection, and Mick turned slowly, half-expecting to see the same greasy punk he'd paid for one last ride the night the tornadoes blew past. But it wasn't.

"Hey, mister," the kid said, and his cupped hands opened. "You forgot this."

It wasn't the punk kid, not him at all. Or maybe it had been, but it wasn't now.

"Hi, Mick," the kid said.

"Hi, Jerry," Mick answered, and saw the black spider that crawled on Jerry's fingers.

"You did this y'know," Jerry said. "You got me killed."

"I'm sorry, Jerry. I didn't mean to."

"But you did," Jerry said, and the spider crept into his mouth, twitched into his mouth, legs curling around his lower lip. The spider made him sound like he was sucking on a gob of Charleston Chew. "What I got to know is—why?"

"I don't know," Mick said.

"That's no help to me now."

"I'm sorry."

"Mr. Kidd wants to see you," Jerry said. "That's what I'm sss'possed to say. Mr. Kidd will find you."

The carnival man stood waiting in silhouette against the blinding midway.

"I lied," he said. "It's not the last show."

"It never is," Mick said.

"Join me," the carnival man said, arms outreached as if to offer a hug. "You like my name so much, you can have it."

"Why can't you die?"

"Good question," the carnival man said, and like Santa Claus, he laid a finger aside his nose. "Come close, I'll tell you. You really do want to know, don't you?"

"I know well enough."

"The big answer you don't know—I'll tell you that, too. All the bad things that happened, the bad things you caused, the bad things to come. I'll tell you why."

Mick came close enough to smell the man's breath, burnt sugar and kerosene. He saw himself as a boy, reflected in the many colors that were trapped like fireflies in the carnival man's eyes.

"I'll whisper," the man said.

Mick's hands closed around his throat. Eye-to-eye, he took the man's throat. The carnival man gave no resistance.

Mick's thumbs crushed in, breaking skin, deeper, spilling hot blood over the bow tie, the white lapels. But he couldn't keep the carnival man's wide-open mouth and cat-white teeth away from his ear.

He couldn't save himself from the carnival man's whispered secret.

All he could do was shove free.

The carnival man tidied his tie, straightened his hat, wiped his stained mustache, spat red.

"Don't forget your lessons," the carnival man said. "Take it from O.U. Kidd, kiddo. Read the midway."

Looking down, Mick saw it.

The shoe. Little pink shoe. Torn.

Care Bears shoe.

"Annie!"

"Don't worry about her," the carnival man said. "She wasn't yours, anyway, and you've already made a better one."

P   *hantasmagoria!*
          As billed.
          As promised.

Mick ran, calling Annie's name, calling Cheryl's, and the lights and sounds congealed around him. He was mired in lights, dulled to slow motion, as the carnival dropped its disguise.

They watched him through new eyes, all the carnival people—raised and swiveled their snake heads and predator heads to watch him through reptilian eyes, old forest eyes.

The figures he remembered from the breakfast tables took new shapes, scaled and many-legged shapes, mutations, taloned, razored, howling laughter, coming after him. Tearing at him.

Mick ran to the hard pound of his breath, to the sound that became a double-rhythm as another set of legs kept pace behind him, gaining on him, cold breath against his neck—ice forced into words.

"You think you can get rid of me?"

Dave's words.

"You think you can get rid of me?"

Dave's huge, orange hands closed like rock over Mick's face, wrenching back. They fell together, Mick on top of the orange bulk—the crushed body, the shattered mannequin.

The dummy's orange arms had separated from his shoulders in a fray of brittle fabric. The hollow chest had crushed in and no one but Mick would have seen the rib cage. No one else would have seen the lips move above the hanged man's constricted throat, or heard the rasping voice, the dying words of the long dead:

"Don't end up like me."

———

He neared the boat ride, the crowd around the boat ride, the safe little boat ride, and Cheryl at the boat ride, bending over a blanketed shape on the ground.

"Mick, where have you been," Cheryl said, tear-streaked, drawing him down to the ground. Down to the open bag, the spilled vials, tape, bandages.

Annie!

"It's my fault," Cheryl said, "my own damn fault, I never should have let her—"

Never should have let her be the next one, Mick thought— the next to get too close to him.

Ginny was there, and Bob Wortham, the town's happiest engaged couple, as white-faced as they had been that dim-dark afternoon in Ginny's basement, the day they found out monsters are real.

"All you good people, back it up a way," the sheriff said from somewhere high and behind. "Let this be taken care of."

"Hi, Mr. Mick-the-dad," Annie said. "I goofed."

"She fell out of the boat," Cheryl said. "I thought she had a broken ankle, but she doesn't, we don't need the ambulance, but a twist like this is bad enough. I can deal with it. We need to get her home. Why can't they make these things safe?"

Mick lifted, stood, to carry his girl.

He picked her up with weak arms that couldn't have lifted a feather, with strong arms that would carry her through all eternity if only she never grew up, never left, stayed just like she was.

"Christy," she said, and Ginny handed her the dripping doll that Annie hugged so tight that water wrung out of it.

He didn't feel like a monster. He'd never meant to call up monsters. He'd been wrong, been mean, drunk, distant, unreliable, but not . . . not evil.

But not right, either, not good to be around. There was something at odds about him, wrong in the head, different with some sort of weird talent, short on human touch.

And if he wasn't a monster, but he knew about monsters, too much about monsters, then—

Maybe that odd thing about him could be useful—might somehow have kept Annie from being hurt any worse than she was. If he understood better, then maybe she wouldn't have been hurt at all.

Nice try, no cigar. No angel's wings for you, kiddo. You're fresh out of golden trumpets, and you lost your terrible swift sword along with your lunch money.

He walked steadily, whipping through high grass. Behind, there was a scream with no fun to it, a wounded animal sound, a pop-crack that could have been gunfire.

Better go see, don't you think? Nahh, not you. You're nothing extra, just another chump. Hiya, hiya, try your luck!

Mick led the way out of the carnival, back to their car, and the procession that followed him this time wasn't of old fears, but of friends and neighbors, the town of Tanapah.

He walked with Annie's comfortable weight, with Cheryl beside him. The carnival man's whispered secret, that he thought he couldn't bear, seemed to lighten with every step.

The bad things that happened. The bad things he caused.

The bad things to come, and everything else to come, and the reason why.

"*Because . . .*"

"*You are . . .*"

"*Alive.*"

AFTERWORD

Trying to write about the first book you ever sold is a little like running into an old girlfriend. You're vaguely embarrassed, a bit ill at ease, and you wonder what in the world you're going to find to talk about.

Of course, you could always take her to the movies.

That's what we—the "we" being Ron Wolfe and me, along with our agent, Harold Schmidt—almost did with *Old Fears*. And the story of our encounters with the film industry reinforces, I think, the fact that it's not the outright rejections that hurt the most in this business. It's the near misses that really twist up your psyche.

"Highgate Signs Craven to Direct 'Old Fears'" shouted the headline in the June 12, 1985, issue of *Variety*. The text went on to note that "New York-based Highgate Pictures has signed Wes Craven, whose recent film 'A Nightmare on Elm Street' is still in successful release, to direct the upcoming feature 'Old Fears.' . . . Bob Kelly is writing the screenplay for executive producers Rosalie Muscatt and David Smith . . ."

It was great to have our book and our names in *Variety*. We felt validated—anointed, if you will, with ink from the show-biz bible. But we already knew about the plans for *Old Fears*, because Harold had snagged us the option earlier in the year.

Ron and I were horror-movie fans, so we were especially excited about Craven doing the picture. We'd both dug *Nightmare on Elm Street*, *Swamp Thing*, and *The Hills Have Eyes*—although our enthusiasm for the *Last House on the Left* wasn't unanimous—and we knew Craven was both a big genre figure and a comer. In a letter to us dated April 23, Rosalie Muscatt had tipped us about Craven's attachment to the project "of course contingent upon his availability and the outcome of our script. Although Wes hasn't done something that wouldn't ordinarily be termed a 'slice and dice movie,' he is currently up to direct *Flowers in the Attic* and some *Twilight Zone* TV episodes, and is very anxious to direct 'classier' films. Hopefully, we'll make a movie this year!!!"

But as you, gentle reader, undoubtedly know, despite Rosalie's optimism—and exclamation marks—the movie didn't get made. Highgate stayed with it for a while, giving us some more option money, and, as I recall, bringing in David Ambrose (*The Final Countdown*) to do a draft of the screenplay. But Wes Craven ankled the project, choosing to do *The Hills Have Eyes II* instead. Many years later, when I interviewed him in my capacity as an entertainment writer for the *Tulsa World* newspaper, I mentioned *Old Fears* and he said, "Oh yeah. Sure. Did that ever get made?"

A few months later, his *Scream* became the top-grossing horror picture in the history of le cinema.

Meanwhile, back in the '80s, *Old Fears*, dropped by Highgate, bounced right back, this time through the venerable gates of Paramount Pictures. It seemed that Paramount was looking for a picture to attract director Jack Sholder, a Craven protégé who'd just directed the second *Nightmare on Elm Street* picture. He'd told studio reps he'd be happy to come aboard if they'd get *Old Fears* for him. They did, and he did, and by New Year's Eve of '86 we'd signed a new option with Paramount. Again, we were excited. Again, we had big hopes. Again, we dug the fact that an up-and-coming genre director was interested.

And again, we didn't quite push past the goal line.

It certainly wasn't Sholder's fault. In fact, when I interviewed him several years later as part of a *Fangoria* magazine piece I was doing on his new picture, *The Hidden* (which I still think is a fine and underrated movie, by the way), he told me a story that bears repeating, if only for the light it throws on the sometimes bizarre ways decisions are made in the movie box.

When I told him I was the co-author of *Old Fears*, he asked, "Hey, whatever happened to the movie?"

I replied that I'd hoped he'd be able to tell me.

"Well," he said, "I had my meeting with the executives, and they asked me to do a treatment. I came back with the treatment, and they told me, 'We don't believe you've captured the essence of the book.'

"I knew the book, and I liked the book, and I felt that I had captured the essence of the book," he continued. "But I went back and did another treatment and gave it to them, and they said they still felt I hadn't captured the essence of the book."

"So I did another one, and I got the same response. Finally, I said, 'Look. I know this book and I like it, and I think I *have* captured its essence.'

"And do you know what they said to me?" he asked, a hint of amazement in his voice. "They said, 'Well, we'll read the book then, and get back to you.'"

With Sholder no longer involved but the option still in effect, *Old Fears* kicked around Paramount for a while longer before the studio gave up on it. We heard all sorts of things during those few months, including the notion that Parmount wanted to use the book as the underpinning for a new spin on the old-fashioned "monster rally" idea that Universal had done with its horror-film icons back in the '40s. This one would involve Jason from Paramount's *Friday the 13th* series, Freddy from the *Nightmare on Elm Street* pictures, Leatherface from *Texas Chainsaw Massacre,* and, if memory serves, Michael Meyers from *Halloween.* We were also told, much later, that screenwriter Jeb Stuart did an *Old Fears* treatment for Paramount directly before going to *Die Hard.*

Old Fears did, in fact, *Die Hard.* Miraculously, Harold got us a third option on it, this time with a guy in Hollywood whose name mercifully escapes me. The option money was smaller than the few thousands we'd gotten from Highgate and Paramount, but the young man told Harold he was knocked out by the book and really wanted to do it right, and all three of us on this end thought that was just a lovely idea. This was before he took out a second option after the original expired and stiffed us on money so he could buy himself a television set.

We did, however, get a chance to see his completed script. Or maybe "get" isn't the correct verb. In it, our two protagonists, Mick Winters and Dr. Cheryl Stanton, became the kinds of characters that make those crooks in *Reservoir Dogs* look like the Care Bears. Ron and I were especially taken with this snatch of dialogue, which gives you a pretty good idea of the overall work.

MICK: F—you, Cheryl!
CHERYL: No, Mick. F—you!

It was just about here that we abandoned all hope. Or, put another way, we thought about this guy actually making the picture and said, f— that. Eventually, so did he, and that's how it ended, at least for the time being.

Ron and I learned a lot during those years of options. We learned that whoever options the book isn't very interested in any input the book's writers might have about the script; they've got their own ideas, and they'd prefer that you didn't stir things up by offering your own. We also learned that the big money stipulated by a contract (in the case of our agreement with Paramount, it was a minimum, I believe, of $165,000 that we'd get the moment that cameras rolled) is kind of like those giant numbers you see on scratcher tickets from state lotteries: They may say $100,000, but you'll be lucky to win two bucks or a free ticket to play again.

Still, those years were a good and exciting time for us. Our option money invariably appeared a few weeks before Christmas, which was fortuitous, and the sweet smell of wild hope hovered always in the air around us, no matter what the season.

One of my all-time favorite observations comes from Samuel Johnson, who said that second marriages were the triumph of hope over experience. I've come to realize that his statement applies also to writing, and especially to writing books. So, with that in mind, I remind anyone out there who reads this novel and thinks this would make a swell movie that a film option is once again available. If you can afford to pay a small amount of option money—and you already have your own TV set—well, you know where to find us.

—John Wooley
Foyil, OK

Note from the author: The above piece was written in 1999, when *Old Fears* became one the first books reissued by Bill Bernhardt's HAWK Publishing Group. Since then, I'm happy

to say that despite my rather snide observations re: a fresh
option, our little horror yarn has refused to lie down and expire
quietly.

In fact, as I write this—in the spring of 2021—*Old Fears* is
in active development at Sony Pictures Television.

ACKNOWLEDGMENTS

For this special 40th anniversary edition of the Book That Refuses to Die, we gratefully acknowledge the work of our editor, Lara Bernhardt; our publisher, Bill Bernhardt; and our copy editor, John Hamill, along with cover designers Maria and Victoria at BEAUTeBOOK, and the crackerjack Wooley media team of Lourdes Alcala, Joey Hambrick, and Steven Wooley.

ABOUT THE AUTHORS

Ron Wolfe co-wrote three horror novels with John Wooley— Old Fears, *Death's Door,* and *Full Moon.* Wolfe is a retired newspaper feature writer and cartoonist turned freelance writer and illustrator. His work includes the graphic novel *Knights of the Living Dead* (illustrated by Dusty Higgins), the Nebula-nominated fantasy novella "Our Friend Electricity," and a cartoon-illustrated state history book, *Arkansas in Ink: Gunslingers, Ghosts and Other Graphic Tales.* He wrote for the original comic book series of *Clive Barker's Hellraiser,* creating the Cenobite sisters Bright Eyes and The Voice.

His most recent work is a children's picture book, *Otto the Otter and the Great Arkansas Mystery.*

John Wooley made his first professional sale in the late 1960s, placing a script with the legendary *Eerie* magazine. He's now in his sixth decade as a professional writer, having written three horror novels with co-author Ron Wolfe, including *Death's Door,* which was one of the first books released under Dell's Abyss imprint and was also nominated for a Bram Stoker Award. His solo horror and fantasy novels include *Awash in the Blood, Ghost Band,* and *Dark Within,* the latter a finalist for the Oklahoma Book Award. With Robert A. Brown he wrote the three novels in The Cleansing horror trilogy, *Seventh Sense, Satan's Swine,* and *Sinister Serpent.*

Wooley is also the author of the critically acclaimed biographies *Wes Craven: A Man and His Nightmares* and *Right Down the Middle: The Ralph Terry Story*. He has co-written or contributed to several volumes of Michael H. Price's Forgotten Horrors series of movie books and co-hosts the podcast of the same name. His other writing credits include the 1990 TV film *Dan Turner, Hollywood Detective* and several documentaries, notably the Learning Channel's *Hauntings Across America*. Among the comics and graphic novels he's scripted are *Plan Nine from Outer Space*, the authorized version of the alternative-movie classic, as well as the recent collections *The Twilight Avenger* and *The Miracle Squad*. In 2020, with Brett Bingham, he wrote the definitive history of Cain's Ballroom, *Twentieth-Century Honky-Tonk*.

CPSIA information can be obtained
at www.ICGtesting.com
Printed in the USA
LVHW031001240423
745165LV00013B/730